The Last Audition

Tom Bainton

Cover design by Amy Lucas

Copyright © 2024 Tom Bainton

All rights reserved.

ISBN: 978-1-0685789-0-8

For my family.

JANUARY

That's great, Charlie. I loved you in The Mocking Half. Really, I thought it was an incredible performance. Especially for one so young. You're fourteen next week, right? Incredible.

So Jess and I have been speaking, and we've seen a lot of boys for this role. A lot. But we keep coming back to you. We would like you to play Tim. If you want to, of course. No pressure.

Fantastic. We're going on a journey, you and I. I'm not saying it's not going to be tough at times, because it will be. There may be times where you're going to hurt, but you must trust me Charlie.

You do trust me, don't you?

Because what we're going to achieve will be golden.

Bob is out when I drop round, which is just about fucking typical. He said he's going to be in after five, but in the whole time I've been buying weed off him, I've never known him to be in when he says he will be. You'd think I should know better by now.

So instead, I'm eyeballing his flat from across the street, cradling a coffee and half reading the paper. Two years ago, this place was brand new, and there was a palpable excitement from the overgrown Trustafarian in her late thirties as the shutters went up; this was going to be the one, the hot spot that everyone in West London came to – they were going to have couches, and papers, and plinky-plonk music that sounds like a Tibetan headache.

And for a while it was, the cool kids and fashionistas dropping in for an overpriced jolt of caffeine and to check each other out. But then a new place opened on Portobello just round the corner from Elgin Crescent, and this neglected corner of Golborne began to lapse back into disfavour. The crowds dripped away, the coffee got weaker, and the smile slowly fell off the face of Lamentia, or whatever the fuck her name was. Now she just sat there, half hiding behind the counter, embarrassed. This place would be closed in a month. I'd put money on it.

But in the meantime, it gives me somewhere warm and dry to stake out Bob's flat until he comes back, even if the honk of whale song is getting on my tits. Rain flecks the window. Winter is here, the nights are short, wet and cold; and the only sensible thing to do is hole up and make sure you have enough puff to blot out the frost and boredom.

I sip my latte and flick through the Times. That's another thing about this place; the coffee always seems lukewarm, like she's been blowing on it for half an hour for fear of getting sued. Coffee is supposed to be hot. This isn't like fucking America where the idiots call a lawyer if they push through paper wiping their arse in McDonalds. Give me a hot coffee. I think I can handle it.

There's nothing in the paper that I don't already know. 2015 and we're off to a flying start. The Middle East is still fucked, the economy remains extra fucked, and if you didn't buy a house twenty years ago, you're super-duper fucked.

Basically, we're all fucked.

Then I see him and a chill runs down my spine. Leering out from the cover of Times 2. James Laurenson, Genius Film Director; sat behind a camera like the Master of the Fucking Universe. I open it up to the double page spread on pages 4 and 5, and he's there again, smirking out of the pages like he's God's own fucking gift to cinema. He's wanking on about his new film, and the sycophantic journo is clearly buying it as she's letting him get away with spouting seven sorts of crap. About his working process, about how he likes to work with actors. My jaw tightens as I take it all in, and I just want to scream. It's such bullshit.

There's a knock on the window. It's Bob, his coat pulled over his head to keep the rain off. Probably doesn't want anything to happen to his hair. He's the only guy I know who spends more on his hair than any woman I've ever met. And no matter what he puts on it, he's never going to disguise the fact that he's going bald.

I ditch the paper and walk out.

"Are you ever on time?" I shake his outstretched hand. It's sticky.

"Sorry, Charlie. Had a meeting about the site. It overran."

Bob's been talking about the site for the past two years and trying to get someone to build the fucking thing for at least half that long. He's done a couple of courses in website design, but the dopey twat smokes so much puff that his short-term memory is completely blown, and he ends up spending most of the time confused, trying to work out what the hell the teacher is on about. As far as I can understand it, which is not much, the site is some kind of social networking community for skaters. There's some kind of twist involved, but it's so contrived that it's pointless, and it's not just me who thinks that as no other fucker seems to want to touch it with a bargepole. Even the other dopey tossers who spunk a small fortune to chuck themselves about the ramps underneath the Westway don't seem to want a bar of it. If he didn't sell them all weed Bob would probably been out on his arse years ago.

I follow Bob out onto Golborne, and we hit a sharp right into one of the blocks. Bobs on the third floor of a shit tower that estate agents are no doubt peddling as the next Trellick to clueless Swiss bankers, but the staircase smells of piss and skunk, and the yoot who seem to live there all eyefuck us on the way up.

We're out on the landing, and Bob lets us in. The teenagers smoking out the staircase don't seem to realise that they're probably doing Bob a massive favour in creating a diversion if there was any police interest – the stink on the stairs means that you don't catch it so much outside Bob's, but you do the moment you're inside. Walk down the small hallway towards the living room and it grows stronger; by the time you're sat on his flea-bitten couch with MTV on the 50-inch plasma you can't smell anything else.

Bob pulls out a big Tupperware box about the size you would get a shitload of ice cream in as a kid, before it began to be marketed as a sex aid and sold in dinky pots that take about a half hour to get soft enough to eat. It's full of hash and weed, and I don't need to tell him what I'm after. It's the same every time; a quarter of Charas. There's no way I'll touch skunk. That's for the yoot who don't want to be able to think or talk. Mind you if I was hanging out on a concrete stairway in North Kensington for the duration of my teenage years, I'd want to be pretty fucking anaesthetized too.

I gave up skunk about four years ago after a night in the flat when I just blacked out. I'd been at it pretty heavily the night before, and when I woke up late the next afternoon, I couldn't remember a fucking thing that had happened. Dick all. And when that happens then you know it's time to change your narcotic. That stuff will give you brain damage. It's fucking horrid.

Bob is quite possibly brain damaged, but he probably wasn't starting with primo equipment in the first place. He looks a bit bewildered as I hand over two twenties, and I'm momentarily tempted to pocket the cash and thank him loudly for the change as I don't think he'd know the difference, but I don't.

"Forty, right?" I ask.

Bob looks at the money for a second. "Yeaaaah," he says, in a slow exhale. It's always the same, like he's kind of gutted to be taking the money, like we should all be smoking for nothing in this non-existent fucking hippy Utopia that only exists in his puff-addled brain. I've been to Glastonbury a couple of times, and from observing at close quarters I've come to the reliable conclusion that most hippies are cunts.

The Charas smells good, and it's squidgy between my thumb and forefinger. Bob puts the telly on and flicks through the channels while I skin up. It's always a delicate business with hash this soft, as if you burn it the way you would with shit soap-bar it'll just end up all over your fingers. All you need to do is touch a flame to it and it'll come away perfectly. I load up a Rizla and fire it up. It's my first for three days and it tastes fantastic. I was thinking about knocking it on the head for a little while – partly the misinformed zeal that a New Year brings, and partly because sometimes I don't think puffing is perhaps helping with auditions – but then I thought fuck it, life's short and shitty, and I could do with a draw.

There's some chavvy girl group parading around in their underwear on the telly, and Bob is clearly into it, the old perv. He's old enough to be their dad, but then so am I. I'm not sure, but I could swear I've seen one of them knocking around Portobello. It wouldn't exactly be a shocker if I had. I pass Bob the spliff and he takes it, inhaling deeply.

"So what you up to at the moment?" he asks.

I shrug. "You know. Same old, same old."

"Anything in the pipeline?"

"Waiting to hear about a couple of things," I lie. The truth is I haven't had a sniff of anything for nearly three months. Fuck knows what my agent is doing. The last thing I was up for was a series on the Beeb about a bunch of young lawyers, and that was in the dim and distant past. The script wasn't great, but then most of them are shit. Carol thinks I might be showing too much of an ambivalent attitude in auditions. It's easy for her to say when she's pimping me out for that level of crap. Where have all the fucking decent feature scripts gone? That's what I'd like to know.

Bob's attention is firmly back on the fanny stack that's unravelling on the screen. And he wonders why he's still single. The man looks like he could do with a wash and a slap, and it really doesn't matter in which order.

"Nice one, Bob. I'm off." I stand up quickly, lest the slight stickiness of the couch should pull me down again. Bloodshot eyes squint up at me.

"Okay, Charlie. Cheers."

The draw is in my pocket and I'm out the door, head down as I turn right away from the back stairs and head towards the other main staircase and the lift. The last thing I need is some yoot taxing me, now I've just scored.

I trudge back along Golborne. It still amazes me how all these little Arabic shops manage to hold their own amongst all the overpriced boutiques that seem to breed here. This corner of West London is incredibly tribal; everyone quietly ignoring each other. You can always spot some tit who's just moved into one of the overpriced bedsits above the shops here; they're the ones buying their vegetables a little too loudly from one of the bemused guys whose stalls line the gutter. There's plenty of hoorays among the Arabs though, along with the teenage mothers who've been knocked up by some psychotic yoot, the media halfwits braying over their Marlboro outside the pub, the bankers who are busy buying up the property down towards Notting Hill, and of course the estate dwelling fuckwits who parade their death dogs up and down. I pass the café on the corner of Wornington and one of them is doing his best to fuck up a Pitbull on a short leash, and you can feel the pitying glances for the animal from the horrified models outside Lisboa on the other side of the road. Not one of them will call the police though. They can't be arsed with the hassle and there's no fucking point.

It's winter and the cold is still biting. Christmas came and went over three weeks ago in a big blaze of 'meh', and now it's just cold and damp and downright fucking depressing. Thank God for that Charas. I went to see Pat on Christmas day, although by the time we'd kicked back for the big afternoon movie I was already asking myself why I'd bothered. Molly turned up for lunch with my two nieces, both who I'll bet are on course for a teenage pregnancy. Molly's marriage went the way of Pat and Dad's at the end of 2010, and she's been trying to hold it together ever since. Personally, I think she could scale back the anti-depressants a little; every time I see her, she always reminds me a little of McMurphy at the end of One Flew Over the Cuckoo's Nest. With Pat playing the role of Nurse Ratched.

I'd been there barely half an hour when the passive aggressive nonsense started. Neither Molly or I can do anything right, and in all honesty we've long since given up trying, and so there was very little to do all day but get shit-faced and eat the M&S Christmas dinner that she'd heated. Sky and Flower (normally those names might be considered a hindrance but based where they are in Hammersmith they're positively run of the mill) opened their toys and started fighting before lunch. They used to think it was glamorous having an uncle who was an actor, but that was back when I was working, and as they haven't seen me in anything for a while and they're getting older they've both clearly decided I'm a loser.

It might have been nice to spend Christmas with Dad, but he's now all loved up and busy with his new family, so we don't even get a look-in. I've not heard dick from him since we spoke briefly on Christmas morning, but I'm not losing any sleep over it. He knows where to find me.

So we're into January. It's dark, it's wet, it's cold, and the summer seems a long way away. I'd fuck off somewhere warm if I could afford it. As I cross the Grove onto Chesterton it starts drizzling again, and I pull my coat up around my ears to try and stave off some of the misery. I narrowly miss a cyclist coming down the hill as I cross, who swears at me, and I have to jog across the other side to avoid a bus who I swear speeds up to try and hit me. Perhaps he recognised me. Everyone's a critic.

I let myself in to the main hall and trip over a bunch of pizza menus that have been dumped through the letterbox in the hour or so in which I've been out. There must be getting on for twenty plus menus there. How many people do they think live in this fucking building?

I'm in one of two first floor flats of a fair size converted Victorian on St. Quintin's Avenue. I bought it at the turn of the Millennium, and since then it's probably vastly increased in value; it certainly feels as if it should as the mortgage payments feel like a monthly haemorrhage. It seems to be getting worse each month and I've now maxed out all my credit cards and since everything kicked off with the credit crunch, they're not giving away free money anymore and everyone seems a lot keener to try and claw some back.

I chuck my keys on the side table by the door and ignore the unopened envelopes that I picked up this morning. Bills, bills, and more fucking bills. I could really do with a job.

I toy with the idea of ringing back the Visa people who've now left me two more messages on the machine but think better of it and kick back on the couch to roll a spliff instead. The idea of trying the new pizza place is appealing, but I'm low on cash after picking up the puff, and in all likelihood, it's probably run by some scrote who's been spending all day scratching his balls. I've got a pizza in the freezer, so that will have to do.

There's no sign of Nick. He's been my flatmate for four years, since I met him on a low budget feature I was doing at the time about a vampire detective. He was the props man, and we got on as we had a shared interest in weed and women, although now he's let the side down and gone and got himself a girlfriend. They used to stay here a fair amount, but he seems to prefer her flat as I hardly see him these days. He's changed since he met her. He already seems to have lost his bollocks and they've only been going out six months. Alex. Short, brunette. She's fit and everything, but there's no way I'd put up with her shit. She's a lawyer, so immediately she thinks she's ten times fucking smarter than the rest of the world. It must be hard looking down your nose at people when you have to stand on tiptoes to reach five foot. Nick seems happy though, so good for him. Be good to see him once in a while though.

There's nothing on telly, so I fire up the Xbox and pick up where I left off in Empire of Blood, raging havoc through the lovingly recreated virtual New York of the 1930s. Antonio di Fratelli's the only part I've played for the last three months, and he's considerably better drawn than half the characters I normally get sent. I jump on the duckboard of a stolen cop car as it heads up Broadway and let loose a volley of bullets at my pursuers with the Tommy Gun. The car screeches to a halt and I'm running across towards 6th Avenue, taking out passers-by with my pistol just because I can. There's something wholly satisfying about gratuitous and nihilistic killing.

I pause the game around an hour later to stick the pizza in the oven, and skin up while I'm waiting for it to cook. I flick through the channels, but there's nothing on. I jump a little when I hear the front door open; two spliffs in and I'm actually thinking that there might be someone breaking in.

Then Nick pokes his head round the door. It's obviously chucking it down outside, as he's soaked. "Hey man," he says.

"Nicolarse. Long time," I reply.

"What you up to?" He wanders off to his room and comes back seconds later rubbing his hair with a towel.

I shrug. "You know. The usual. A little bit of 'Blood. You want some pizza?"

"No, you're alright." He slumps onto the couch next to me. "I had a massive chicken pie on set a couple of hours ago."

"You're filming? You're back early."

He nods. "The director tripped over some cables and fucked his ankle up. They took him to the hospital. So, we're back tomorrow."

"What a nob."

He reaches into the ashtray to pick up the spliff as I head back to the kitchen to get my pizza. When I come back, he's flicking through the channels like he always does, like he hasn't been living in someone else's flat for the past God knows how long.

"How's things with Alex? Good?" The pizza tastes fucking terrible.

Nick turns to me and bats his eyelashes. "Why? You miss me?"

"Always."

He stops flicking as he comes to World's Most Retarded Car Chases in the higher numbers. Perhaps he hasn't changed that much after all. This certainly feels like Groundhog Day, watching seven-year-old footage of chav twats tearing up and down the motorways in stolen Escorts.

"Yeah, things are good. She's got some kind of business thing tonight. Chambers. Drinks. Something."

The pizza's just too dry. I ditch half of it in the bin back in the kitchen. I cram the box into the rubbish. They're trying to encourage recycling, but I just can't be fucking arsed.

"You're there all the time now. I mean it's not a problem. I'm just saying." As the words leave my mouth, I realise I'm sounding like a total fucking homo. Like we're fucking married or something.

I walk back into the living room, and Nick's there looking over at me with a serious look on his face.

"Actually, there's something I wanted to talk to you about." He drags on the last of the spliff and chucks it in the ashtray.

"Alex and I have been talking, and we think we're going to move in together."

I bite my lip to stop myself from telling him not to do it. Not because I want him to stay or anything, but because I think Alex is a fucking bitch.

"That's quite soon," I tell him.

He shrugs. "What can I say? I'm crazy about the girl."

Crazy is right. She's a gobby, chippy cow, and despite working out four times a week is still clearly losing the battle against some pretty obvious fat genes.

"Cool," I say. The golden rule; never slag off a mate's bird to his face. It will only lead to a whole big world of shit. "So, when's that gonna happen?"

"I don't want to drop you in it. Is six weeks' notice okay? Should give you time to start looking for someone else." His attention flicks back to the screen, and he's chuckling away at some drunk driving cunt from Batshit, Idaho or wherever.

"Well, skin up then," I tell him.

He reaches for the tin without looking, and peels off a Rizla. Someone else. It's been hard enough living with him for the past six years, and I actually like Nick. The idea of living with someone else is pretty much impossible. My thirties are fading about as fast as my career, and the last thing I want is some stranger sharing my living space.

But then I don't really have an option. Nick's rent has been shoring up my debts, and without that I'd be well and truly fucked. With the benefit of hindsight, it probably wasn't the best idea to get a second mortgage on this place when the money started to run out, and I've only just been able to afford the repayments with what Nick has been paying me a month. Then there's the credit cards, my overdraft, and all the other shit from a whole number of greedy fuckers breathing down my neck.

I look at Nick. Find someone else? Cunt.

He finishes building, and lights it, puffing quickly twice, like he always does, before passing it to me.

"You'll be alright, won't you?" he asks.

"Be glad to be rid of you, you skanky twat," I tell him. "Perhaps I'll find someone who knows how to rinse a fucking bath out after using it."

He grins. "Perhaps you'll find someone who won't mind the odour of stale semen that wafts from what you call a bedroom every morning."

"That's you smelling your own burps." He laughs. So he's moving out, even if it is to go and live with a fucking dragon. It's the end of an era. We should go out with a bang. Celebrate. Not tonight obviously, as it's fucking dismal. But soon.

I pass him back the spliff. "You up for a night out? Been ages."

"How about Friday? Alex is out with her mates, so I'm home free." He laughs at the TV, where some twat is falling into a ditch halfway through a roadside sobriety test.

"Friday it is."

All I have to remember is to keep it buttoned and not wax lyrical about what a fucking bitch I think his girlfriend is, and we should have a good night. Besides, Nick will be coming off four days plus on a commercial shoot, and without the angry hobbit breathing up his neck he may pull his finger out and spot a gram or two so we can make a proper evening of it. Just like the old days.

I look at the screen where a yellow Yank school bus is zigzagging up the wrong way of a motorway scattering panicked cars in every direction.

"Nick, you cunt," I tell him. "We've seen this one before."

He drags on the spliff and chucks it back at me. "So?"

I pick the spliff up from where it's dropped on the rug. There's so many blim burns on it, it's beginning to resemble some kind of hippy smock.

"So let's break out Mortal Kombat and fuck each other up."

Nick is long gone by the time I finally surface around half nine. He was due on set at seven in the morning, and after the two bottles of cheap red we tucked away, on top of all the puff we smoked, that can't have been easy. Not to mention that I kicked his arse all over the shop in Mortal Kombat. I should stick virtual Ninja skills up on Spotlight, I'm that fucking good.

I crawl into the kitchen and stick the kettle on. I grab the coffee from the fridge – some good Colombian stuff from Sainsbury's. I know the stuff I like now, and I'm prepared to walk up to the top of the Grove to get it, rather than have a bunfight with all the pikeys in the Tescos on Portobello. Every time I go in there it feels like the end of the fucking world. I'm running low again, so make a mental note to pick some up later in the day. I doubt somehow that I'm going to be rushed off my feet.

I take the coffee into the lounge and switch on the laptop. It's an old G4 Ibook, and the once gleaming white plastic is looking very scuffed and is beginning to turn a shade of grey. It whirs into life very slowly, and as I fire up Safari it makes a nasty clicking sound. The internet runs so slowly on this thing it's like being back in the bad old days of dial-up. If I had the cash, I'd be straight down Regent Street to pick up a shiny new MacBook Pro.

I've half-drunk my coffee by the time I've managed to get into my mail. Nothing from Carol, but then there's nothing new there. In fact, there's nothing from anyone. Not a fucking sausage. Bar the usual spam from the Viagra and Rolex pimps, and that doesn't count. Time was when I would have been cruising around on Facebook, but I deleted my account a couple of months ago. Part of it was the realisation that although I had 196 friends, the only one I ever saw was Nick.

The rest appeared to just be detritus that I picked up from various shoots. Part of it was that I was getting continually bombarded with friends' requests from no-mark twats who I had never met. But the clincher was when I drunkenly did some vanity surfing and discovered that there was a bunch of people in a group called 'Whatever happened to Charlie Reed?'

I check my watch. A quarter past ten. Carol will be in by now, sat in front of her desk with a Starbucks skinny latte leaving a coffee ring on some script or other.

Even as I press the call button next to her name on my phone, I hate myself for it. I'm turning into one of those desperate fucks I always used to despise.

The phone rings four times before there's a clunking sound as the handset is fumbled in answering. Annette. I don't even have to hear her voice to know it's her – just the way she fucks up a clean phone grab gives her away.

"Hello. McKinley's Performing Artists. Can I help you?"

Annette sounds like she looks. Plump, and a bit thick.

"Hey Annette, how you doing? It's Charlie. Charlie Reed. Is Carol there?"

"Hi Charlie, can you hang on a moment?"

I'm put on hold, and thirty seconds later Annette is back on the line, telling me blatant lies.

"Hi Charlie, she's not in just yet. Can I get her to give you a call?"

I pause for a moment and grit my teeth. I know Carol's there. Annette is such a bad fucking liar; you can hear Carol's there in her voice. What's doubly insulting is that anyone can hear how bad a liar Annette is, not least someone whose stock and trade is all about the finding of emotional fucking truth. You'd think that if Carol was going to fob people off, the least she could fucking do would be employ a decent liar to cover for her. But then, maybe it's just my calls she's not taking.

"Sure, no worries." I try to sound breezy. I can do breezy. "It would be great to speak to her if she's got a minute."

"Okay, Charlie. Sure. I'll pass that on."

The phone clunks back in the cradle at the other end in the same ham-fisted way it was picked up. The girl really needs to get to grips with handling a phone. It's not that hard to pick up a lump of plastic, even for someone with fingers as fat as hers.

I toy with the idea of putting the telly on but watching daytime TV is too much of an admittance of defeat. My phones rings, and I grab it immediately, thinking it's going to be Carol.

Big mistake.

"Hello?"

"Hello, is that Mr. Reed?"

Busted. If unsure, leave it for voicemail. I broke the golden rule. Too late now.

"Speaking."

"Mr. Reed, my name's James Adams, and I'm calling from Keldon's Financial Services about your Visa account. I've noticed that you've missed this month's payment and was wondering if I could take a payment over the phone from you now?"

I've got to front it out. This is only one of the guys who've been hounding me for payments, and if I don't throw him some kind of bone now it's only going to lead to a bigger headache.

"Sorry," I lie. "I've been away on business." I fish my debit card out of my wallet, and hope and pray that I'm within my limit to make a payment. I read out my number to the guy and wait for what feels like an eternity to see if it authorises.

"That's fine," he says. "I notice that you've cancelled the direct debit payments with us. I can set one up again with you now if you like. Make things easier in the future?"

"Thanks, but I'm having some problems with my bank at the moment. In the process of switching accounts."

There's a tiny pause.

"Sure," he says.

That second of silence says everything: right, another fucking deadbeat who's reached the end of his credit run and is fobbing me off with a heap of crap. "Well, when you've set up your new account, perhaps we could set something up then."

"Definitely," I say.

"Have a good day, Mr. Reed," he says, and hangs up.

After a call like that it can only improve. I really need to get a job, and the stark reality is that if I don't land something soon, I'm going to have to look at something besides acting. Casting directors aren't exactly beating down my door. The last time I registered with a temp agency they set me up with an office job with a bunch of normal people. I lasted a fortnight doing data input before I walked out for an audition and landed a part in a miniseries on Channel 4. I vowed then never again, but that was before I started getting all these moody phone calls.

There're all sorts of scams out there about trying to make money through the internet, but I wouldn't trust half of the shit you hear. Most of them seem to be about making one guy rich – and he'll be the one placing the ad in the first place. There must be some things that I could start sticking on eBay. I'd even do bar work, if it weren't for the fact that too many people recognise my face.

I could sell the flat and move somewhere else, but then why the fuck would I want to do that? This is my home, and even though the Grove is chock full of tossers, it's still my manor, and I can't even think about living anywhere else. Not even Kensal Rise, and that's only up the road.

I've toyed with the idea of getting involved on the other side of the camera and trying to get some work with crews. I've spent enough time on film sets to know what everyone does, and I'd be more than happy to get stuck in. But I know that once I'd done that, there would be no going back in front of the camera. You can go in front from behind, but once you join the crew there's no going back again. Even temp work is preferable to fucking myself over permanently.

The one thing that's going to keep me afloat for the foreseeable future is the fact that Nick has agreed to cancel the direct debit and pay me cash instead for the last month, so at least I'll have some actual money to play with, rather than it just trying to stem the constant haemorrhaging of my bank account.

I piss about on YouTube looking at videos of weird Christian fundamentalists, waiting in vain for Carol to call back. Enough is enough. I skin up a little reefer just to ease me into the day and trundle off down towards the library. Normally it would be straight down to Portobello to grab a coffee at the Electric and watch the girls floating past, but I really need to watch the cash. It's a nice enough day, and if it holds, I might kill some time in Hyde Park. I'm turning into a fucking pensioner.

The library is quiet, and warm. A winning combination. I grab the paper and sit down and work my way through the news. It's something I've done for as long as I can remember and is always a good mental exercise to keep going on the days you're not working. Find a story in the news and imagine yourself as the character telling it all from their perspective. Colour it as much as possible. If the average Sun reader could see the number of paedophiles I've played in my head, I'd be strung up from the nearest lamppost. It's all in the imagination though. It's not like I'm going to go and fuck kids for research.

Today's dream team involve a Polish scientist working on a cure for cancer, a builder who's just won the lottery, and an MP who's just been discovered cheating on his wife. Before I know it, an hour has gone by, and I'm beginning to feel a little peckish. Pulling on my jacket, I check the back pages to see if there's going to be anything worth watching this evening.

There it is. 10.35pm, BBC One. 'The Twelfth of Never.' It even gets a Pick of the Day. The write-up describes it as the feature debut of one of our greatest directors (their words, not mine); a slow burner that examines the confusion of adolescence over the course of a summer. And one that features a stand-out performance from a young Charlie Reed.

Me.

It's a good film; I can't argue with that. But I would question whether James Laurenson is one of our greatest directors. He's definitely one of the biggest cunts that England has produced, and I can vouch for that from personal fucking experience. The film was a slow burner; it made me the most famous teenager in Britain for a while and gave me a career, but that doesn't change the fact that Laurenson is a shitbag and will remain one 'til the day he dies.

Still, there may be some good comes out of it. Maybe some casting directors will see it and wonder what I'm up to now, and maybe I'll get a bite on a couple of juicy roles. One thing is cast iron guaranteed: that by the end of the week Carol will be swamped with a ton of scripts from 'low budget filmmakers'. Each of these will be poorly written, cliché-ridden melodramas from public schoolboys who all fancy themselves as Quentin fucking Tarantino just because they've read a couple of books on how to knock up a screenplay and Daddy's bought them a camera. They'll be watching the film (because, you know, it's a classic), and they'll all suddenly be struck with what they each believe is a wholly original thought; that I'd be the perfect lead for their own little masterpiece. They are going to be the guy who resurrects Charlie Reed's career, just like QT did for Travolta in Pulp Fiction. They'll wing their scripts over to Carol, and besides being mostly cack, there will be one other crucial factor that unites every single last one of them.

None of them will have any money.

They'll all plead poverty, that they're putting their limited budget into getting the movie on screen. It's all crap. I could throw the Reservoir Dogs DVD out of my bedroom window, and I'd probably hit two or three of the cunts striding down St. Quintin's braying into their mobiles, ordering in some coke for Friday night (which they always seem to have plenty of fucking money for, by the way.)

'The Twelfth of Never' was last on telly about sixteen months ago, on Film Four. Carol received over twenty scripts. Every single one of them was fucking diabolical.

I can only hope that there may be someone watching who sees that I'm not a bad actor, as I wouldn't like to see out the remainder of my life dwelling in ever increasing obscurity.

It's just a shame that my career seems to have peaked at it's very beginning, and equally a shame that I've got such bitter fucking memories from the whole experience. But then that did give me something to draw on.

The sun ducks behind the clouds as I make my way up the Grove towards Sainsbury's. I'm out of coffee, and I need to pick up some food for later. Maybe even push the boat out and stretch to a bottle of wine.

My mobile rings. It's Carol. I answer.

"Hey Carol."

There's an audible intake of smoke down the other end of the line, and a growling cough as she exhales before speaking.

"Charlie, darling. How are you?"

A lot better than you by the sounds of it, I think. Carol has smoked forty a day ever since I've been with her, and proper full fat fags at that. When I smoked, she used to take the piss out of me for smoking Marlboro Lights, as she'd light a fresh B&H with the dying embers of one on the way to the ashtray. No smoking ban for Carol. The window in her office is now permanently open as she puffs away next to it, with a tiny fan heater underneath her desk on full blast to try and counteract the cold that's blowing in. There's no chance of Carol making it up and down the stairs for every fag; not with the amount she smokes. And not with her frame either. She's a big lady and shows no sign of shifting any of the pounds soon.

I made the mistake of following her up the stairs back up to the office once after we'd had a coffee, and it was like chasing an asthmatic hippo. Right now, she seems like my one last connection to the world of acting, and if that goes, I'm well and truly fucked.

"I'm good, babe," I say. I'm 'darling', she's 'babe'. 'Twas ever thus and shall forever be. "You know, keeping busy."

"Good, good. You seen what's on tonight?" The phone moves away from her mouth as she makes a god-awful hacking sound. She should really think about quitting.

"Yeah. I'm already preparing myself for the deluge of dross from all the wannabe auteurs who are going to make me Lazarus."

"Now, Charlie, be nice."

"I need a job, Carol. Seriously. One that pays."

"I know darling, I know." She's got her soothing voice on. I've been with her fifteen years, and I have to give it to her. She knows how to handle people. She certainly knows how to soothe. "But then, tonight could be perfect timing. There's something coming up with Salt and Acre for the Beeb. A hospital drama. There's an interesting part which has you written all over it. I'm trying to get you a meeting. They're going to start looking at people next week. I've just mentioned that your debut gets a screening tonight, and Meg's interest was piqued."

Get. Fucking. In.

Salt and Acre are one of the bigger independents, and if they're looking at people then that means they've got a commission, and the one thing they do well is drama series. I don't think I've met Meg, unless our paths have crossed on another production in the past. It's more than possible. But that doesn't matter. I'll just have to use my charm.

"What's the part?" I ask Carol.

"He's a young surgeon. Well, youngish. Married, but embarking on an affair. A 'dishy shit', was the quick pitch, if I remember."

"Nice. Do I know Meg?"

"She came over from Armada."

Fuck. Meg. I think I have met her. If I'm right, she's the uppity cow who knocked me back for a job a couple of years ago. It was a murder mystery thing for ITV that Armada were putting together, and if I'm right, she was assisting the producer on that project, and I got the distinct impression that she didn't like me. I didn't get the job. She probably did me a favour, mind you. I saw the finished thing and it was total fucking shite. Still, Salt and Acre do some good stuff, and I need the work.

"Yeah," I tell Carol. "Maybe our paths have crossed. Let's chase her tomorrow once the film's been on, see if we can line up a meeting."

"Will do, Charlie darling. Speak soon."

"Bye babe," I say, and she's gone.

Thank fuck. I'm feeling good again now, like I'm back in the game. I march into Sainsbury's like I run the fucking place and swoop up a load of veggies that I can stick in the steamer, along with a piece of salmon. A yummy mummy gives me a nod like she knows me, and I grin back, knowing that when it finally dawns on her where she knows me from, she'll probably be squirming with embarrassment for the rest of the afternoon.

It's an odd thing, having a face that people recognise. Note that I don't use the word 'famous', as I'm pragmatic enough about my position in the world of entertainment not to think that I'm Jude Law. Nor am I, and I would never describe myself, as a 'celebrity.' Firstly, I actually have a talent, and one that I've worked pretty fucking hard for over the years. 'Celebrities', on the whole, are bellends who splash their tits all over the red tops, or second division footballers. And, while I'm generalising, I've flushed bigger talent after my morning coffee.

Most of the time people will see me and kind of double take, in a "where do I know him from?" way. Not so much round here though, which is another reason why I'd never consider moving. The civilians round here can deal with seeing a familiar face.

I pick up a bottle of white wine that will go with the salmon, and float everything through the self-swipe checkout. I toy with the idea of trying to palm the wine through without paying, but I don't want to end up like one of those ageing TV hosts still trying to explain that one after ten years, so over the reader it goes.

The sun is shining as I walk back down the Grove, and I take the right onto Barlby Road after the bridge. The weather is almost good enough for a game of tennis in the courts on St.

Marks, but then everyone I know who'd be up for a game is probably at work. By the time I get back it's time for lunch, and there's a shit load more mail for me in the hallway. None of it looks good; far too many official looking envelopes with URGENT plastered all over them. I dump them unopened on the table by the front door, and heat up a tin of soup, then flop on the couch with Empire of Blood and a fat reefer.

It's dark when I wake up, and I'm hungry. The clock on the TV says 10.55, and that's when I realise that I've been asleep for around five hours. I paused the game momentarily to shut my eyes, and just went out, sparko.

I flick on the TV to BBC1, and there I am. A lifetime ago, and I can remember it as if it were yesterday. I'm standing in Richmond Park, looking at the woman playing my mother as she walks away holding her new boyfriend's hand. Twenty minutes in, and it's coming up to the end of the first act. Sally, my mother, is now with Mark, her new boyfriend, and I can sense the truth that she can't see; that he is in fact a total wanker. My dad died in the first five minutes, so Mark is obviously going to be a wrong 'un.

I'm watching my teenage self as a tear rolls down my cheek, and I have to give myself credit; it's quite a performance. As the warmth of the early evening sun falls on my face, the shot holds and I look hurt, angry and confused, all rolled into one. This was a shot that we did early in production, and there's a reason why my performance looks so fucking convincing.

Because when the camera was rolling, I was hurt, angry and confused.

James Laurenson had spent most of the afternoon gently preparing me for this scene. We'd talked about what was going on in Tim's, my character's, head, and how he was going to light it and shoot it.

It's the beginning of June. It's a warm evening. All the crew are milling about waiting for magic hour so that James, the fucking wunderkind, can get his shot. We've played the scene where Mark talks to me and ruffles my hair, and they've got the coverage of them walking away into the setting sun.

We're all set up for my close-up. James comes over to me, talks quietly, and we're ready to go.

All is quiet. He calls 'action.' The camera has been turning over for about fifteen seconds when he calls 'cut.'

And he starts screaming. To the producer, to the crew. About whose fucking stupid idea was it to get this fucking adolescent? This – cunt – who can't act his way out of a fucking paper bag?

He's pointing at me and screaming. And I'm standing there, feeling like someone's ripped my fucking stomach out, and I feel a tear roll down my cheek.

Out of the corner of my eye I see one of the grips smile, and my cheeks flush with shame.

The only sound in Richmond Park is the gentle whir of a camera turning over. Somewhere in the distance a cuckoo calls.

Laurenson calls 'cut.' And that's it for the day. The lady from wardrobe with a kind face, Moira, comes over and puts her arm round my shoulders. I manage to keep it together until we reach the trailer where I collapse in floods of tears. She hugs me and tells me not to worry. That everything will be okay.

Laurenson doesn't come to see me in the trailer. Doesn't apologise. Doesn't explain. I'm a fourteen-year-old boy, adrift in a world of adults who make no sense. My mum comes to pick me up that evening, and Laurenson speaks to her. In the car on the way home she asks me how the day went, and I tell her fine.

It took all my energy to wake up the next morning and go back to the set. It's the last place I wanted to be. The thought of facing the crew, looking Laurenson in the eye after the humiliation of the night before was too much to bear. I tried to pretend that I was feeling sick, that I couldn't make it; but Mum wasn't having any of it and kicked me out of bed in time for the driver to pick me up at half 6.

I arrived at the house where we were doing the filming, and it was as if nothing had ever happened. One of the sparks nodded to me as I got into the trailer. I pulled on the clothes that Moira had laid out and sat waiting in my chair for Lorraine to come and do my make-up. She walked in after a couple of minutes still finishing her bacon sandwich, squeezed my shoulder, and started applying foundation to my cheeks.

Then James Laurenson came into the trailer.

"How you doing Charlie?" he asked, grinning.

"Alright," I mumbled. I could feel my cheeks going scarlet again, despite making myself a silent promise in the car on the way in that I was not going to let him upset me ever again.

"You ready for today's scene? Finding Mark's letter to Sally?"

I nod, keeping my eyes fixed between Lorraine and I in the mirror. He must know I'm upset; I'm thinking. Any minute now, and he'll apologise.

"Good lad," says James, still grinning. And he leaves the trailer. There was no apology. And none ever came.

I felt like shit for the rest of the shoot, so much so that one morning I was sick. I couldn't work out why James wanted me in the fucking film if I was such a shitty actor. And the butterflies in my stomach turned to writhing maggots, and I spewed. All over the trailer. Moira held me as I shook and told her that I couldn't do this anymore.

I saw her, later, talking to James in hushed tones at the side of the set. She looked angry, pointing her finger back towards the trailer.

That was the last day she worked on the shoot. The next day her assistant took over for the last ten days, and she was never as kind to me.

I ran into Moira about ten years later when I was playing a narcoleptic cop on an ill-advised comedy feature. We hugged for a good five minutes, and then I asked her what she said to James that day. She smiled at me and pinched my cheek.

"I told him to stop behaving like such a cunt, darling. He didn't like it very much."

'The Twelfth of Never' wasn't a massive hit when it came out, but it did good business, especially for a low budget British movie. And the critics loved it. I had to admit, it looked fantastic; Roger lit the thing beautifully, and Laurenson knows how to tell a story. With the benefit of age, I can look back and acknowledge that he knew what he was doing; as he got a performance out of me that I remain proud of, despite everything.

It's said that a director needs a tiny sliver of ice in his heart to do his job. James Laurenson has a fucking glacier in what passes for his. He was fucking with me to get a performance; the perpetual state of terror and confusion that he manufactured for me was perfect for the film, and it burns through on every frame.

But he never apologised for what he put me through. And for a while I thought I'd never act again.

Belinda, who plays my mother, puts her arm around my shoulder, and the camera stays on my face. There's a slow fade to black, and the credits roll over a lone cello.

There are tears in my eyes, but they're not for the joyous reuniting of Tim with his mother. They're tears of mourning for a part of myself that I lost over that summer, and I don't think I've ever got back. Prior to that film, I had a lust, a joy for acting that I didn't think could ever fade; after that, when I finally started again, there was always a low-lying dread whenever I approached a film set.

It's gone half 12 as the credits roll on the screen. I'm tired. Mentally fucking drained through reliving that once again. I draw on the last of the reefer in the ashtray and kill it before taking myself off to bed.

Friday night.

It's been a good week.

Carol was back on the phone the day after 'The Twelfth of Never', and the meeting with Meg at Salt and Acre is all set up for the end of next week. I'm supposed to be getting a copy of the pilot script sent over on Monday, so I'll just keep my fingers crossed it's not a complete turkey.

As predicted, a couple of 'low budget' screenplays have already started trickling into the office, and I'm not going to hold my breath about the quality.

But right now, I'm fresh out of the shower, Nick's pumping out tunes from the Ipod, there's beers in the fridge, we're two spliffs in and he's racking out a couple of fat lines on the table in the lounge.

It's a good party table; one I picked up from Golborne Road about five years ago when I was feeling flush. It's five foot long and two foot wide, and the surface is all mirror. I don't hit the beak anywhere near as much as I used to, but on the occasion that we get nasty, this table is still the way to go.

Nick picked up a couple of grams from one of the sparks on the commercial he's just come off, and it's pretty poky stuff. That's one thing about working in the film business; on the whole you'll get better quality drugs. We did the first line about half an hour ago, and my teeth are still tingling now. The shower felt fantastic, even more so as it followed a fat coke dump – always a good idea to get it out of the way early in the evening.

I rifle through my wardrobe, swigging on a beer as my head bobs up and down to Jay-Z. I could really do with buying some new clothes, but that's not going to happen until I earn some real money again. Every one of these shirts has seen better days, and in the end, I go for a darkish blue linen number from Paul Smith that still cuts the mustard. I haven't shaved since last weekend, so there's now a good smattering of stubble on my face.

I run my tongue over my teeth, and rub my jaw, leaning over the mirror to get a good look at myself. A few lines coming in, but I still look pretty fucking good for my age, even though I say so myself. Still a full head of hair, greying at the edges but with a tinge of boyish curls that somehow works. Not bad looking. I may never be a matinee idol, but I do okay.

I swagger back into the living room where Nick is busy carving out a couple of beasts on the table. I lean in to grab a skin and begin to roll one up for later.

He looks up at me. His jaw is already going. "Good gear," he says.

"Too right." I take a fag from the packet and spark it up as I empty another one into the Rizla. That's the thing about my namesake drug; it makes me want to smoke. Not just smoke, come to that. It makes me want to scream, to fight, to drink, to run, to fuck like a madman.

It's probably not very good for me. But I fucking love it.

I drag deeply and blow the smoke high in the air. I'm flaking the Charas off into the Rizla now, and my foot is dancing its own little fucking jig as I do so. Fag in the ashtray for a second, and I'm picking the Rizla up, a lick (where the fuck has my spit gone?) and it's rolled.

And in the meantime, Nick is still pissing about on the table with his credit card, running it up and down the coke like fucking Rain Man.

"Come on, you cunt," I tell him. "I'm itching to get out."

"Alright, Charlie. Fucking hell."

I look at him. He always looks like this at the start of a night, but he'll soon settle into it. He always gets uptight and fucking twitchy off the first couple of lines, but he's fine once he's out and in a fucking boozer.

He picks up the rolled up twenty on the table, and leans in, takes the whole line in one big sniff. He chucks the note across the table to me, and I come over to his side. I lean over, and up it goes.

He grins at me. The world draws sharply into focus.

"Let's fucking have it," I tell him.

We're out of the door, and in the taxi that's been idling outside for the last ten minutes. There's never any question of where we're going to go. We always start at the Mason's Arms. Kensal Green may be a fucking toilet, but it does have a very good boozer going for it.

Not a word is spoken for the five minutes it takes to ferry us up to the Harrow Road, and the only sound we make is an occasional deep snort to try and make sure none of the precious powder escapes. I can sense the driver eyeballing me in the rear-view mirror, and it could be because he recognises my face, or it could be because I'm off my fucking tits; either way, I don't give a fuck.

He pulls up outside the pub, and we pile out. Nick leans in to hand him a tenner, and a quick nod to the big fucker on the door, and we're in.

It's busy. Friday night, and this place is still revelling in its position as the top dog of West London pubs. There's a host of familiar faces in the place, but after a quick look round we decide to check out what's upstairs.

I'm straight to the bar and order us in a couple of pints. It's busy already, but then there's nothing new there. Most of the faces in here will have been in straight from work and won't be going anywhere in a hurry until they call closing. I'm on nodding terms with the guy behind the bar; we were introduced once but I'm fucked if I can remember his name. I turn and give Nick his pint, and true to form, his jaw has begun to settle down a bit now we've made it out.

All the couches are gone, and we sip our beers for a while, looking around to see if there's a likely table we can crash. A few familiar faces here and there, but no-one you'd want to sit down and have a fucking drink with.

Then Jimmy D cruises past. I nudge him.

"Oy, oy" I say.

"Charlie!" He grins, takes my right hand and leans in for a chest bump. "How's it going?"

"Alright, Jimmy. Not bad. You know Nick, don't you?"

The pair of them nod to each other. "Hello mate."

"So how's the cocktails? Night off?"

He turns his head, looks over at a table where a blonde sits nursing a vodka and tonic. I've seen her around, but then that goes for most of the people in the room. He grins.

"Got a date. But business is good."

Jimmy D runs a private bar business, providing cocktail makers and shakers for events and parties. I got to know him from sampling his wares myself at a couple of his parties, and he's always taken care of me whenever he's seen me on the other side of the bar. He's also pretty generous when it comes to doling out late night liveners, and we bonded properly over a couple of fat ones at a country house do about three years ago. I'm sure it doesn't do his business any harm to be seen with the almost famous either, but he genuinely seems like one of the good guys.

"Do you want to come join?" he asks. "Squeeze on our couch?"

I grin at Nick. "Why not?"

We follow him over and are introduced to Poppy. Even sitting down, you can tell she must be well over six foot tall in the killer heels she's wearing. Jimmy D comes in at around five eight, and it's not the first time I've seen him with a girl who towers over him. Must be some kink of his to be lorded over by Amazonian blondes.

Poppy turns out to be an occasional journalist stroke model; the translation for that being she's a trust fund baby with a laptop and a coke habit. She immediately sniffs the drugs out on Nick, and charms him into passing her the wrap, and she's off to the bogs to tuck in. There's a glimmer of pain in Nick's eyes as he watches her go and looks over to me; we both know that the likelihood is that there will be very little change out of that wrap once she's back from the bathroom, as she will have tried to cram as much up her nose as is humanly possible. To be fair, it's probably what I would do in the circumstances.

Jimmy D tells us all about how they met while she's off tooting. They hooked up at her uncle's house in the Cotswolds where he'd been running the bar for a party a fortnight ago, and it all got a little out of control, with a bunch of them all ending up in a Jacuzzi in the basement watching a friend of hers sucking someone off. I can well believe it – it's always the wealthy ones who are the worst behaved.

She comes back a while later, her eyes popping out on stalks and passes the wrap back to Nick. He grins, tight-lipped, and shoves it back in his pocket.

"I'm gagging for a ciggie," says Poppy, licking her lips. "Who wants one?"

"I'll come," I say. "We'll pick up some drinks on the way back. Same again?"

Nick nods. Jimmy winks, raises his glass. "Vodka and tonic."

I follow Poppy out onto the roof terrace. It's still fucking freezing, and so we crouch under a patio heater. I fish out my packet of fags, as I've learnt the hard way that I always end up smoking on a night on the gak. At least if I bring a pack out with me, I don't end up being one of those no-marks who ends up poncing off everyone else all night. I offer the pack to Poppy, and she takes one. I light them both, and we smoke in silence for a moment. She's shivering.

"Have we met?" she asks. "You look familiar."

I smile. "I get that a lot. I don't think so. You might have seen me in something though. I'm an actor."

She looks at me, and then her eyes open wide in recognition. "Oh my God! It's you. From that film! The one that was on the other night."

"The Twelfth of Never."

"That's it. God. That's a good film."

"Yeah. It is."

"I thought you were very good. Honestly. Really good. It was James Laurenson's first film, wasn't it? He's such an amazing director. My friend Angelica worked on the publicity for the studio that released 'Cinnamon', and she said he's really a genius. An absolute genius. You're so lucky to work with him. Angelica says he's a lot funnier than most people would think at first. But then, she's hysterical herself…"

I zone out, and smile and nod. The only thing that's worse than listening to someone on a coke rant is listening to a fucking idiot Laurenson fan on a coke rant. Poppy is pretty, I'll give her that, but I've known her for about fifteen minutes, and she's already taken all our drugs and now she's boring the fucking shit out of me.

Smile and nod. Smile and nod.

I stand there pretending to take in what she's saying until I finish the fag. I drop it on the floor and grind it out with my heel, then do a little mock shiver and lead Poppy back inside. She's still banging on about Laurenson.

We go to the bar to pick up some drinks on the way back. It's too much to fucking hope that Poppy's going to stick her hand in her designer handbag and spring for a round – girls like her never do. They'll talk about themselves all night while doing all your coke, but there's fat fucking chance of them getting the drinks in.

She's still dribbling on in my ear as I catch the bartender's eye and place my order. There's a tiny half smile of recognition from him; not because he's seen me in anything, but because no doubt he's been on the other end of a coke-fuelled rant from a Trustafarian and he can see I'm beginning to lose the will to live.

I pass a couple of glasses to Poppy, and we make our way back to the table.

"Did you know Charlie was an actor?" she asks Jimmy D, who fakes surprise and looks at me.

"Yeah, but not a very good one," he says.

"Fuck off," I tell him, and sink into the seat next to Nick. I feel like talking to a normal human being for a while, rather than some rabid blonde who is probably already working out an angle on me that could in some way further her 'career'.

I lean into Nick. "Terrible cunt," I murmur.

"Tell me about it. She's more or less cleared out that wrap."

"I wouldn't worry. Jimmy's usually carrying."

Poppy's away now, whaling on Jimmy with all the wit and wisdom that powder brings, and he's smiling and nodding, smiling and nodding. You have to hand it to him; the man is a pro. He's prepared to put up with no end of drivelling nonsense if there's the chance of a shag at the end of it.

Nick and I sit there for a while, taking in all the movers and shakers that West London has to offer.

"Thanks for that rent thing," I say, breaking the silence.

"No worries, man. My pleasure. You thought about who you're going to get in yet?"

"Not yet."

"I can ask around if you like? Put a couple of good guys forward?"

I turn to him. "You sure you want to move out? You can keep your room for a while if you like. I'll do you a deal."

He shakes his head. "The time has come, Charlie. You know when you know, right? And Alex and I are serious."

"You love her." I'm trying not to, but I can't help sounding a little cynical as I say it. It ends up coming out sounding far more poisoned than I intended.

Nick turns to me and nods. "Yeah, I do. I'm sorry it's not working out for you personally, Charlie, with the flat and everything, but that's just the way it fucking goes." There's a flash of anger in his eyes. Never come between a mate and his bird. "I mean, you've never made any attempt to disguise just how much you don't fucking like her."

Shit. And I thought I was at least putting a brave fucking face on the whole affair. Of course I don't fucking like her. She's a hobbit witch. Imagine the poison dwarf from the end of Don't Look Now with a more expensive taste in clothes, and you're coming close to Alex. But then, the antipathy is very mutual. She clearly thinks I'm a cunt and has made no attempt to disguise that, so it's no wonder that I don't fucking like her. But I can see that Nick is getting fucking twitchy, and I don't want to lose one of the few good mates I have.

"It's not that I don't like her," I lie. "It's just that I always get the impression that she doesn't like me very much. And, well, I guess I just feel a little defensive."

Crisis averted. I've clearly hit the nail on the head, as the flash of anger has gone and is now replaced by a shiftiness evidently born out of deep discomfort. Alex, you cunt, I think. She's clearly been pouring poison in his fucking ear for some time. At least I've got the fucking decency to not slag her off to Nick's face.

"She does like you," says Nick. "It's just that you're very different people."

He's a fucking terrible liar. He needs to get that sorted if he's going to last the duration with Alex, because she's so high maintenance that it's inevitable he's going to have to tell the occasional fib. Now I just feel like playing, to see where this will go. Nick's a pretty honest and forthright guy, and coke has the magic effect of loosening anyone's tongue.

"I know," I say, nodding solemnly. "I know we're very different people." And I just leave it hanging there, waiting to see if he'll take the bait. He jumps straight on the hook.

"Alex went to a public school and studied really hard," he says. "Not that there's anything wrong with not going to university," he adds quickly, "but her background is just very different. She's very academic."

"Mmmm," I say nodding.

"She studied hard, you know Charlie. Really hard. She got a first. From Cambridge! That's an incredible achievement."

"Wow," I say nodding. "Sometimes I wish I'd gone to university."

That's not bullshit. That's true. I do wish I'd gone to uni. A little piece of me can't help feeling like an inferior thick cunt because I never went, even though it's manifestly obvious to me that three years of drinking, drugs and fucking with a degree at the end of it does not make anyone a genius. But the main reason is I think it would have been a fucking good laugh.

"She doesn't think you're stupid," Nick adds. "Far from it. She thinks you're a very bright guy."

Be still my beating heart, I think. I smile and wait for him to continue.

"She's just been brought up with this incredible work ethic. She's always studied really hard, and now she's at the chambers and has got her head down there."

I can read the subtext here. "So, she thinks I'm lazy?"

"No, god no," says Nick, as his face tells me I've scored a bullseye. "It's just that, well, I don't think she understands the life of an actor, that's all."

Meaning she thinks I sit round on my arse all day long, doing fuck all. Fair enough, at the moment that's true, but when I'm working it's hardcore. I bet even Alex would be hard pushed to do some of the hours that I've put in on set – sixteen-hour days, alternating between day and night shoots? She should give that a go before deciding my life is just one big fucking picnic.

"You know how hard it can be, sometimes," I say. "It can be very tough, when you're working. It's just that you're not always working."

"I know," he says. "Believe me, I've tried to explain it to her. But I just don't think she gets it."

"Is she happy with what you do?"

"I think she'd like it if I got something a little more permanent. And sometimes I'm tempted myself. I don't need to tell you what it's like."

Too right. Recently I've felt like I've been losing my fucking mind for want of a job. But that could be all about to change.

"I forgot to say," I tell Nick. "I've got a meeting next week about something that could be interesting. You know Salt and Acre?"

He nods. "Yeah, they did that cop thing for the Beeb last year, didn't they?"

"Towards the Edge. Yeah, not bad. They picked up a couple of Bafta noms."

"Cool. So, what's the part?"

"I'm still waiting for the script, but it sounds like it could be a bit of a winner. A surgeon. Lead. Bit of a bastard."

"Perfect. You wouldn't even have to act."

I can't help but grin. "Fuck off cunt."

Nick grins back. "See? It's like the lines write themselves."

Jimmy D leans over. "Fancy a change of scene? We were going to try Kensal Road."

The Blag. That could be good. I've been looking around while Nick and I have been talking and there's not much in the way of available women.

Jimmy grins as he sees me take in the room. "Poppy's meeting a couple of friends down there," he says with a wink.

"Why not? You up for it?" I ask Nick.

"Sure," he says.

We down our drinks and follow Jimmy out. If he didn't have an office upstairs then there's no chance we'd bother, but he's got a desk in one of the units on the second floor. This is good for two reasons; firstly it means that we can get straight in without any bollocks from the door bitch who would otherwise be more than happy to keep us outside for half an hour, and secondly it gives us somewhere discreet to all go off and do a cheeky line or two, rather than cramming ourselves into one of the nasty cubicles with the other plebs.

We walk out of the Masons and Jimmy manages to flag a cab down straightaway. We all pile in, and we're off for the short hop, cutting down Kensal Road after the Bridge, past what used to be Virgin records and is now a set of flats for Hedge fund managers. Even if I was Brad fucking Pitt you couldn't get me to live there; it's way too public. Like living in a fucking goldfish bowl.

Seconds later and the taxi's pulling up outside. Jimmy drops a tenner through the window, and we waltz in as he flashes his key fob and points out the four of us.

We're in, and Poppy spies three good looking women, and with a little squeal runs over to join her mates. Jimmy keeps walking past the bar, towards the door that leads to the offices.

"Jimmy. Wanna drink?" I ask him.

He winks at me and beckons his head to follow him. He holds the door open for Nick and me, and then we're in. The noise from the bar immediately drops ten decibels.

"Let's leave her to it for a minute," says Jimmy.

We troop up the stairs and onto the second floor, and Jimmy lets us into his office.

He sublets a desk from a mate of his who makes T-shirts, and the walls are lined with designs, past and present. They mostly feature animals with speech balloons, all very ironic and West London, but still cool. Beast. They retail for around forty quid a pop, which is a small fortune for a T-shirt, but they look good. I own a couple myself. Jimmy goes to the fridge and pulls out a bottle of vodka, and some tonic to go with it, and fixes the three of us a drink at the sink.

Nick takes this as his cue, and gets the second, full wrap out of his pocket and starts chopping out some lines on Jimmy's desk. I get the spliff out of my pocket, and spark it up, opening a window so we can smoke out of it. Jimmy brings the glasses over, and we all chink.

"Cheers," he says.

"Cheers." I say back and pass the spliff over. I look at Nick, who's already showing all the dedication to chopping out coke of an autistic ten-year-old with a Rubik's cube. I raise my eyebrows to Jimmy D. "This could be some time."

"Fuck. Off." Nick's gaze never wanders from what he's doing as he says this, and there's something about the way he delivers it that creases me up. He looks up. "Seriously though, this is fucking rocky gear. This dedication ensures a smoother ride."

"You're a nob," I tell him. Jimmy is puffing away on the reefer when his phone rings. He looks at the call display and ignores it.

"Poppy," he says to us by way of explanation. He raises his eyebrows. "Treat 'em mean, keep 'em keen. Besides, she's just on the sniff."

Nick grins as he rolls up a twenty and leans in to hoover up a line. Cutter's choice. Sure, his looked like the biggest of the three, but it's nothing that Jimmy or I would have done differently. He offers the note to me, and I come over to hover. I must deliberate over the two for a second too long, as Jimmy quietly says behind me,

"Choices, choices."

"I'll have both if you're not careful," I say, and take the left one in one fell swoop. It's been a while since the last line back at the flat, and this one kicks everything back into gear. My nose burns, and the drop is already making its way down the back to where it's going to make me feel like I'm about to have my tonsils out.

I pass the note to Jimmy and as he leans in to do his, his phone starts ringing again.

"She's keen," I say.

He comes up smiling and wiping a finger over the surface rubs what's left of the gear above his shining white teeth. "What can I say? She's had a little of the Jimmy D magic."

"More like Paul fucking Daniels," I say. I sniff hard and swig long on the Vodka and tonic to try and wash it all down.

"Nice," says Nick.

"Come on then," says Jimmy, draining his glass. "Let's get back downstairs and see what's going on."

We're all quite charged as we wait for the lift to take us back downstairs, but clearly, we're not going to take the stairs.

Nick's foot is going like Michael Flatley with Parkinson's, and I can feel myself itching to get amongst it.

We walk back into the bar, and it's still heaving. Poppy spots us, and rushes over to Jimmy D, dragging him over to where she's sitting with three other girls, every one of them a little too cool for school. Nick and I are introduced, and Poppy's clearly already briefed them that I'm some kind of famous actor, as they're already checking me out. I sit down next to one of them, a brunette called Chloe. She's five ten, dresses well, and is cute, even if she's all too aware of the fact.

"Hi," I say.

"Hi," she says, with a smile that tells me that this is pretty much in the bank, and I don't have a lot to do if I want to take her home with me tonight.

"So, what do you do?" I ask her.

"I teach yoga," she says.

I smile. And nod. Because I honestly don't know what to say. What I want to ask is 'Are you fucking serious? Another yoga teacher?' because it's not like there seems to be any kind of shortage. Every other girl I've met over thirty seems to be a yoga teacher, which can only beg the question, who is left to actually take any of these fucking classes? Or is it that they all just rally round on some kind of infinite loop, attending each other's sessions until they're so all flexible they can literally disappear up their own arse?

I don't say that. Rather I say, "I like yoga. I find it really relaxing."

This roughly translates as 'I took a couple of classes last year but found it deeply fucking irritating.' But then I'm quite happy to feed this girl a load of bollocks, as I'm not planning on seeing her past breakfast tomorrow.

She smiles, leans forward and touches my hand. "I saw that film you were in the other night." She looks down, leaving her hand there. "It made me cry."

My cock twitches. This is about as clear a come-on as I've ever had, and between her laying it on with a trowel, and the coke making me feel deeply fucking groovy, I'm feeling like fucking Superman.

"Thanks Chloe," I say, and as I look at her, I'm picturing her naked. "That means a lot." I touch her hand with mine, and out of the corner of my eye I can see her harpy mates nudge each other. "Can I get you a drink?"

She smiles. "Vodka and tonic please."

I stand up, look around. "Anyone else?"

I've timed this well. The girls had clearly got a round in while we were upstairs, and so it's just one for Chloe, and Jimmy. I look around, but there's no sign of Nick. This wouldn't be the first time he's sloped off mid evening, but then I might have done a runner if I was forced to talk to the other two dragons on the table.

I wander over to the bar. I can sense a lot of glances being cast over towards my right. I take my position at the bar and use the mirror to check out who the focus of the attention is.

It's Lucy Fontaine. And my heart sinks just a little. Since I worked with her on a 'The Trampoline,' a little low budget feature about five years ago, our careers have gone in polar opposite directions. I didn't even think she was still in London, as the last I heard she was making studio pictures in La-la land. It's no wonder everyone's checking her out as the girl is looking good.

I look just a little too long, and she clocks me. I smile and nod, and she grins a little too widely and mouths a big "Hi!" Great. So now I've got to go and find out just how fucking fantastic her life is.

I get the round in, and am thinking about swerving saying hello, but Lucy clocks me and beckons me over. I squeeze over to her, and we do the kissy cheek thing.

"Hey Lucy. How's things?"

"Great, Charlie. How are you? Busy?"

There's no-one else I recognise, which probably means they're old acolytes or studio twats from the States. Either way, I'm being routinely ignored, and Lucy shows no sign of introducing me; so I guess this is a flying visit to her table to make her look even more popular and interesting.

"Not bad. You're doing well I see."

Since the Trampoline she's been in a couple of big summer hits that she's been smart enough to ballast with two or three director lead character projects that show her acting chops, and she routinely gets great reviews. Plus, she's absolutely gorgeous; big Bambi eyes peek out from underneath a long choppy fringe, and she's got a smile that can stop traffic. I tried it on myself with her at the wrap party for the Trampoline, but unfortunately, she knocked me back. Not that I can blame her, as her refusal is one of the few things I can remember about that party. I was extremely pissed.

She raises her eyes, and half shrugs her shoulders in a vain attempt to appear self-deprecating, but we both know that she's on a great run and are both trying to avoid to fact that my career is, comparatively, floundering in the toilet.

"Yeah, she says. It's good at the moment. I'm speaking to Woody Allen about possibly doing something next year."

I can't help but smirk at this, as if anything is going to arrest her career it'll be working with Woody. He's phoned in the last couple of things that I've seen. Fucking atrocious.

"Wow," I say. "Woody Allen? Cool."

She takes a sip from the champagne flute she's holding, and looking round the table to check no-one's listening, she then leans in close to my cheek. My heart does a little flutter, and I'm already picturing walking out of here with Lucy Fontaine and throwing her about my bedroom. I bet she tastes amazing. Like spiced honey.

"Don't say anything, but I had a meeting with someone you know about something very exciting," she says.

"Oh?" I say, trying not to sound deflated.

"James Laurenson. God, he's amazing, isn't he? Just so fucking intense."

There's a nasty taste in my throat, and it's not just the coke. Why is it everyone always ends up talking about fucking Laurenson?

"Yeah, he's definitely intense."

"What's he like to work with?" she asks.

And I know I shouldn't, but I can't help it. She's asked me, and even as I open my mouth, I know this isn't a smart move.

"Actually Lucy, he's a gigantic cunt."

"Oh," she says. I'm trying to read her expression, but she's not saying anything. She's just looking at me, studying me, not really giving anything away. And then she hears one of the guys on the table say something, and she turns and laughs.

And our conversation is over.

"Nice to see you Lucy," I say, a little too loudly, and I walk back towards Chloe and the table holding the drinks. I hand Jimmy D his Vodka and tonic, and then I sit back down next to Chloe, a little too clumsily.

"What took you?" she asks, smiling.

"It's a nightmare getting served in here."

Chloe looks at me, and the tiniest of furrows forms in her brow. "You okay Charlie?"

I turn and give her my best wolfish grin. "I'm just dandy. And how are you?"

This is just fucking unbelievable.

I lie back on my bed and try to work out why it all went wrong. Chloe and I got back about an hour ago. Nick was here on the couch, a reefer in his mouth and the rest of the gear on the table. I fixed us all a drink, we each had a line and a smoke, and then Chloe asked to see my bedroom.

She kisses me, and we fall onto the bed. In no time we're under the covers and we're down to our underwear, and she's wearing some very nice stuff that shows off her yoga-toned body to perfection. I rub my hand over her stomach, and I realise that there's absolutely no reaction from my cock whatsoever. It's like it's fucking flatlined down there. I try to prolong the foreplay for a while, sucking on her tits to see if that might spark something, but there's nothing. She reaches down to grab hold of my erection and discovers there isn't one.

"I'm really sorry," I say. And then I trot out the big lie, and I'm betting it's not the first time she's heard it; "This has never happened to me before."

"Don't worry, Charlie," she says, but I can tell she clearly thinks I'm a total fucking loser. "These things happen."

"It's probably the coke," I say.

"Probably," she says. And she's leaning back in the bed. I'm looking at her face, and I may be paranoid, but I think there's the faint glimmer of amusement there. Perhaps she's already rehearsing revising the story of how she once fucked Charlie Reed, the actor, to one of Charlie Reed can't get it up.

She swings her legs out of bed. I reach out and stroke her back. I try to sound masterful, and like this really doesn't bother me as I say: "You don't want to hang around for a bit? Have another go?"

She turns and smiles at me. "I've got a lot on tomorrow. Need to go and see my parents. Another time, eh?"

I smile. "Sure."

But we both know I'm not going to call her. We're both silent as she dresses, and I spark up the rest of the spliff that's sitting in the ashtray by my bed. She's all set in next to no time.

"You don't want me to call a taxi?" I ask.

"I'll be fine. It's not too far to the Grove from here. I'll grab one there."

I nod. "Sure. Okay."

She smiles but doesn't bother coming over to kiss me or anything. I'm not even going to embarrass myself by asking for her number.

"See you Charlie." And she's out of the door and gone.

I listen to see if there's any sign of life from Nick next door, but it's dead to the world. I'm fucking relieved, as the last thing I want to go through is any explanation as to why Chloe has just undertaken a moonlight flit when I should be nuts deep.

No. Now it's just me with my whirring brain for company.

Of course it's fucking happened to me before, although it's been a very long time since the last time little Charlie let me down. I'm racking my brains trying to work out how and why. It's not just the fucking coke. There have been plenty of times in the past when I've fucked like an angry donkey for hours on the stuff with no detrimental effects on my cock whatsoever. It was that fucking conversation with Lucy Fontaine, and the fact that she's going to be working with that cunt Laurenson. And that she should then cut me dead for telling her the truth about the man. That, and that my life is in a state of flux. Nick's moving out, I need a job, and every other fucker I've ever borrowed money from is ringing my phone off the hook to try and claw it back.

I don't know where the fuck my life is going.

I'm thirty-seven years old, and I'm behaving like an adolescent. I finish the spliff and stub it out.

And I get a flash of Callie. She would always skin up a post-coital reefer, and would always, always pass it to me to light and smoke first. Unchaining the dragon, she'd call it.

Callie. Five foot eight, auburn hair, green eyes, perfect. And I blew it.

It's been five years since we broke up, and she was the closest I've ever come to settling down. We were together for nearly eleven months. She was working in a dubbing studio where I went to do some ADR on 'The Trampoline', and she started flirting with me. I had come in at the end of the session and so took her out afterwards for dinner. It was a perfect evening – one of those times when the universe comes together, and everything just clicks. I managed to get a cancellation at this swish little Japanese place I know, and we plied each other with sake until we could barely stand. We ended up in a cab back here, and barely left the bedroom for the rest of the weekend.

Callie was beautiful, but there was far more to her than that. She was smart - smart enough to see through my bullshit, and she just got me. She'd call me out, especially when I was being cynical; she'd say that it was just a defence mechanism. That I was worth more than the negativity I was showing. I fell for her in a big way, and she for me. We'd probably still be together now if I hadn't fucked it up. She'd arranged to come down to the set of a TV thing I was filming. I knew she was coming, and that was probably in the back of my mind when I decided to fuck the naughty little wardrobe minx who'd been coming on to me for the past week. So, when Callie walked into the trailer the first thing she saw was this skank going down on me. She just looked at me. She didn't even bother to say anything. Didn't get angry, didn't scream, nothing. What always stays with me is this look of pity that she shot me – that she knew she was worth way more than this; that she knew that it was a clumsy act of sabotage on my behalf, perhaps to test her to see what she would do. But most of all, it was a look that told me that she knew that I would remember this moment in years to come, and bitterly regret the moment I let her go.

And she was right.

I wonder, from time to time, where I would be now if Callie and I were still together. Perhaps we'd have got married, perhaps we'd have moved out of London, perhaps we'd have kids.

But I know I'd have been happier.

I went back to the ADR studio about this time last year and ran into one of the engineers who had worked with her. I tried to sound nonchalant as I asked him about her. He told me he'd been to her wedding a couple of years ago. Turns out she'd married this 'lovely guy' she'd met snowboarding, and she was now expecting twins. It was like a knife in my guts. It could have been me. I know that Callie loved me. Deep down, I loved her, more than I've ever loved anyone else. But I'm such a fucking idiot that I never realised that at the time.

The wisdom that hindsight brings.

I've not had that many regrets in my life but letting Callie go is one of the biggest. There's plenty of jobs I've gone for and didn't get, but that's part of working in this industry. You win some, you lose some. But that's all out of your control. What I did that day was a conscious act, albeit one born of massive stupidity, and it led me to throw away something precious and valuable. And that was self-destructive.

I lie back in my bed for a while, looking at the ceiling. There's fuck all chance of me getting any sleep any time soon, what with the combination of coke and self-loathing that's coursing through my system. I begin to skin up another reefer and it occurs to me that I'm running low, and I should probably pay Bob another visit at some time soon. The last thing I want to do is end up without any puff. It may mean that I actually have to deal with reality, and right now that's a terrifying proposition.

I spark up the joint and lay back in my bed and pick up my book. Even as the pages fall open, I can feel it's going to be a pointless fucking exercise as my mind's got all the focus of a drunk tramp with a bag of chips. I drag deeply, shut my eyes and try to tell myself not to think.

FEBRUARY

I want you to cross the kitchen. Open the fridge door.

Stand there a moment.

Do you feel sad?

Look sad.

Sadder.

Good.

Cut.

I come out of Oxford Circus on the Apple Store side of Regents Street, figuring, as I'm early, that I may as well kill some time lusting after shit I can't afford. It's a short walk from the tube to the store but it's still like the fucking Krypton Factor dodging Italian tourists who seem to have forgotten how to fucking walk the moment they stepped off the plane at Stansted. I get it, that you're in a foreign city, and that you're going to want to slow down and look around, but some of these halfwits seem to have lost all motor skills and just dawdle around slack-jawed; sheep in dayglo fucking backpacks.

I should be used to it living where I do; anyone who's ever been near Portobello Road on a Saturday knows that it's a fucking Mecca to continental teenagers into candles and scented soaps. They'll either get off at Notting Hill and work their way up to Portobello Green, or off at Ladbroke Grove and back down the other way; either way if for any reason you need to get something, or meet anyone on Portobello at the weekend, then forget it. There's been a couple of occasions when I've tried to meet people for a coffee at the Electric on a Saturday, and I'm always, always late; and more to the point totally fucking exasperated by the general twattery on display.

But it's a short walk from the tube to the Apple store, and I can live with it for a short while. It's nice and toasty inside and gives me a chance to warm up a little before venturing outside again. The snow subsided two days ago after a savage few days, but the beauty and newness of a snowbound London has now given way to a hungover grey slush that covers everything, and that seems to suit the character of the capital so much more. It's still cold though. Bitterly. And as I want to turn up to the Salt and Acre meeting looking halfway presentable, I've gone without wearing a hat as whenever I do it always fucks up my hair. I'd like a good shot at this and turning up with shit hair wouldn't be very surgeon-like, so I decided on hatless. A good idea about forty minutes ago when I left, but not so much now I've been out in the cold for a while. I'm fucking freezing.

I cross over to the new iPhone and start playing around. Nick's got the 6; practically everyone I know has got one for that matter; except of course, for me. It's top of my list once I nail this job and start to bring in some much-needed cash, but right now I'm still getting by with a shitty iPhone 3. I've been trying to front it out for a while, pretending it's a deliberate choice, that I'm happy with this piece of crap as I only need a phone to make calls, but it's all bollocks. I need a new phone.

But not today. "I'm alright mate," I say to one of the store's Stepford kids as he bounds towards me with an idiot corporate grin. My message to the Apple guys? We get it, Apple is a fun company. But that doesn't mean that all your staff needs to bounce around like Tigger with a cure for fucking cancer. I peruse the laptops, and the MacBook Air is the second on my wish list. They look great, and are fast; and right now, anything would be better than the archaic monster I'm currently using.

I quit the Safari page I'm half looking at to check the time in the top right-hand corner. 11.50. That gives me five minutes to make my way to the Salt and Acre office just off Carnaby Street, and I'll still be early.

The one thing that's always stayed with me is something that Brian Townsend said when I first did 'The Mocking Half' in the West End. Being the classically trained old Queen that he was, he was fond of making grand gestures, and he seemed to want to take me under his wing and give me the benefit of his wisdom. Part of me suspects that he wanted to give me quite a bit more than that, but as I was well under the age of consent, he managed to contain himself.

We would always end up in make-up at the same time. He would peer at me in the mirror, a little bleary eyed, and hold forth in stentorian tones, bestowing me with the benefit of all his worldly wisdom. His beard always looked like there was something living in it, and his nose glowed red with a lifetime of boozing, but he was a funny old soak, and he could always have me laughing.

Charlie my boy, he would say, one must always – always - be early.

You'd often be able to smell the red wine that he'd been on since lunch coming through his pores, and he certainly wasn't as fussy about always being sober, but his need for punctuality is something that I've always adhered to.

I'm outside the entrance to Salt and Acre in no time. They've clearly got pots of money, as they've taken up residence in one of the little houses in one of the lanes that peels off Carnaby. I've been to an edit suite in one of these buildings not so long ago, and you need buckets of cash to pay out rent on one of these places. I hit the buzzer. There's a muffled sound through the intercom.

"Hi, Charlie Reed for Meg."

The buzzer sounds immediately, and I push the door. The stairway up to the first floor is lined with posters of past productions, along with some awards. Standard stuff for a successful prodco. There's a big open plan room where a receptionist sits behind a desk. She looks up and smiles, and I smile back. She's in her early twenties, and I'm betting she's fresh out of Uni and is called Amaryllis or Chrysanthemum or something similar. She's wide-eyed and very cute, and still has an air of innocence about her. It won't be long before that goes; it'll all be over when some coked-up director swans in here full of shite and promises and ends up bending her over in some Soho toilet and fucking her senseless.

"Hi," I say. "I'm Charlie Reed. Here to see Meg?"

"Hi Charlie," she says, brightly and full of beans. "Do you want to take a seat? I'll let Meg know you're here. Can I get you anything to drink?"

"Some water would be lovely. Thanks."

She smiles at me and turns to head for a kitchen at the other end of the floor, and it gives me a chance to check out her arse, which is fucking perfect.

"Charlie? Hi."

I turn to see a brunette with short hair looking down at me. Fuck. It is Meg from Armada, and if she didn't like me much before, the fact that she's just caught checking out the blonde's arse won't have improved things much. Not good.

"Meg. Hi." I stand up, and take her hand, shaking it warmly. I've really got to lay on some charm to try and claw this back now. "How's life over here? I bet they're missing you at Armada."

"Daisy's looking after you, I take it?"

Daisy. I knew it would be a flower of some kind. There's something snide in the way she asks the question, the subtext being 'get enough of a peek at her arse, saddo?'

"She is, thanks. Yes."

Daisy returns with a glass, and hands it over. I take it with a smile. Meg is checking me out to see if I do any more letching.

"Do you want to follow me?" She's all business. I'm already thinking that this is fucking pointless. I may as well try and charm a corpse. She walks into a small office where a guy in his early thirties sits with his expensive trainers up on a table. He's wearing a Beast T-shirt underneath a plaid shirt, and his glasses are achingly trendy.

"Giles, Charlie. Charlie, this is Giles Ford. He's directing ep one."

"Charlie, hi. Good to meet you." He flashes a smile at me, and

I'm nearly blinded by the dazzle. He must have spent a fortune getting them whitened.

"You too. Nice T-shirt."

"Cheers."

Meg sits down next to him, indicating for me to sit down opposite them. "You've read the script?"

"Yeah, I love it. I think it's fantastic. Hugo's such a great character." The script wasn't bad at all - definitely better than most of the shit I end up reading, and Hugo seems to have more than the single dimension that a lot of TV characters seem to display. I found myself grinning on more than one occasion as I read the script and could feel myself getting under the skin of the guy.

"It's an unusual take on the hospital drama," I continue. "Seems a lot more psychological than a lot of things I've read."

Giles is nodding, Meg is just looking at me.

"How's things Charlie? Tell us what you've been up to." There's that tiny flicker of cruelty in her smile again as she asks this, like she already knows the answer only too well. What does she expect me to say? Well, actually pretty much fuck all over the last six months since I did a commercial voiceover, but I have been keeping myself busy getting stoned and wanking furiously to internet porn.

"A few things," I say. "I'm talking to a couple of people about some low budget features." Again, this is true. Carol has been wading through the deluge of idiot auteurs who have been sending in their scripts, and a couple have shown some promise. I've had a look, and they're okay. One of them concerns a librarian who is covering up the guilt caused by the accidental death of his brother when they were children, the other one is about a soldier back from Afghanistan. Again, neither of them has any money, but that is par for the course. It's probably something to do with the fact that anyone under the age of thirty thinks that it's their God given right to go on the net and just download whatever they want for nothing. In the real-world people should get paid. Try sauntering into Gucci and waltzing off with something without paying for it and see how easily you get away with that. And, for the record, last time I checked everyone else in the fucking country was getting paid for their jobs, so why the fuck shouldn't I? I'm not seeing many brain surgeons busking on the tube.

"That's great," says Giles, with a total lack of sincerity. "So, you've got the script? We'd like you to read from the top of page twelve, where Hugo is preparing to go into theatre." He leans over to tinker with the small camera that sits on a tripod next to him while I prepare myself.

I take a breath and put on Hugo.

I like this script, and I've been doing quite a lot of homework for this audition. I've been reading stuff on the net, checking out medical textbooks, getting my head in the space of someone who literally has power of life and death over another human being, and the power and arrogance that that must give you. I'm thinking about the intensity of character that can focus for ten hours plus on all aspects of an operation, and the drive that makes you want to do that in the first place. The script makes Hugo's arrogance clear, but he's also charming as well as occasionally cruel. The scene from the top of page twelve sets things out nicely: he's breaking off an affair with a junior surgeon while they both scrub up for theatre, ready to begin a different affair with a hospital administrator later in the episode.

"Just because this is over doesn't mean that you should lose your focus…" I begin.

And then my phone rings.

For a second, I can't quite believe what's happening, but sure enough, my fucking phone is ringing. Meg casts a sly little look to her right at Giles like "can you believe this guy?", and I can't fucking blame her. I always turn my phone off in auditions, always.

Just not today.

I delve into my pocket and pull it out, switching it off. "I'm really sorry about that," I say, mumbling.

"That's okay, Charlie. Whenever you're ready."

The pair of them are sat behind the table looking at me like I'm the world's biggest chump. And I proceed to choke. The phone has thrown me, properly, and for all my efforts to get it together, I'm all over the place. The reading I give wouldn't get me a two-line walk on, let alone Hugo the sexy surgeon. I try and claw it back, and Giles is courteous enough to give me a note which I try and follow, but I know it's not just me but all of us who can breathe a sigh of relief when Meg finally thanks me for coming in.

I pull on my coat, attempt my best smile, and leave the room. Meg doesn't even bother to show me out. Daisy is on the phone as I pass her on the way downstairs, and waves goodbye as I hurry out.

It's fucking freezing outside, and I suddenly have an urge to smoke a cigarette.

McKinley's isn't that far from here, a short walk across Soho to Charing Cross Road, and so I hurry over to see if I can beat Meg before she makes the inevitable phone call to Carol. I keep my head down as I pace across Wardour Street and onto Old Compton, as the last thing I want to do right now is run into anyone even vaguely familiar.

I take a right onto Charing Cross Road, and suddenly it occurs to me that I haven't even checked which fucker just put the kibosh on me getting a job. I pull my phone out and get through to the answerphone.

"Mr. Reed. This is James Adams from Keldon's Financial Services. I'm calling about your Visa account. We need to take the minimum payment from you as soon as possible. Could you call me back on this number at your earliest convenience? Thanks."

You cunt. You total fucking cunt. The rage is all consuming, and my knuckles are white with anger. How the fuck am I meant to make a minimum payment if you call me up when I'm in the middle of trying to get a fucking job?

I'm outside McKinley's. I'm about to hit the buzzer on the door next to one of the bookshops when I check myself. This is not a good idea. Don't go up while you're like this, I tell myself. Breathe. Take a minute.

I walk around the corner and pick up a packet of Marlborough Lights and a box of matches. Taking up smoking again, properly, when I'm being hounded for money might not seem like the best idea, but even as I put the first cigarette in my mouth, even before I light it, I'm getting that reassuring tang of tobacco and chemicals. I light a match, and drag deeply, getting a little nicotine spin as I inhale. And I feel ten times better. Fags are fucking brilliant for that. Long term I know it's a shitty, expensive habit. But the short-term gain is that you feel fucking ace.

I stroll around the corner puffing furiously before I find myself back outside McKinley's. I hit the buzzer, and there's a crackling sound as Annette fumbles the handset off the wall.

"It's Charlie," I say, and there's a buzz.

The inside of the hallway of this building looks like it hasn't seen a lick of paint in about twenty years. I've been coming here that long at least and there's nothing been done to it in all the time. McKinley's is on the first floor up a dark flight of grubby stairs, with lino peeling dangerously away in places.

One wrong move here and you could end up in a tumbled mess at the bottom.

I'm up and on the first floor in no time, and I push the door open and walk in. Annette has left it open and is already back behind her desk and on the phone, and she waves to me and mouths "Hello". I grin back and walk across to Carol's office and poke my head around the door.

She's on the phone jabbering away as a lit fag curls smoke from the corner of her mouth. She's wearing a coat and has a scarf wrapped tight around her neck to counteract the biting wind mixed with exhaust fumes that sails in from the Charing Cross Road. If there was any hope of respite from the cold by coming in here, then I can think again. Carol raises her eyes at me, smiles, and beckons me to sit down opposite her. I do, pulling out my fag packet as I sit down and leaning across the desk to borrow her lighter. She shakes her head in a 'naughty boy' gesture and interrupts whoever is talking on the other end of the line.

"That's great, Nigel. All sounds very interesting. If you can send over a copy of the script, I'll make sure she gets it." She listens for a moment, then interrupts again. "Right, ho, darling. Understood. I must go now; my meeting has just arrived. Alright then, alright. Yes, alright. Bye. Bye. Bye."

She drops the phone back in its cradle with a flourish, and taking a long last drag on the cigarette, stubs it out in the overflowing ashtray on her desk.

"Charlie, darling. Back on the fags I see."

She makes a move to get up, and I make it easy for her by coming over to her side to do kissy cheeks. She drops back in her chair again, and I could swear she's out of breath from the effort of just trying to climb out of it.

"I can't help it," I tell her. "I just love them too much."

"Hmmm," she says, looking at me. She's one of the few people who knows me well, and she can sense there's something not right. "So, what happened?"

"I fucked up, Carol."

"It can't have been that bad?"

"Trust me. One of the all-time worst. I'd only just started the audition when my phone rang. Total crash and burn. Absolutely fucking awful. I just thought I should give you a heads up before you get the call. Because you'll be getting the call."

"Never mind, sweetheart." Carol reaches for another fag and clicks the lighter. There must be at least forty butts in that ashtray on her desk and I'm willing to bet good money that it was empty this morning. Her lungs must look like a couple of oily rags, not to mention that her heart is working overtime to pump blood around a frame her size. She could at least give it a fighting chance and cut down.

"So, what else have you got for me, babe?" I'm trying not to sound desperate, but things are approaching fucking crisis point, and I really need to earn some money. "Is there anything else in the running? Any interesting looking theatre I should know about?"

Carol shakes her head. "We know you don't do musicals, so unfortunately that rules you out of the new Guys and Dolls at the Almeida. Shame. The National aren't looking until September now, but I'll be sure to put you out there when it comes around."

September? At the rate I'm going I'll be a penniless husk by June.

"I really need something babe. Anything. No commercials?" She shakes her head. "I'm always listening out, Charlie darling. You know that."

"What about these low budget features. Are they offering anything? I'll work for scale."

"There is something that's come in. I haven't had a chance to look at it yet, but you're welcome to take it away and read it first if you like?"

"What is it?"

"Another micro budget feature. First-time writer-director. I spoke to him on Monday, and he seemed a little bit more switched on than most. He asked for you personally, thought you'd be perfect for the role."

She scrabbles through the pile on her desk and pulls out a pristine looking script from just underneath the top. She hands it over to me, and I look at the title. FINDING JESSICA. Not a bad title.

I flick through, check the page count: 112. It's written in Courier 12 point rather than crayon, and seems to be formatted nicely, action all aligned in four-line blocks. A flash of optimism comes to me momentarily; maybe this is the one, this could be a work of unparalleled genius that puts my star well and truly back in the firmament and has everyone beating down my door again.

Then the flash goes. I'm in my agent's freezing office without a fucking hat, and my head is turning numb. All I can hope for is that what I hold in my hands isn't a piece of total shite, and that they are able to offer me some money so I'm not starving and homeless by the end of the fucking month.

It takes a whole four hours for the call to come through, by which time I'm at home trying to shake the cold out of my frozen bones. Carol calls me as I'm huddled around the electric heater that I've pulled down from the top of the cupboard; the way my finances are looking the last thing I need is a fuck-off heating bill to contend with. Although right now I don't honestly think it would make the slightest difference. I don't know how I'm going to afford to pay for anything.

The phone's been ringing off the hook for most of the afternoon, but I've been dodging them all and letting the machine get it. Time after time it's muppets from the financial services department from whatever company's turn it is to hound me, but they all seem to be stepping up the pace. I'm deeply in arrears; quite literally up to my arse in it, and what with the call I've just had from Carol one of the few chances I had of sorting things out seems to have just flown out of the fucking window.

They passed. They wanted to thank me for coming in, but they've decided to go with someone else for the role this time. I can only imagine the satisfied glee on Meg's face as she put the call in, and she probably finished with a smart arsed comment about leaving my phone on, even if Carol never mentioned it to me. She tells me not to worry, that there's no point beating myself up about it. I've been doing it so intently all afternoon that I just don't have the energy left to do it anymore. But I'm fucked. Seriously fucked.

All the puff is gone, and I've already put a call in to Bob to go round and pick up some more. There's no way I'm going to get through the rest of the evening without getting severely stoned. I've still got a little bit of cash left from Nick's rent fund. He's going to be out at the start of March, so there's something else that I need to sort out sharpish.

It's just gone 5, and it's starting to get dark. I fucking hate the winter. It's cold, and wet, and depressing. It's not even like I've got a fucking girlfriend who could keep me warm. I shudder as the thought of the aborted night with Chloe jumps into my head. What a fucking nightmare. I've been keeping my head down ever since, just in case I bump into anyone I know. Being skint is one thing, being fucking impotent is something else entirely.

My stomach grumbles. There's not much in the cupboards, and once I've been round to Bob's I should really pick something up from Tesco and try and avoid my usual lavish tendencies and get something cheap. I need to eat. I shouldn't really be spending the little I have on dope, but fuck – there's very little else to live for at the moment than get deeply twatted.

I check my phone again. Bob probably won't be back yet, but I'll take the chance. Anything's better than being in the fucking flat.

I drag my hat down over my forehead and wrap the scarf tight before setting off, and pace quickly with my head down all the way up to the Grove. Onto Golborne and the traders are all packing away their stalls. I move quickly past the coffee shops just in case I see anyone I know and take a sharp left after the bridge and I'm outside Bob's building. I hit the buzzer, and no fucking surprises. He's not there.

I stick my hands in my pockets and head up towards Kensal Road to kill time by walking round the block. I pass the end of Bob's building, and I hear a door open behind me. For the life of me I don't know why, as I should know better by now, but I turn round to see where the noise has come from.

And I make eye contact with one of the yoot. There's three of them, no more than 15 at most. But they look fucked up, and full of aggro. I turn back and keep walking towards Kensal. The footsteps are quick behind me. I'm looking around in front of me, and the streets are empty. Great. This is looking like the perfect end to the perfect day.

"Got a cigarette?"

I turn to face the three of them. One of them, standing in the middle, is eye-fucking me dead on, and I'm trying to be cool as I look back at him with no aggression whatsoever. Either way you could be in a lot of trouble – show fear and they'll fucking eat you alive, judge the look back wrong and it's a challenge and you're showing them disrespect.

His mate on his right – my left - is looking at me coldly, and the guy on his left just looks shit-faced, and that he'd rather be somewhere warm and dry than robbing someone.

"Sure," I say. And I slowly pull out the fags. Perhaps starting again was a good idea after all. I open the packet, and they all help themselves. The one in the middle takes a spare and puts it behind his ear, and his mates quickly follow suit. He holds on to the box and looks me in the eye. I hold on to it for a split second before letting it go.

"Got a light?" It's the same guy asking, so I get out the box of matches and hand them over. He takes them, lights his cigarette, and chucks them to his mate on the right.

"Blad, empty your pockets."

Great. Here we go.

"I don't have any money."

"Shut the fuck up. You're gettin' eaten ras clat."

I swear to God I don't understand a fucking word they're saying. I doubt they get half of what they're on about. I didn't bring my wallet out with me, and I've only got about £45 in cash on me, and forty of that is earmarked for a very specific purpose and giving it to these little toerags is not part of the plan.

The one in the middle raises his voice. "Blad, set me your money, and your phone."

If anything is going to convince them I'm skint, it's my phone. I pull it out and offer it to the guy in the middle.

"Seriously mate," I say, "if it's money you want, you're talking to the wrong fucking guy."

He looks down at the phone, and takes it, then chucks it to his silent mate on his right. He looks at it, then looks at me and speaks for the first time.

"Blad, what the fuck is this?"

"It's my phone."

"Man, we should boy you up for this. I know you blad, you're an actor. I seen you in that film. Actors are bare boilers man, innit. Set us your money."

So, he recognises me. And if I'm understanding, he thinks that because I'm an actor, I must be loaded. I could laugh out loud if it didn't mean I'd end up with a knife in my ribs.

"Yeah," I say. "I'm an actor. But I haven't worked for a while. I'm totally fucking brassic. I've probably got less money than you."

The one in the middle is looking twitchy, but this is one of the best performances I've done in years. It fucking should be; grounded as it is in truth. I'm just trying not to feel any fear, as these guys will smell it on me and then I'm fucking dead in the water. The eye-fucking is losing some conviction.

"You an actor, Hollywood? You're telling us you got no green, Mr TV Man?"

"Straight up." I shrug my shoulders a little. "Take my fags, have my phone if you want it, but I got nothing else."

The guy on the left turns to the guy in the middle. "Look at the phone, blad. He's got nuffink."

The guy in the middle takes a half step forward, and now he's right in my face.

"You ran into the Bad-mine dem, blad. Next time we gonna get paid. This time, we let you go actor man."

He strides away, followed by the mute guy on his left. The pair of them are moving as quickly as they can while holding up the crotch of their trousers with one hand. All three of them have got their pants hanging out. The guy on the right who recognised me jogs on after them. The other two are way ahead, already crossing to disappear into the park. The third guy turns back and chucks me my phone.

"Thanks," I say quietly. He stands there for a moment, looking like he wants to ask me something.

"Blad, how do you get to be an actor?"

I put my phone back in my pocket. I try not to show that my hands are shaking and do a long calming breath before I answer him.

"Why, you wanna act?"

He shrugs. "Maybe."

The kid's got something. He can certainly fake disinterest with the best of them, but then living in West London he's going to have apathy down cold as his default setting. "It'd be nang."

"Nang?" I have to ask. I don't know where this conversation is going, but I'll have a head start if I at least get a grip on what the fuck he's on about.

"Heavy, man." He pulls the cigarette from behind his ear and lights it. There's still one behind the other ear.

"Got a spare?" I ask him.

He grins. "You got balls, blad. You're alright." He chucks me the cigarette, followed by a lighter. He's checking me out now as I smoke. "What's your name, Hollywood?"

"Charlie. Charlie Reed."

"Yeah, Charlie Reed. What was that film you were in? From the other night?"

"The Twelfth of Never."

"Bad film, blad. Raw."

"I didn't think you'd like it."

He shakes his head. "Nah, bad film. My dad died, innit."

"Oh," I say. "I'm sorry."

"So how do you get to be an actor?"

"Luck, mostly. I could hook you up with someone, if you like."

"Serious?" He's momentarily wide-eyed, but distrust quickly clouds over. "Nah, man. You just try and fix me with five-oh, innit. Fuck me over."

"Why would I do that?"

"We was gonna tax you blad. You could fuck me up."

I shrug. "Maybe, but you gave me my phone back. So, I haven't got a lot to complain about, have I?"

He's looking at me, wary.

"Look, I'll give you my number. If you want me to help you, then you can call."

"Fuck you, man. You batty."

I laugh. "I'm not fucking batty. And if I was, I could do better than you, you cunt."

The moment this flies out of my mouth I'm already questioning the wisdom of taking the piss out of someone who's just tried to rob me and disrespecting them by calling them a cunt could be nothing short of suicidal. He looks shocked for a second, then grins at me. "You got raw cohones, actor man. Set me your digits."

I read it out to him while he programs it in his phone. "What's your name?" I ask him.

"Elijah," he says. "I'll be seeing you, actor man."

He turns, and leaves, following his two mates in the direction of the park. I stand there for a moment, smoking the rest of my cigarette.

Bob is in when I ring on the bell five minutes later, and he buzzes me up. By the time I sit down on the couch I'm properly shaking with the adrenalin that's now coursing through my body, as I'm replaying what's just happened, and imagining all the alternative outcomes that could have played out.

"You okay Charlie?"

Bob is looking at me strangely. I realise that I'm staring at the television, gently shaking while rocking backwards and forwards.

"Kind of," I say, and proceed to tell him all about it.

He wanders into the kitchen as I'm halfway through, and after some clanging and banging he brings back a couple of mugs of tea. I sip it gently as I finish the story.

I've already told him that they didn't get the cash off me, so I can't quite believe it when he turns round to me halfway through skinning up and says, "Fuckers, man. Robbing a man for his cash. Don't worry about paying me now." He hands me a fat quarter of Charas and grins. "Get me next time."

This is too good to be true. I knew that Bob was pretty dopey in every sense of the word, but now he's giving me puff on tic. Which given how long his memory holds out, is effectively giving it to me for nothing. Still, with my finances in the state they're in, I'm not going to argue with him.

"Cheers, Bob," I say. "Nice one."

"No probs Charlie. I know you'd do the same for me."

Pretty fucking doubtful, but it's not like I'm going to point that out. I lean forward to skin up. The way this is panning out, I may even get fed if I stick around here. Normally I'd get off as quickly as possible, but there's nothing to rush back for at home, and after what's just happened, I'm still a little jittery about hurrying back outside. Probably just as good to hole up here, watch telly and get fucked up; even if it does mean having to listen to Bob dribble on at intervals.

I'm halfway between relieved and fucking pissed off about the mugging, even if it did peter out into nothing. I've lived here for years and nothing like that's ever happened before. That kind of shit is normally for the tourists and nervous North Londoners, but if you're a local you carry yourself differently; generally you'll be left the fuck alone. So now I'm questioning myself as to whether something's changed in me, whether there's some perceptible weakness that the yoot can now smell on me. Like I'm some kind of wounded animal.

Bob told me once that the origin of the word 'assassin' comes from 'takers of hashish', and that the first assassins were generally off their tits on puff or opium. It made no fucking sense to me at the time, as a smoke has always made me feel pretty fucking mellow; but on looking into the eyes of that middle yoot tonight the penny suddenly dropped. He was ripped to the tits, but there was no mellowness there at all. He was ready to go; ready to take something sharp out and rip open my stomach.

Until his mate stepped in. Elijah. The wannabe actor. Although with a penchant for knife crime, stealing and ruthless violence he may find himself more suited to producing. Still, the kid had something; he could certainly do the eye-fuck thing with a great deal of confidence, and there was a wry intelligence in his face. I'd be prepared to hook him up with Carol for a meeting. Why not? It'd be good to try and give someone else a break. The karma might be good for me. Of course, she'll want to know how I got to meet him in the first place, but I'll just have to think of something. I doubt she'd be bending over backwards if she knows he's a mugger.

I'm brought back to Earth by the ringing of my phone and have a look at the caller display. I don't even need to look. It's gone six, which is prime time for all the wankers who start the harassment calls, probably thinking as they do, that I'm a normal civilian with a normal job, rather than some layabout ne'er-do-well who lays around getting stoned all day. I ditch the call. I really don't feel like going into one of those conversations right now. I should really get back to some of them tomorrow though. The calls seem to be getting more and more urgent and intense every time they leave a message.

Bob is saying something, and I tune back in to hear him ask: "Do you fancy some Thai, Charlie? It's my treat."

Good old Bob. Hang round for long enough and he comes through.

There's a poster on the wall of a man with his head in his hands, with the word 'DEBT' above it in big capital letters. If this is meant to make me feel any better, it's not working.

I finally caved in and came to see the Citizens Advice Bureau underneath the Westway about my financial situation, and to see if there's anything that I can do about the constant fucking phone calls. I've brought the letters with me, and Penny has just gone off to photocopy everything. I've known Penny for all of about ten minutes, and she's already irritating the shit out of me. She's got an aura of well-meaning do-goodery about her, in that soppy, wet, knitted manner that comes with not having been fucked for about fifteen years and owning one too many cats. She's been simpering at me with perfectly arched eyebrows and a protruding bottom lip since I've been telling her what's been going on, and it's all I can do not to lean over the table and give her a slap. I feel a great swell of self-loathing rising in me with the realisation that I'm asking for help for someone I would normally cross the road to avoid.

It's a tiny poky office. There's a computer on the desk in front of me, and the wall is lined with a smorgasbord of posters for a range of complaints, any one of which might be appealing to the person who's sitting in my position. Problems at work, problems at home, child abuse; and they all look like they've been knocked up in about half an hour by some junior tosspot in an agency who will have charged the government a small fortune for the privilege.

Penny comes back into the room, and even the apologetic way in which she creeps back to her position behind the desk and meekly sinks in her chair is fucking irritating.

"Okay, Charlie. I've just had a chat with Margaret about your situation, as I'm not an expert…"

"If you're not an expert, shouldn't I be speaking to Margaret directly?"

I'm trying not to sound chippy, but this woman is seriously starting to get on my tits. Just looking at her now, I'm wondering what she might be an expert in. Tofu bakes, probably.

She throws me that sympathetic smile again. "Margaret is tied up with another client just at the moment, so I'm afraid you're stuck with me. Given that you have two outstanding mortgages on your property that you're having trouble making payments on, we think the only realistic option for you is to sell your flat."

I grit my teeth. It's not like I'm surprised, but the reason I'm here is to try and see if there's a way round that.

"I was hoping that there might be a way of avoiding selling my property."

Penny simpers at me. "I can understand that Charlie, but given the correspondence that you've received, there could be a grave danger of your flat being repossessed anyway. I'm sure it would be better to sell and get something back. You may even make enough to try and settle some of your credit card debt as well."

"Is there nothing else I can do?"

Penny looks at the paperwork – my paperwork – in the folder in front of her. "The only real alternative in your situation would be bankruptcy, in which case your assets, your flat, would be sold anyway." She looks up at me, the eyebrows arched in sympathy one more time. "I am sorry, Charlie. I can imagine this all must be very distressing for you."

I stand up, picking all the letters off the desk.

"I would get in touch with all your creditors and let them know what you plan to do," Penny adds. "You may find it could buy you a little more time."

I nod and walk out. I would have thanked her, but the silly cow has been about as much use as a chocolate teapot. If I'd known the meeting was going to be quite that pointless, I really wouldn't have bothered. I can't believe that I'm going to have to sell the flat, although it's looking like I don't really have any other option. I've been looking on the net for alternatives, but there was very little else I could see, which is why I ended up at the Citizen's Advice this morning to see if they had any ideas. And look how well that panned out.

I stand outside the estate agents opposite the tube for a while, checking out the prices of property. I should be grateful that I'm selling here at least; if I was trying to shift a flat in Leeds or some other shithole I could be royally fucked. But there's no sign of a crash round here. There's some uppity cow on the phone sitting behind the desk nearest the window, and a guy in a thick pinstripe with his feet up on his desk towards the back. He's reading the paper, and I'm guessing that either he's the boss of this little crew, or that the boss is out.

I push the door open. He clocks me and the feet swing off the desk and suddenly he's all business.

"Hi," he says. "Can I help you?"

"I'm looking to sell my flat. It's on St. Quintin's."

"Great!" He's all smiles, but then he fucking would be if he thinks he's going to get a sniff of 3% of a small fortune. "Shall we drive up there and take a look at it?"

He thrusts his hand forward for me to shake. "I'm David."

"Charlie."

"Good to meet you, Charlie. Shall we?"

Most people fucking hate estate agents, and although it's not like I deeply respect them or anything, I do recognise that they've got a job to do. I can watch them and appreciate all the forced chumminess and empathy for what it is: a performance. If you were trying to buy a property during the heady days of 2005 or so, I could see where you could develop a loathing for them; as house prices seemed to double every five fucking minutes, but if you're looking to make money out of property then you've really got nothing to complain about.

I follow David out to his car over the road, and it turns out to be a Renault Clio. Five years ago, and this would probably have been a BMW 7 series or a Merc, but conspicuous consumption went out with Lehman Brothers, and so now a small runaround is more contrite.

I climb in next to him, and he pulls a U-turn and drives down past the gym and takes a sharp right onto St. Marks.

"I've got to ask," he says, looking in the mirror before turning to glance at me. "You look very familiar. Where do I recognise you from?"

"I'm an actor," I tell him. I've got the envelope with all the letters on my lap. I'm betting that I'm not the first person to walk out of the Citizen's Advice with a similar envelope to walk straight into the estate agents.

"That's right. You were in Nicholas Nickleby, weren't you? My Mum loved that adaptation."

Nicholas Nickleby. A blast from the past. I could do with another job like that right now. The BBC pays well for its costume dramas. That was over ten years ago now and playing Smike did me a world of favours at the time. Poor unfortunate Smike my arse. Going retard did quite a bit for my career.

"Thanks," I say as we turn off St. Marks onto St. Quintin's. I'm not really into getting into a big one about my career, but then I doubt this bloke is that thick that he might not piece together the fact that he's not seen me in a lot recently with the fact that I'm selling my flat. "It's this one just here. On the left."

He pulls over and he follows me through the front door. He looks around the hallway and checks out the state of the carpet on the stairs that lead up to the first floor.

As I open the door, I'm already beginning to wish that I'd waited a couple of hours and come back to clear up first. There's a couple of roaches in the ashtray, the kitchen is a state, and the whole place could do with a hoover. David is too keen to get his mitts on the place to mention any of this though and looks studiously at the ceilings as I whisk the ashtray into the kitchen to empty it into the bin.

I come back into the lounge and he's nodding to himself. "Good high ceilings," he says. "Good size lounge." He wanders into the kitchen, takes a look round.

"Washing machine and dishwasher?" he asks.

"Just the washing machine," I say, and he nods.

He checks out the bedrooms, nodding, and casts an approving eye over the bathroom.

"Very nice, Charlle. Very nice flat. Well maintained. I don't think you're going to have a problem selling this. Not at all."

"What do you think it's worth?"

"Two-bedroom, good size rooms? Period property? I'd happily put this on the market for you at half a mill. Probably take offers just under to avoid the hike in stamp duty."

Half a million. That would clear the mortgage debt and leave a hundred thousand spare. And that would clear all the other debt and still leave me a bit of money to play with. It could be worse. The key thing is that I need to turn this sale around pretty fucking sharpish. The most recent letter I got from the lenders seemed to hint that I needed to sort this out in six weeks otherwise I was going to be out on my arse. And that would be spectacularly shite, as I really have nowhere else to go.

"Great," I say. "What happens now?"

By the time I get back from sorting everything out at their office it's getting on for 5 o'clock, and someone will be coming round first thing in the morning to take a load of photos so that I can get the ball rolling. David seemed to think that it wouldn't be a problem to turn a sale round fairly quickly, as apparently property here is still highly desirable.

I plonk a pint of milk down on the kitchen counter, stick the kettle on, and have a root around underneath the sink for some cleaner so that I can begin to try and make the place look halfway presentable. It would be nice to think that Nick might make an appearance so that he could give me a hand tidying up, but it's pretty fucking unlikely. There's a bottle of Jif cream cleaner that's all gunked up around the opening, and as they renamed it around the turn of the Millennium it's clearly seen better days. I squirt the little that's left in the bottle on the surfaces, when the phone rings.

I've been dodging calls for weeks, and now promise myself that I will sort it out first thing tomorrow and let the myriads of people that I owe money too that it's all going to be coming back to them, and soon. I've given up answering the landline completely, and always let the machine get it; and over the last fortnight the messages have been getting progressively less courteous. Not that they were that chummy to begin with.

But it's my mobile that's trilling, and as I fish it out, I see it's Carol, so I drop the sponge and answer.

"Hey Carol."

"Charlie, darling. How's things?"

I'm tempted, but I don't go there. Better to try and fake some degree of positivity. "I'm fine babe. Just having a spruce."

"Wonderful," she says, and she just manages to get the end of the word out before she wrenches the handset away from her mouth as she breaks into a series of hacking coughs. I can hear the brown gunk being cleared from the depths of her lungs as she does this, and there's a split-second silence, which I'm guessing is her dumping whatever she's just coughed up into a tissue.

"Sorry darling," she says.

"No problems babe," I say, and listen for the tell-tale click of a lighter sparking up a new fag. There it is, regular as clockwork.

I go over to my jacket and fish out my own packet and take them back into the kitchen, where I light one off the stove. If you can't beat them, join them.

"What's going on Carol? Martin Scorsese been pestering you again?"

"Unfortunately not, darling. No, I'm calling about 'Loving Jennifer'."

It takes me a minute to place it, but then I remember. The script is lurking unread somewhere in the lounge. I felt so fucked off about the Salt and Acre audition, and then so freaked out by the attempted mugging, that I forgot all about it.

"Oh yeah?"

"What did you think?"

"Not bad on a first reading," I lie. If there's even a sniff of money out of it, then right now it's a work of fucking genius. "I'll have to have another look."

"I suggest you do, darling. I had a call from the director today, and he's very keen to hear your thoughts. Wanted to know if he could buy you a coffee this week. He's based in your neck of the woods."

Of course he is. They all fucking are. The Grove is rammed to the rafters with low budget filmmakers.

"What do you know about him?" I ask.

"Charming young man. Absolutely charming. Donovan Taft. Do you know him?"

"I can't say I do," I say. But then that's not saying much. For the past twelve months I've been feeling increasingly adrift, and I feel like I don't know fucking anyone. I'm sure that's part of my problem.

"Extremely talented, by all accounts. He was short-listed for the Bafta short film award last year, and just got pipped. He's written this screenplay and seems to have raised a lot of the financing, even without anyone attached. And he seems very, very keen on using you, Charlie dear."

"That's nice," I say. "What part?"

"Charlie, really." Carol sounds a bit pissed off. "If you'd read the script, you'd know there's only one male role in it. Well, there's a couple of small extra parts, but it's the main role he's talking about. I have to say darling, I think you'd be perfect for it. I told him that you'd taken my only copy, and the sweet man made sure another one came straight over. He wanted me to read it to help try and persuade you."

I can't help it, but despite all my better judgement, I'm beginning to feel a little excited. Carol doesn't normally enthuse quite like this.

"I was just testing you," I say, winding her up.

"Just read the script darling. And get back to me with some good times for you to meet."

"I will. Oh!" I shout down the phone as I remember, and just manage to catch her before she hangs up. "There's someone I'd like you to meet. Maybe. At some stage."

"Meet? Really? Who?" This is the first time I've ever asked Carol for any kind of favour like this, so it's no small wonder that I've piqued her interest.

"This kid. I don't know, I just think there might be something about him."

"A kid?"

"Teenager. Black kid, about fifteen? He's quite ghetto, but he's definitely got some kind of presence."

"Really?" There's a wheezing sound as Carol takes a deep, contemplative drag on her cigarette. "How did you meet him?"

"He stopped me in the street, recognised me from 'The Twelfth of Never'. He wanted to know how to become an actor."

"What did you tell him?"

"Give up now while there's still hope."

Carol chuckles down the other end of the line. "Okay darling, I'm happy to say hello if you think he's got something. Give him my number. What's his name?"

"Elijah."

"Elijah. Good. Biblical. Read the script darling. And call me tomorrow."

"I will. Night babe."

She hangs up, and I quickly finish wiping down the surfaces in the kitchen, drop the fag butt in the sink, and then go to find 'Loving Jennifer' in the lounge.

It's half eight when I finally finish reading, and my stomach is rumbling. One hundred and twelve pages, and it's not bad. The character – my character – Roy, is a late thirties sports teacher who finds himself at a loose end in the holidays, and decides to trek across the South Downs, on his own. He books himself into this guesthouse, and for the first time in his life, falls head over heels in love. But there's a catch. She's a big woman, a good fourteen stone or so, and he has to battle his own superficial demons about what society, and his friends expect him to have in a relationship. He suffers doubts, and a crisis of confidence; rejecting her around page 92 before realising that she's made him the happiest that he's ever been and so they end up back together. It's funny in parts, poignant in others, and I can see it working; it says something about the superficial nature of attraction in modern society, and that hoary load of old bollocks.

Both characters are three dimensional and jump off the page, and I can see myself playing Roy. The truth of it is, I'm flattered to be asked. It's a great role.

I fire up the laptop and google Donovan Taft. He's up there on IMDB, so he's clearly not a total bellend, and there's a link to his site, so I go and take a look. The short that nearly made the Bafta is up there, and it's not bad. Shot well, and he gets a good performance out of the two leads. There's some depth there, and the music works well with the story. This guy may well have something.

I put down the script, knowing that I'm going to come back to it later. But first I need to eat something, and I also need to clean up the fucking flat if I'm ever going to have a hope in hell of selling the fucking thing.

I'm strolling down Portobello on my way down to the Electric to meet Donovan Taft. He's a member there, as a lot of up-and-coming media are. I've never bothered – I've been tempted on occasion, but then I've always managed to blag it in on whoever's membership we're going in on, and with the recent state of my finances I'm glad that's one less phone call I've had to make; pleading poverty to the member services at that place would probably be the ultimate in humiliation.

I could be finally coming out of the woods – David sent round a photographer to get some good snaps of the flat, all the measurements were done, and I went down to sign all the paperwork. My flat is now on the market. I was initially gutted, but once I called all the people back who've been hounding me for money and explained to them what was going on they all immediately became a whole lot nicer. I got a series of addresses of people to write to with evidence of correspondence with the Estate Agents, with the understanding that they would hold off until I got the money back from the sale. There are going to be people viewing the flat from here on in, so it helps that I'm out and about; one annoying part of this means that I'm having to puff out of the bathroom window so that the flat doesn't smell of drugs, and it's still fucking freezing outside. But at least it seems that my money problems are gone. Now I just need to think about where I'm going to live.

But right now, the sun is out, and I'm on my way out to lunch with a director about a film. He's obviously keen as when I said to Carol that today could be good, he practically bit her arm off, wanting to buy me lunch and everything. I've read the script a couple more times since, and it's good. I think there could really be something there, and I'm looking forward to meeting the guy to see if he's half as switched on as he seems on his website.

I go into reception and tell the fox on the desk that I'm meeting Donovan Taft in the bar, and she smiles sweetly and pushes the book in front of me to sign, and then I'm straight upstairs. I see him immediately as he stands up to greet me, all smiles as his hand is outstretched. He's tall, especially for a director. Coming in at a little under six foot I'm looking up at him and trying to work out just how big he is, but I'm guessing six five at least. I've usually been a good head taller than most directors I've worked with, who on the whole seem to have developed Napoleonic complexes which they then work out by entering a profession where they get to tell everyone else what to do. Donovan is dressed well in jeans with expensive Adidas that look box fresh, and a black shirt that I'm guessing must be tailor made to fit his lanky frame quite so well.

I grin as I take his hand, and we shake.

"Good to meet you, Charlie. Thanks for coming."

"My pleasure Donovan."

"You hungry? I thought we could grab something straight away. You know, order early, then talk about everything."

"Good idea," I say, and follow him through to the restaurant where he's already reserved a table. He's got that cool confidence that a few of the guys I've worked with have had, with a sharp intelligence in the eyes.

We sit, and chit-chat about the Electric and mutual acquaintances – he knows Jimmy D – obviously - and has recently come off a commercial with Bob Taylor who shot 'The Trampoline', so I mentioned Bob's unique talent to pull an available woman on the crew within about five minutes, and Donovan laughs, as apparently nothing has changed, and he did exactly the same on their brief four day shoot. The waitress comes, and he orders the Dover Sole, and I go for the risotto. I'm pleased to notice that he's not only keen to make sure to order wine for our lunch, but also that he casts an appreciative glance at the waitress's disappearing arse.

He leans forward conspiratorially. "The women get better looking every time I come in here. I swear to God."

"Tell me about it," I say, nodding wistfully.

"You seeing anyone at the moment Charlie?"

I shake my head, not least to banish the flash of memory of Chloe's retreating back leaving my bedroom from a fortnight ago. "Not right now."

He nods. "Me too. Far too busy for any of that bollocks."

I raise my eyebrows. "I had the impression from your script that you'd be a lot more romantic."

"You like the script?"

"I love it. I'm flattered that you're thinking of me for Roy." I pause. "Obviously, you're a very astute director."

He laughs. "That I am, Charlie. But then I doubt I'm the first director to chase you with a script for their debut feature. Not after your performance in 'The Twelfth of Never'. And that didn't exactly harm James Laurenson's career, did it?"

I'm impressed. This guy is obviously a lot smarter than your average bear. "No, you're right. I do get a lot of scripts from first time directors. It's just that a lot of them are…"

"Shite?"

"Exactly."

The wine arrives, and he tastes and approves it quickly, without any kind of elaborate pantomime, so that gets another tick of approval.

"So, what are your thoughts on the script?" he asks.

"At first, I wasn't sure about the believability of their relationship. You know, why would Roy decide to go for a woman like Jessica? I mean, she's funny and everything, but wouldn't he immediately discount her because of her size? But when I re-read it, it all began to make sense." Donovan is nodding, listening to me. "It's the fact that she's happy with herself and he's so unhappy with himself, right?"

Donovan grins. "Something like that."

"She's like this big warm fire that everyone is drawn to. That's the reaction that she inspires in the village, and he sees it, and gets sucked in."

"Tell me more. What do you think of Roy?"

"Don't get me started. Seriously. I could give you the background of his last ten relationships. How he never got over the loss of his mother…"

"His mother died?" Donovan looks surprised.

"Definitely. That's why he's been so unsuccessful in his relationships until Jessica. Because he was scared of commitment, and he couldn't function. And that's the difference with her, because part of what she offers is an unashamed return to the maternal love he was denied as a child."

He sits back in his chair. "Fuck me, Charlie. I spent two years on that script, and no-one has ever mentioned that to me before. It's never even occurred to me before. But you know what? That makes perfect sense."

I grin. "Normally I charge a fortune for these kinds of insights, you know."

"I can well believe it. I'd really like you to play Roy, Charlie. I think you'd be perfect for it."

"I'd love to. Really."

"You know we haven't got a lot of money, right? You're happy to work for scale?"

"For this, I'd be delighted. Have you any other casting ideas yet? What about Jennifer?"

"You know Izzy Myers?"

Izzy Myers. She was written out of long running soap Buckingham Avenue in spectacular fashion when she was held hostage by her crazed ex-husband and eventually murdered. She's a great choice to play Jessica, both because I would think Donovan will almost certainly be guaranteed some hefty coverage in the tabloids, but also because she's on the larger size.

"Nice," I say. "That should help get a distributor on board."

The waitress arrives with the food, and I try not to fall on my risotto with indecent haste. There was nothing left for breakfast this morning, and I'm totally skint. Nick is supposed to be coming round later with the rent, which will mean I'm actually able to get some provisions for home.

"Have you got a date for filming yet?" Soon, I'm hoping, as any sort of income is going to help right now.

"First of April. Rehearsals start in about three weeks' time. Don't worry, all the casting will be in place by then."

"Fuck! That's a month away. Why so soon?"

"Tax reasons. If we go into production on that date, then we get the money back. I'm not quite sure how it works, but it's all set to go. I had the impression from your agent that you'd be okay for those dates?"

"No, I am. It's great. I'm up for it." I take a sip of wine. "I'm just impressed that you managed to pull the financing together so quickly."

He pushes his glasses up on his nose. They look expensive. "Yeah. Well, getting shortlisted for the BAFTA certainly helped."

"Loved that film, by the way."

"Thanks. That, and having a good exec producer who was able to pull some strings, call on some favours. All very helpful when it came to securing the money."

"I thought you were producing it yourself."

"Kind of, yeah. But having James on board has opened up a lot of doors."

I've just put a forkful of risotto in my mouth, yet suddenly all I can taste is bile. He can't mean who I think he means. Surely not.

"James?"

"Laurenson. I thought you knew. He was the one who suggested you'd be right for Roy in the first place."

I force a grin and swallow the risotto that's still in my mouth. "Cool," I say, and reach for the wine.

That's just fucking weird. I've no idea what goes on in James Laurenson's twisted brain, but the idea that he's had me in mind for anything is deeply strange, not least because he makes a film at least every other year, and I've not had a sniff of a casting for anything since 'The Twelfth of Never' over twenty years ago. Why I should suddenly be in the running for a lead in a low budget film from a rookie director, I have no idea. Maybe he's already been whispering in Donovan's ear about what a prime candidate I am for a good mind-fucking, and how I can be best exploited to get a good performance.

Or maybe, he just thinks that I'm right for the role; that after all this time has passed maybe it's time for the sun to shine on me once again. But then maybe it's just because I'm fucking dirt cheap.

Donovan has just said something to me, but I've no idea what it is. Just the mention of Laurenson's name, and I'm already showing all the signs of turning into a major fucking basket case.

"Sorry, miles away. Just thinking about the last time I saw James," I say.

"You okay, Charlie? You look spooked." Donovan is looking at me carefully, like he's trying to figure me out.

"I'm fine. How did you get James on board?"

I'm looking at him now, and he's either a fantastic actor, or he genuinely has no idea of what happened on 'The Twelfth of Never' shoot. All I'm getting from him is that he's keen to work with me, and that I'm the right guy for the job. I need to stop being so fucking paranoid.

"At the Baftas. We got talking at the after party, and I told him how much I liked his work, and one thing led to another, and so I started talking to him about 'Loving Jennifer.' He said he liked the sound of it, asked to see the script, and next thing I know, he's offering to exec produce it for me. He's effectively backing the whole thing himself."

"That's fantastic," I say. The fucker can certainly afford to, I think but don't say. "And he thought that I would be good for Roy?"

"Yeah. He said you had the right mix of diffidence and vulnerability."

Whatever the fuck that means, I think. "Shucks," I say. "You're embarrassing me."

Donovan laughs. "And you're a piss taker. You are a good choice."

The rest of the lunch floats by in a cloud of white wine and boundless enthusiasm. Donovan orders in another bottle and tells me about the locations he's lined up to shoot along the South Downs, as well as the crew. Bob Taylor is on board to shoot, which is great, as I've worked with him before, and someone called Sally who I don't know is doing the production design as she worked with him on his short.

I like the guy, and we get on well. He's switched on, knows his script and characters, and he tells me that he's storyboarded every single frame. It's going to be a tight twenty-day shoot, but he's confident that they'll be able to get everything done in that time. It's getting on for half four when we eventually leave, both of us a little the worse for wear, and a handshake turns into a manly hug as Donovan tells me he's psyched and looking forward to seeing me in rehearsal in a couple of weeks' time. He turns and saunters off up Portobello towards the Gate, and I turn and walk the other way, tingling with a warm glow that things may be finally turning around. Then I think of Laurenson again, and my smile vanishes. I can't work out why he would recommend me for Roy. We haven't seen each other for the best part of twenty years, and it's not like he's been beating down Carol's door to cast me in anything since.

So why now?

I know I'm being ridiculous but having been subject to his mind games before I still have this underlying panic that it's some kind of elaborate hoax; that with a week to go Donovan is suddenly going to call me to let me know that he's sorry, but he was wrong; and that he's going to have to go with someone else for the role.

I need to stop thinking like this. Donovan is great; a talented, smart director, and we're going to make a film together.

So why do I have this underlying dread gnawing at my stomach?

MARCH

We're waiting for you again Charlie.

The camera is still running.

We're going to wait here all night if we have to.

Until you get it right.

Nick has arrived with a car and dragon in tow to clear his room out. As soon as he walked through the door, he was gobsmacked at just how tidy the place was looking and was a little surprised to find out that I was selling the place. There've been a couple of people around to see the flat, but no-one's biting just yet. David says that this is perfectly normal for the time of year, and that there is no need to panic. I'm not panicking, I just want to sell the fucking place quickly so that I can sort my debts out, and because I don't want to have to be dealing with all of that bollocks when I've got a job coming up that should take up all of my focus. The last thing I want to be doing on a film set is dealing with an Estate agent.

So right now, I'm in the living room smoking a reefer, getting Antonio nuts deep in some whore in old New York with the volume turned up, as I know it will annoy the fuck out of Alex.

She's barely even managed to fake being pleasant since she arrived, and Nick looked deeply fucking uncomfortable being in the same place as the both of us, so I guess once he's gone that'll be it, and I won't see him again. She really is a chippy little bitch. I've no fucking idea what her problem is, but I can't imagine her walking around work with a face like a smacked arse, her lips all pursed like someone's just pissed vinegar in her face. She'd be out on her ear in about fifteen seconds flat. No, I guess it's just something that she saves up just for me.

Rather than actually confront her, I've taken the deeply mature move of acting out virtual loud sex through the television, as I thought that might be sufficiently irritating. There's some banging around in the bedroom, so I'm sure she can hear it.

Nick comes out with a box of books and shoots me a look to say 'You twat', but in truth he looks more amused than bothered.

"Want some of this?" I ask him, offering the spliff.

He shakes his head. That probably means that Alex won't let him.

"Need a hand?"

"Thanks, Charlie. That'd be grand. There's another box in the bedroom that needs to come down to the van."

"No problem," I say, and I turn down the volume, drop the spliff in the ashtray, and walk over to his bedroom.

Alex is sitting on the floor, folding all his clothes and packing them tidily in a suitcase. She doesn't look up as I enter, and I stand there a second to see if she'll acknowledge me. She doesn't look up but carries on folding clothes in silence.

"This box here?" I ask, moving to pick up the one by the door that's full of books.

"Looks like it," she says.

I pick the box up and ferry it out of the flat and down to the car where Nick is playing with the seats, trying to maximise the space so he'll be able to cram everything in. I crouch down and leave the box on the kerb.

"She's in a good mood," I say.

Nick looks up. "Fuck Charlie, are you going out of your way to wind her up? What's with all the sex noises on the fucking telly?"

"What?" I ask, all fake innocent. "I'm just playing Empire of Blood."

"Being a twat is what you're doing. Seriously, you know it's winding her up, so why do you do it?"

"I think you've answered your own question there."

"Can't you at least make an effort?"

I shrug. "Nick, I might if she didn't make it quite so obvious that she thinks I'm a gigantic cunt."

He's getting all flustered now, as he does when he's caught in the middle of something and doesn't know what to do.

"Look," I say. "I'll try, but it would be nice to think that we might still get to hang out occasionally once you move out. That I might be able to come and see you in your new flat without being on some kind of vetted list."

"'Course you can," he says. "It's not like that, honestly."

The trouble is that that's exactly what it's like, but I don't think that even Nick can see that yet. And good friend that he is, I don't think he's strong enough to tell Alex that he'll do what he wants. And I think she's going to run him ragged.

I smile. "OK. Let me know if you need any more help." I turn and walk back up to the flat. I turn off the game and put the TV on to half watch Friends and smoke the rest of the spliff.

I leave them to it, and the rest of the stuff goes down to the car over the next hour. Despite my offer to help, the pair of them seem to have it under control, and slowly Nick's bedroom becomes a shell bar the bed - which was mine to begin with.

The last load goes down, and I watch out of the sitting room window as they manage to cram the last of Nick's stuff into the back of the car. Then the pair of them proceed to have a discussion, and although I can't hear what's being said, it looks like Nick is pleading with Alex to do something, and she's shaking her head. Finally, she relents, although she's looking pretty fucking grumpy about it.

And then Nick walks back to the flat, and I realise as Alex follows that the reason she's just been so fucking moody with him is that he's just asked her to come and say goodbye.

I flop back on the couch, and Nick comes in. He puts his key down on the table.

"So," I say.

"I know," he says. "It's weird, isn't it?"

"Deeply fucking strange."

Alex is standing in the doorway like she'd rather be anywhere else in the known universe.

"Bye Alex," I say.

"Bye Charlie," she says. But the uppity cow can't even bring herself to look at me as she says it.

"I've got to ask, you know," I say to her, trying to remain calm. "Because I've always fucking wondered. Just what is your fucking problem with me anyway?"

Nick's face goes white as a sheet, and Alex looks up and grins malevolently like this is the chance she's been waiting for. Like I've just handed her a fucking invite on a silver platter.

"Oh Charlie," she says. "Where would I even begin to start?"

"Just fucking try me. Seriously. What have I done to you?"

"It's not what you've done to me, Charlie. It's just your shitty fucking attitude to life in general. Your sexism, your laziness, your inability to see that no-one's going to just fucking hand you a job. The negativity that infects everything around you. Your hapless solipsism."

I have no idea what that means, but it doesn't sound very good. "Don't hold back Alex, say what you think."

"Is it any wonder you won't face reality when you're stoned all the fucking time? That's why you're selling your flat, isn't it? Because like some kind of childish fucking idiot, like some kind of star, you thought that someone was just going to swoop down and solve everything by offering you a job. Well grow up Charlie, because that's not how things work in the real world. Is it any wonder that you're not getting any fucking work when you clearly hate everyone and everything?"

"Interesting you should say that" I tell her. "Because funnily enough I've just been offered the lead in a feature film. We start shooting in less than a month. You think I'm lazy? Fuck me, Alex, I've worked harder and longer than you've ever had to. You think you're all fucking that because you went to Cambridge? Well, you're fucking not."

"And you think you're hot shit because you've been in a couple of things on the telly? Fucking grow up, Charlie."

"Oh, and by the way, I don't hate everyone and everything. But I do think you're a gigantic twat." I turn to Nick. "Good luck mate, because I hope you realise that this is a glimpse of your future."

Nick stays schtum and stares at the floor, and I'm getting the impression that right now he'd rather be anywhere else in the known universe than stuck in the middle of this developing row. But addressing him is a guaranteed way of winding up Alex even further, so I carry on.

"Seriously pal. I'd fucking watch it if I were you, because I wouldn't wish this on my worst enemy let alone one of my good friends."

"Friends?", Alex snorts. "You don't know what fucking friendship is, Charlie. How many friends have you got, really? Fuck all. Because you're too fucking self-centred to make any kind of sacrifices, which is what a normal friendship entails. Having someone provide you with coke and rent does not a friendship make. Not even close."

I look at Nick, and he's still looking at the floor. And I feel like I've been kicked in the chest. So that's how he feels. Like I'm just the worst kind of free-loading cunt, and one who doesn't actually give a shit about him.

I stand there for a moment, looking at him. "Right. I suggest you both fuck off out of my flat then."

"My pleasure," says Alex, and walks out of the door. Nick can't even bring himself to meet my gaze as he shuffles out after her.

I slam the door and go back to lie on the couch. I feel shell-shocked, like the last five minutes were just dropped on my head like an emotional anvil. I had no idea that Nick felt like that, and I honestly thought we were pretty good mates. I've always been friendly and considerate (at least, I thought so), but the way she was pitching it you'd think I was just some kind of self-centred drug thief.

It was the fact that he just stood there, letting her rant at me. His silence spoke volumes. So that's the end of that friendship.

I lean forward and delve into the tin to skin up a fat reefer, as I'm feeling like getting properly fucked up right now. My hands shake as I flake the Charas off into a Rizla.

I've got loads of friends. Loads. I always get on with everyone on a shoot. It's just that when the shoot finishes it's kind of hard to stay in touch with people. But I've still got loads of friends. There's ten people I could call right now and suggest we hook up for a pint. It's just that I don't really feel like it.

Then a thought occurs to me, and while I'm skinning up, I switch on the laptop and wait for it to whir into life. I light the joint, and drag on it deeply, then open up Safari and go to the online dictionary. I need to know what solipsism means. It turns out that Alex thinks I have an "extreme preoccupation with and indulgence of one's feelings, desires etc – an egoistic self-absorption."

Well, fuck her. At least I'm not a fucking midget witch.

It's a beautiful morning. One of those bright blue days that should fill you with the joys of spring and all that shit, but I'm feeling like I'm on my way to the fucking gallows.

Things aren't that bad; I keep telling myself. Rehearsals for the film start in a couple of weeks so it will be good to start working again, and I just need to hold out until the first day of the shoot when there will finally be some money in my bank account. Not much, but then anything is better than nothing. Carol gave me a call this morning, and everything is all set to go. So, I should be feeling chipper.

No, the reason that I'm feeling down is where I'm going. It's always pretty fucking depressing at the best of times; the view out of the front window of the top deck of the 52 as it winds its way up the hill towards Willesden Green, but especially so when I'm on the way to visit my mother.

I think back to what Alex said to me a week and a half ago, about my negativity, and it's something that's been hanging round my neck ever since like a giant millstone. Even if she is a horrid cunt there must still be some truth in that, and there's no prizes for guessing where I will have picked up that particular trait from.

Pat. Patricia Reed. The woman I have to thank for my career, in many ways. She met my dad when she was twenty, and had me very young, only two years later – and so ever since I've been paying the price for denying her her chance to become an actress herself. No, instead of becoming an actress Pat decided to channel her latent aggression into becoming a pushy stage mum, and so began her lifelong skills of withholding affection to express displeasure. I swear it was a desire as a kid to make her happy that made me work so hard to become good, as I thought that if I got this audition, made it into that play, then she would be happy. Pleased. And she would love me.

It worked, to some extent. When I got the role in 'The Mocking Half' in the West End, she was delighted, at least for a while. But then she gradually grew cold, and to this day I'm still not sure why. I guess because my success just accentuated her feelings that she could have made a go of it herself, and that I was denying her her chance. By the time I got the role in 'The Twelfth of Never', she seemed to have gone properly cold on the whole idea of me acting at all; but by then of course it was too late, and I was set on a course which is still playing out now.

So, it's no wonder that part of me dreads these little visits, and this one especially, as I'm going to have to tell her what's going on with the flat. I can't see any other way of getting around it – I'm going to need to be out of the flat in case it's sold while I'm away shooting the film, and even though I've been racking my brains trying to think of an alternative for the past week, there really isn't one. Dad has got his hands full with his new little family; there's no room at Molly's, and I can't afford to pay rent anywhere until I sell the house.

Fucking horrible though the idea is, I'm going to have to ask to move back in with my mother. It's no wonder I'm feeling fucking negative.

My phone rings. I pull it out of my pocket and check the screen. Not a number I recognise. I'm not really in the mood to talk to anyone, so I ditch the call and go back to staring out of the window. A random dog pauses on its way down the hill to dump a fat turd out on the pavement. There doesn't seem to be any owner in sight.

My phone beeps a voicemail, so out of curiosity I ring through. There's a pause before I hear a voice, like he's not sure whether to leave a message. "Hollywood. You gonna help set me up to be an actor? This is Elijah, man. You remember me."

Nice. It sounds more like a threat than a request, but then I'm sure that's just being a yoot in West London. Maybe he's just nervous. Maybe he thinks I'm going to call the cops on him. Whatever, I said I'd hook him up with Carol, I'll hook him up with Carol. But I'll let the little fucker sweat for a bit before calling him back. Right now, I've got other things to worry about.

We turn left off Chamberlayne along the avenue that leads to the library, and I look left to see if anyone's in their upstairs bedroom. Puerile though it is, I'm always hoping to catch someone topless, seventies porno style.

I get off at the library and turn left along the High Street in the direction of the little house I grew up in on Churchill Road, and the sinking feeling hits me. I fucking hate this part of London; it's only a couple of miles from the Grove as the crow flies, but it may as well be another fucking planet. Up here it's all Australian backpackers next to bewildered Muslim families, and there's a combination of drunken exuberance and resigned despair that never seems to reconcile. And in the middle of it all lives Pat, rattling around her house like a bottled spider, quietly resenting everyone and everything in her immediate vicinity.

Churchill Road hasn't changed that much since I grew up here. Property prices have shot up, while if anything the place seems dirtier and more turgid than it ever did. But the overriding feeling I get from the place is that it feels small. Part of that may be that I've grown since leaving here, part of it may be the enormous houses that surround me on the Grove; but I think a lot of it is just a total lack of ambition on behalf of the residents of this street that seeps from every brick.

I walk through the gate and ring the bell. The window boxes still sit on the front windowsill, and the flowers are in bloom, basking in an attention that's never afforded anyone who steps inside the house. I wait the usual fifteen seconds it takes for her to pull herself out of her chair at the kitchen table and trudge towards the front door, and then the door opens a crack, and she peers through the chain.

"Oh," she says. "It's you."

"Hi," I say, and the door closes so she can unfasten the chain, then she lets me in, turning to walk back down the corridor to the kitchen. That's the full extent of her acknowledgement. Of course it's me, I'm thinking. You knew I was coming, and it's not like your hectic social life would have you confused about who's dropping in at any time.

She goes to sit down in front of her laptop at the table, and I lean down to kiss her on the cheek. She's got a document open on her computer; probably some translation that she's got going on. Pat grew up in Spain, is practically bilingual and earns her money doing translations for an agency. She's been threatening to fuck off back to Granada for some considerable time, and I honestly think that one of the key reasons she hangs around London is just to prolong her feeling of abject misery, and then dole it out to the rest of us.

"Let me just finish this," she says. "Then I thought we could have some salad."

Salad would be about right. Drab, bland, minimum effort. I sit down opposite her and look over the bookshelves on the wall. There's a range of recipe books up there, but I could confidently say that I don't think Molly, or I have ever tasted a dish from a single one of them. I really have no idea what they're doing on the shelves at all; some kind of set dressing to suggest an enthusiasm for cooking, for life in general, which is clearly, obviously (certainly to the immediate members of her family) just not there.

No, Pat has a fairly limited repertoire, and I don't expect that to change at any time in the near future. And today's staggering jump into the known is a salad. Maybe egg, maybe tuna; maybe, if she's feeling really radical, both.

She finishes typing a sentence, then clears her throat and pushes her glasses up on her nose before greeting me with a short smile that never reaches her eyes. "There," she says. "Done."

She climbs out of her seat and goes straight to the fridge where she pulls out an iceberg and some tired looking tomatoes. She dumps them in a colander under the tap and pulls a small avocado from a bowl on the windowsill.

"So how are you, Charlie?"

The question seems to fall out of her and seems to be directed towards the garden fence rather than me. I can't see what she's looking at, but I'm willing to bet from the weary tone in her voice that it's a glazed look into the middle distance. This is the first time I've seen her since Christmas, and five minutes in and it already feels like a lifetime.

"I'm okay. Not bad. I've got a bit of news. I've just got the lead in a feature. We start rehearsals in a couple of weeks."

She remains motionless a second, then moves over to the sink to turn the tap off. "That's good," she says.

"Yeah, I'm pleased. Great director as well, very bright guy. Donovan Taft."

"Never heard of him," she says, as she dumps the sodden leaves into a spinner and starts hammering on the button on the top as if it were a time machine that might take her back to before I was born.

"Does a lot of commercials. And he was shortlisted for a BAFTA for his last short."

"Oh. That's good."

So far, and nothing has changed. I may as well drop the bomb now, just to get it out of the way, so it's done. If she's going to carry on as if I've just brought the black fucking plague into the house, then I may as well give her good reason.

"Mum, there's something I need to talk to you about," I say.

This gets her attention, and she stops attacking the salad spinner to look at me, eyebrows raised.

"I'm selling the flat."

"You're selling your flat?"

I nod. "I don't want to. It's the last thing I want to do. But I really haven't any choice. I've had a bad couple of years. It happens to everyone, but I seem to be on a bad run. I've come down to the last two or three for a couple of things, but they always go with the other guy. And all the while this has been going on, I've been running up my debts, trying to postpone the inevitable. And now the chickens are all finally coming home to roost."

She turns and looks at me, dead in the eye. "I haven't got any money, Charlie."

"I know," I say, trying as hard as I can to not grit my teeth. "I know. That's not what I'm saying. The only way of sorting out all my debts is to sell the flat, so that's what I'm doing. I've got the Estate Agents on it and everything."

She shakes her head gently as she decants the washed leaves into a bowl. "That's a dreadful shame, Charlie. You'll be giving up your independence. Where are you going to live?"

Fuck, I think. Make this fucking easy, why don't you.

"Well, that's kind of why I'm here. I start rehearsals on this film in a couple of weeks, and then we go straight into shooting after that. A lot of it on location on the South Downs. So, I'm going to need to clear out my flat before I go. And I was wondering if I could stay in the spare room for a bit. You know, until I get myself sorted."

"I'm not sure if it's convenient, Charlie."

"You haven't got another tenant?"

She shakes her head. "Still just the one."

"How is he?"

"Oscar? He moved out. I've got a new one now, Sofia. From Belgrade."

Pat's had tenants for the last five years, but they never seem to last longer than about six months. She hasn't yet made the connection that she might be impossible to live with, and that just about anything is preferable to lodging here with her. They tend to be language students who are here for a couple of years, and once they've been at the college for a short while and made some friends, they're off. Yet another reason why I have to be out of my mind – if you come from a shithole in Eastern Europe and still find it impossible to live with her, what fucking hope have I got?

"So why isn't it convenient?"

She opens the fridge and pulls out a couple of hardboiled eggs. She must remember that I'm not that keen on eggs and is just serving them up in the salad as another way of fucking with me. She slices them up straight into the bowl.

"There's a lot of stuff in the spare room. I don't know where else we would put it."

I'm trying not to get annoyed. "Couldn't it go in the loft?"

She shrugs. "I suppose. Such a shame, Charlie. Such a shame. I know how you loved that flat. And your independence. So important."

Two plates and some cutlery are unceremoniously dumped on the kitchen table. The salad bowl is plonked down in the middle.

"It might be nice to think you would come up and see me because you wanted to, not just when you want something," she says.

For fucks sake, I think. Here we go. Time for the Miss Havisham act. Of course, it's my fault that I never come and visit; it's nothing to do with her being about as welcoming as your average tumour.

"It's not like that," I say. "I've just been busy, you know."

"But you clearly haven't," she says. "Which is why you're selling your flat."

I spoon some of the salad on to my plate, determined to honour the promise I made to myself this morning not to rise to any of her shit. Not to get angry, even when provoked.

"I've been busy trying to get work," I say. "It's not like I've been doing nothing."

"Haven't you got some friends you'd rather stay with? I'm sure you'd rather be with people your own age than back living with your mother."

You have no fucking idea, I think, but bite my tongue. "I'm sure it won't be for long. I just need somewhere to stay until the flat is sold, and the film is over. Then I'll be able to afford to move into somewhere of my own."

"You're welcome to stay, Charlie", she says with a tone in her voice that says I'm anything but. "Of course you are."

"Thanks," I say. "I appreciate it."

"So, when do you think you'll be coming?"

"Not sure," I say. "End of the week? Just so long as it's before I start rehearsals."

"Okay," she nods. "I'll get you a key."

I swallow a forkful of salad. I fucking hate hard boiled eggs, but I don't think now is the best time to remind her of that.

"There's something else I need to ask. A favour?"

She raises her eyebrows again. "Another one?"

"I was wondering if I could borrow some money. I'll be able to get it back to you. Very soon. As I soon as I sell the house, if not before."

"Just how much trouble are you in, Charlie?"

I don't know where to start, so I buy time with a mouthful of salad. She looks concerned now, but I know that's a look that's all about how this is going to affect her life; not that she does or sees anyone anyway. And I know she's got money stashed away. She must have. She never goes out, eats frugally, hardly drinks. She earns good money from her translations and lives like a fucking nun. So, she can definitely spot me some cash.

"I've got a lot of debts," I tell her. "And I've reached the end of my overdraft limit, so until I sell the flat there's very little that I can do. I can't get my hands on any money."

She shakes her head. "I thought you would have money saved. You know how unpredictable your profession is."

"I did have," I lie. "But it all got spent in the lean times, and I've borrowed a bit too much on credit. I'll be back on my feet again soon though. I've a good feeling about this film. It's a great script."

"How much do you need?"

She'll lend me the money. Of course she will. But I know that she's going to revel in making me fucking beg for it, and she's not going to let me forget this in a hurry.

"I'm going to need to hire a van to move my stuff. And I don't think everything will fit in here so I'm going to need to put some of the furniture in storage for a couple of months. Obviously, I need to get about, so if I can borrow some cash for that, that would be helpful."

I pause and look at her. She's looking at me with what can only be described as contempt.

"I'm really sorry. Really."

And I am, if mostly for myself. Having to go cap in hand to her for money is possibly the lowest point of an already fairly shit year.

"I will get it back to you as soon as I can."

"How much?"

"The van and storage could go on your credit card. But I could use a couple of hundred in cash."

She nods, and silently looks back down at her food. I find I've completely lost my appetite.

"I don't suppose you've asked him if he can help?" she asks.

"Who?" I ask, knowing full well who she means. But then I'm not going to make it easy for her.

"You know full well who," she says. Then after a pause, "Your father".

Of course I haven't. I wouldn't even bother wasting my breath. It's been a long time since we got together and being as he never has any money at the best of times, and that he's now got a whole new little family to deal with, asking him for a handout would be just about the most pointless exercise I could imagine.

"I have," I lie, "but all his money's a little tied up at the moment."

She raises her eyebrows. "I'm wondering where you might have got your money management skills from. Well, I can't say I'm surprised."

I'm a little astonished that she's mentioned him at all, as it's the first time his existence has even been acknowledged in the house, as far as I'm aware, since he left it shortly after Molly and I left home in the early nineties. I think he lasted as long as he possibly could, until she finally wore him down to the point where he couldn't take any more. There was a method of torture used in China hundreds of years ago called 'Death by a Thousand Cuts', where a victim would have tiny wounds inflicted all over the body over a prolonged period. The wounds would never heal, and slowly but surely the victim would bleed to death. I was stoned on my couch when I saw the documentary explaining it all, and all I could think of was my dad, and that that must have been exactly what being married to Pat was like.

James Reed was a young man when he met Pat, just eighteen, and she had a good two years on him (if not more, as I've never been a hundred per cent certain she's as old, or as young, as she says she is). They bumped into each other at a pub in Hammersmith, both out with friends, and an instant attraction quickly developed into a blossoming relationship. Dad's work in an advertising agency meant that they could afford a small one bedroom pretty quickly, which came in handy when they got married sooner than expected; only six months before I arrived. She's been downright fucking miserable my entire life, and I can only imagine that for a brief period they were happy together, him entranced by her beauty and her dreams of being an actress, her basking in the glow of his adoration; before it all started slowly descending into a life of drudgery and silent abuse.

There were times when he came home very late, and I would lie in bed listening to the rows that followed downstairs. I'm guessing that he was having affairs then, and I wouldn't have blamed him if he did. Anything to keep sane, to feel something akin to love. But he never left, not until both Molly and I had left home. At least, not physically. For a long period of my teenage years, when I was out almost every night with a performance, on the rare occasions I would see him it would feel like he was just a shell. I don't know why he didn't leave sooner; maybe he thought Molly, or I would have thought less of him if he had, but I kind of wish he'd taken the leap. I'm sure that I would have gone with him.

Within a year of him leaving he'd moved in with Sarah, a teacher around about his age. That all seemed to be going very well, and I'd go round occasionally for dinner, but then four years ago that all fell to pieces, and he moved out to live with his new girlfriend, Iolanthe. I've no idea where he met her, as I've only seen her about three times in as many years, and when I have it's very difficult to get her to talk about anything besides herself. She's an interior designer in her late twenties, and the mother of my two stepsiblings; twins, Sam and Emma. It might be nice to see them a bit more often, but Dad seems to have his hands full and seems to have a knack of picking as life partners women who severely get on my fucking tits. Certainly, the thought of asking him for money is a waste of time, as supporting those three is keeping him broke enough.

Mum finishes the salad on her plate. I look at her carefully place the last forkful in her mouth. I've sometimes wondered why she never tried to get back out there, to find someone new herself. I'm sure part of it is because deep down she's aware that she's got some fairly severe personality issues that would drive away someone with the patience of Buddha, but I guess she's also scared. It's not like she doesn't have the opportunity; she spends all day working from home, and could easily get involved in some online dating, but maybe the thought of someone else leaving her is just too much to bear. Maybe it's easier to stay alone than risk being hurt again.

"You can make coffee," she says. "If you want to use the spare room, you're going to need to clear it out."

I nod and lean over to grab her plate and take it over to the dishwasher. She's always been militant about the rinsing and stacking, and today's not a good day to challenge that. I fill the kettle with water and switch it on.

The back garden is looking good, and like the window boxes at the front, the flora and fauna out here receives a lot more love and attention than Molly or I ever did. There's a little bench leaning up against the back wall, and I make a mental note that that's where I'll be having a much needed spliff when I come back here in under a fortnight's time.

Mum keeps her coffee in the fridge, so I spoon some into a cafetiere and stand there letting it brew for a minute. I bring her back a mug, black like the very depths of her soul, and put it down in front of her. She's already got her laptop back open on the table, so I'm guessing all our bonding is done for the day. I've got time on my hands right now, so even though my instincts are to run screaming from the house as fast as I possibly can, I don't.

"I'll get started on the spare room," I say. "What do you want me to do with everything?"

"It can go in the attic."

I nod. "Okay."

I walk up the stairs to begin clearing. There are a couple of prints hanging, but very little in the way of photos. The only place in the house where there are photos are in the lounge – one of me, one of Molly, and one of Sky and Flower. The one of Sky and Flower is the only one she's even vaguely interested in though, and I think she'd be more than happy not to have ours up at all, if it weren't for the fact that it would just look too weird on the rare occasion that she might have visitors. No, there's very little decoration in the house. Pat keeps all her attention for the garden.

The spare bedroom is in the middle, with what used to be my bedroom now being let out to lodgers at the back of the house. Sofia's not in, so I take the opportunity to see what's been done with what used to be my bedroom. She's clearly tidy – the bed is made and there's nothing on the floor. A couple of photos sit on the dressing table, and there are some books on the shelf, but these are the only real clues that someone lives here. I take a closer look at the photos. There's one of a girl in her late teens in the arms of someone whose own mother would forget what he looked like, who's simpering at the camera. The other one is a posed family shot with the same girl sat on a couch with what I assume are her parents, along with a younger brother. I take a closer look to try and get an idea of her personality and judging from the look of her boyfriend I'd say desperate, and not too picky. Her eyes look a bit too close together, and she's got fucking terrible hair. It's got that dry, fizzy quality, and I wouldn't be surprised if she cut it herself.

I beat a retreat and creep back to the spare room. It's small; and made all the smaller for tons of Mum's crap that's piled up in boxes all over the place. There are books all over the place – mostly Spanish ones that she's translated and that have then just ended up in here. There's a single bed, and I don't think I could get my double in even if I tried. At least if I did then there would be no more room for anything else, so I guess I'm going to have to stay with this. The overall appearance of a cell isn't improved by the fact that there isn't a window, and the lack of natural light makes it doubly depressing. I sigh, looking around. I may as well get started.

It takes a good hour and a half to schlep everything up the stepladder and into the loft. I take the opportunity while I'm up there to leaf through a box of old, forgotten 2000AD's, and relive my youth pouring over Judge Dredd; and make a mental note to check out if they're worth anything on eBay.

Shifting everything about so that I can get all the boxes up there and positioned so they're not going to come crashing down and through the roof takes a level of patience that it would normally take me two or three spliffs to acquire; the only problem being that after I've smoked that much the apathy kicks in and I really can't be arsed. So, I take it slowly, and get it done bit by bit, and it's approaching four o'clock when I finally get the last box up there, and the spare room is empty. It still looks tiny, but I can probably make do for a while. It's not like I've got a choice. I dig the hoover out from the cupboard under the stairs, as I know I'll only pay for it later if I don't and give the room a good clean.

"All done," I say, as I open the door to put the hoover away.

"Leave it out," she says. She's still got her nose in her laptop and hasn't looked up to acknowledge me. "I'll give downstairs a quick going over."

"I can do that," I say.

"If you like."

Not particularly, but I do it anyway, as I'm going to remind her that I need to borrow some cash in about two minutes, so anything I can do to soften that blow is only wise. I run the hoover all over downstairs, leaving the kitchen so I don't disturb her.

"I'd better get off then." She hasn't moved and is still tapping away.

"You've cleared the room out? Everything's in the loft?"

"Everything," I say. "I've been very careful loading it up there."

"Good."

I stand there a moment, wondering if she's going to make this at all easy. I guess not.

"Mum, would it be alright if I borrowed that money? It's only for a while, I promise. I'll get it back to you soon."

She sighs, irritated, and pushes her chair back to go to her handbag on the kitchen counter. She opens her purse with no small amount of drama, clearly signalling just what an affront this is, that her son should come to her cap in hand. She takes out three twenties and holds them out to me.

"This will have to do," she says. "If you need more you'll have to wait until the end of the week."

"Thanks," I say, taking the money. "That's really helpful. Honestly."

She grunts quietly, as if her dissatisfaction hadn't just been made clear enough and goes over to the bookshelves and grabs a set of keys, and hands them to me.

"Here," she says. "I'd appreciate it if you'd let me know when you're coming."

I nod. "I will. Thanks." I lift my coat off the back of the chair and try not to make it look like I'm getting out as quickly as possible. "I'll be off then. Like I say, it'll probably be the end of the week."

"Fine," she says, levelling me with a look that holds no affection. It's getting dark in the hall as I leave, but she doesn't turn the light on, but instead turns on a reading lamp on the bookshelf in the kitchen, throwing a small pin of light over her computer.

The rain is coming down as I walk back to the bus stop, and I stand there getting wet. I'm not really a big one for omens, but I issue a silent prayer as it falls harder that this is symbolic of a baptism, of rebirth and a new beginning, rather than a portent of storms and misery ahead.

By the time I'm back in the Grove, it's properly dark and the wind is blowing bitterly cold outside. There's a lot to do in the flat if I'm going to be out at the end of the week, and so I begin the arduous process of packing everything I own.

The mobile rings. It's Carol.

"Hi babe."

"Charlie, darling, how are you?" She sounds just as raspy as ever, but I can hear she's got a fag on the go. Nothing changes.

"Okay. Busy with some house stuff. I told you I'm moving?"

"Really? I thought you loved that flat, darling."

I do, I think. Carol knows I'm broke, but I haven't been into the exact details with her, as I don't think she needs to know, and I don't want her to think I'm desperate. Even if I am.

"Yeah," I say. "But I need to downsize for a bit. Tighten my belt."

"You're very wise, Charlie. Very wise. I bring tidings from Donovan Taft. We've got a schedule for you. A week of rehearsals from next Monday, then straight into the shoot."

"Great," I say. "Can you email it to me? I don't think I'm going to be able to get in this week."

"Of course, darling. Will do. You'll have to let me know how it goes."

Holding the phone in my hand I suddenly remember that Elijah phoned me this morning, and I haven't called him back. "Babe, you know I told you about that kid I met on the street? You know, the one who recognised me. Wanted to be an actor?"

"Mm hmm."

"When could you see him? I could send him down to the office. Take a look at him, ask him to read something?"

"For you darling, anytime. How about the end of the week?"

"Okay, thanks. I'll let you know."

I hang up, and call Elijah. The phone rings out and goes to voicemail. I hang up without leaving a message. Two seconds later the phone rings. A different number. I answer.

"That you Hollywood?"

I'm not sure about the switch phone thing. Must be some kind of related paranoia to do with robbing people.

"Hi Elijah," I say. "How's it going?"

"I thought you were going to blank me, blad."

"Nah," I say. "So, I said that I might be able to hook you up with someone."

There's silence on the other end of the phone.

"You there?"

"Yes, blad. Who you gonna set me wiv?"

"My agent. Carol. I asked her to take a look at you. She knows talent when she sees it, so it could be a good break for you."

"Serious?" If he's trying to keep the thrill out of his voice, he's failing, and for a second, he sounds like exactly what he is; an excited teenager.

"Serious," I say. "Can you go and see her at her office on Friday?"

"Yeah, man. Definitely."

"You'll need to do a reading."

"A what?"

"An audition piece. She needs to see if you can act. It's not all about looking pretty."

"You funny, man. I ain't gonna do no fucking reading."

I sigh. "Then she's not going to see you. And I'm just wasting all of our time."

There's a pause on the other end of the line. "What do I have to do, blad?"

"You need to read a piece from a play, or a film. It's a good idea to get two together. One modern, one Shakespeare."

"I ain't doing no fucking Shakespeare, Hollywood. That shit's fucking gay."

I laugh. I've never been that much of a fan of the bard myself, but I haven't heard anyone nail it quite so succinctly before.

"Fair enough. But you're going to need to do something. You got a scene you could do?"

"I dunno, man."

"You need some help?"

The pause again. There's a level of distrust here that is probably understandable, but he's not making it easy.

"I'm not going to turn up with the police, you know," I tell him. "And before you ask, I don't want to fucking bum you. It's just I've done this shit before, and I could give you a couple of pointers."

A couple of seconds pass, then "Safe. Okay, Hollywood. We can meet."

Fuck me, like he's doing me a favour now. This kid could go far.

"You know the park on St. Marks Road? There. Tomorrow, twelve o'clock. And by the way, I'm not going to have any fucking money on me."

"Nah man, I can't step there. Some bad men shank me, you get me? You come to the Pleasance, innit."

It's my turn to pause. I'm doing this twat a favour, and it would be nice to feel a little fucking appreciated.

"Serious man, I can't get there. It's easy for you man, innit. You don't know what it's like for me, blad."

There's a pleading in his voice, and I realise that behind the bluster, the front, and all the aggression he's just a scared kid. He's right, I don't have any idea what it's like. Not really. It's different for me. You hear about kids like Elijah getting stabbed almost every day, and usually for nothing more serious than being in the wrong street.

"Okay," I say. "I'll come there. I'll see you in the Pleasance. Twelve o'clock. See you then."

"Safe." The line goes dead. I suppose a simple 'thanks' is too much to hope for, but then Rome wasn't built in a day.

It's just before twelve when I get to the Pleasance, and sit down on one of the few benches, waiting to see if Elijah shows. I spent some of the morning on the net and think I might have a good piece for him. Initially I was thinking about Brighton Rock; about the recording that Pinkie makes for Rose in the booth ("you think I love you, but I think you're a slut"), but then I thought casting him as a young gangster might not be the best way forward. He needs something with a bit of an edge though, so then I thought about De Niro's voice over at the start of Taxi Driver – "someday a real rain will come and wash all this scum off the streets." Fuck knows if he's seen it or not, but then it's probably better if he hasn't, or otherwise he might just end up doing an impression.

I've printed it off for him, and now am sitting on the bench watching someone from the council collecting all the rubbish out of the bins. Then I see him walking up the path towards me – he's on his own and is swaggering along like he's the king of W10.

He slumps down on the bench next to me. To anyone else this is going to look so like a drug deal.

"Hollywood. 'Sup, blad."

"Elijah. How's it going."

He nods, bobbing his head up and down. He's not really looking at me but is scanning the area around us. It takes me a second to work out what he's doing, but then I realise. He's looking around because he doesn't want to be seen with me. Anyone who sees us together is only going to want to know what's going on, and I'm pretty sure that he wants to keep his ambitions private.

"So, you done much acting?" I ask him.

He shakes his head. "Nah, man."

"So why do you want to do it?"

He shrugs. "Looks like fun, innit. Plus you get paid, star. And you get plenty pussy."

Despite every effort not to, I get an image of Chloe popping into my head. I haven't been out since that night, and what with how that panned out, I'm not in a hurry to again. I'm skint. Going out to test Elijah's theory about getting plenty of pussy just really isn't doing it for me right now. There is something in that though; over the years I have found that women seem to be a little bit more interested in getting to know me than some of my other contemporaries – something I can only attribute to having a recognisable face.

"So, you're in it for the money and the women then?"

He sucks his teeth. "Cha. Course man."

"Fair enough. So have you thought about a piece that you could do?"

"What do you do, man?"

"Well, I've been around the block, so they'll normally get me to read from whatever it is they're casting. But you haven't. So you're going to have to do something that shows you can act. You see 'Taxi Driver'?"

His brow furrows. "Nah."

"That's okay. It's probably good you haven't. It's this guy who comes back from a war and he's fucking angry. He hates the world. A lot of the film is him driving around, talking to the audience about how much he fucking hates everyone."

"Nang bruv."

"I've printed off this piece for you. Have a look at it, then read it out to me."

He gives me a sideways look. "Serious?"

"You want to do this? Then try. This is a scene where he's writing in his diary about this woman that he's seen; that he becomes obsessed with. He's parked his taxi opposite her building and has just stared at her so far. She's seen him watching her, but they haven't talked."

I hand him the paper, and he looks down at it. I can tell he's reading it carefully, and the second time he looks over it his lips start to move. He finishes and looks up at me.

"Okay."

"You want to give it a shot?"

He nods. He looks down at the paper again, then starts.

"All my life needed was a sense of direction, a sense of someplace to go. I do not believe one should devote his life to morbid self-attention but should become a person like other people. I first saw her at Palantine Campaign Headquarters at 58th and Broadway. She was wearing a yellow desk, answering the phone at her desk. She appeared like an angel out of this open sewer. Out of this filthy mass. She is alone: they cannot touch her."

He looks up at me.

"Not bad," I say. "She was wearing a yellow desk?"

He looks down at the paper, then looks back at me. "I said dress."

"You said desk, but it wasn't bad. You've not seen the film?"

He shakes his head.

"Good," I say. "You'll like it but wait until after Friday. It's better you don't see it yet."

"Lemme do it again."

"In a minute. Acting is all about convincing people you're someone else, that you've become this different character. So, get your head round the idea that you've seen some really bad fucking shit, maybe seen a couple of your mates blown to pieces in a foreign country, and now you're back home. And no-one wants nothing to fucking do with you. You're driving a taxi around, at night, and everything you're seeing makes you angry. There's a point before this where he says, "someday a rain will come and wash all the scum from the streets." So, he could have grown up reading the Bible, and he's waiting for the wrath of God. But he's not that educated, right? In the film you see him writing in his diary with a pencil, and he's got this spidery writing, kind of like a kid's. But look at what he's saying in that piece. First, he knows he needs a sense of direction. Maybe he's been drifting his entire life. That line, 'I do not believe one should devote his life to morbid self-attention'..."

"What's that mean?" Elijah is leaning forward, and I've got to give him credit. He's listening to me, like he wants to work this out.

"Morbid self-attention? It means that he's only concerned with himself, perhaps he's examining his motives for doing everything a little too much. But it's quite a flowery phrase for an uneducated soldier. To me, it sounds like he's repeating something he's heard on the radio or seen on the TV. Because it might make him sound cleverer than he is. How many guys do you know who refer to themselves as 'one'? Not many, right? Same for this guy. He's repeating something from somewhere else."

Elijah is nodding now, like he's beginning to get what I'm on about.

"Okay, try now."

He looks down at the page again and pauses a moment before doing another reading. It's good; he manages to capture something of Travis's confusion and childishness.

"That's good, Elijah. Seriously. You know one of the things that makes a difference in an audition? Whether you can take a note. That means they're going to want to see if you can take direction, or if you do the same reading every time. So, I've given you some idea of how Travis might think, what his background is, what he might feel. You see at the end where he talks about 'this filthy mass, this open sewer?' I want you to imagine that someone is getting in your face at that point, and I want you to get angry, just for a minute. Then pause a second, relax, and deliver the next line like the memory of this woman is the one thing keeping you calm. Yeah? Try that."

He's looking at me, and he nods. There's the flicker of a smile on his face before he starts, and then he reads. Listening to him, I'm fucking blown away. He gets what I've been talking about perfectly, and he totally nails it, responding to the direction I've given him with empathy and skill. His voice is going to need a bit of work, but if he can scale back the West London patois then he should be okay.

"That was good," I tell him.

He's grinning at me. "Yeah?"

"Yeah," I nod. "Really good. I think Carol will be impressed. Do me a favour though. Try and calm down the bad bwoy ting and ting with her, yeah? She's not going to be impressed with any of your gangster shit. It's fine to have an edge, but she's going to want to know that she can send you out to an audition and not be embarrassed. So be polite. You don't have to suck dick, and it's good to know yourself. Some guys would pay good money to have your fucking confidence. But try and be nice. Because if you fuck off Carol, all this will have been for nothing."

He nods, his face all serious. I can tell he wants this. And if he reads like that for Carol, I think she'll give him a shot.

"And don't watch the film, at least not until you've done this. I just think it's better if you don't."

"Alright. Safe."

"You done anything like this before?"

He shakes his head. "Nah."

"Nothing at school? No?"

He laughs. "You seen my school, blud?"

"Fair enough. So, is there anything else you want to know?"

He shakes his head.

"Okay. Well, break a leg for Friday." He looks at me, momentary aggression in his eyes. I can't help but laugh. "No, I don't mean, actually hurt yourself. It's how you say good luck to other actors."

He stares at me a second. "You is deffo batty, man."

"Whatever. I'll speak to Carol on Friday and find out how you did. You can call me next Saturday if you want."

He nods and folding his piece of paper lifts himself off the bench and begins to swagger off. I'm just beginning to think 'twat' when he turns.

"You alright Charlie, man. You need anyting, holler. You get me?"

He turns, and he's away again. Fuck me. After that, I practically feel like family.

Three days later and I'm finally nearing the end of a marathon session of packing. Everything I own is either in boxes, or in a suitcase, or ready to be dismantled. I've been slowly wandering from room to room with a spliff, taking it all in. This is probably the last time I'm going to be in here after almost seven years. I'm trying not to feel all sentimental about it, but deep down it really feels like a kick in the bollocks. This is my home. My place. I worked hard to pay for this, and now it's going it feels like part of me is dying; and it's the part of me that felt like any kind of success. Letting this go feels like the ultimate admittance of failure. That I'm a piece of shit. That it was all for nothing.

I'm trying as hard as I can to look on the bright side, to see that selling the flat is going to sort me out financially in a way that I never was before; that as one chapter ends so another begins and blah, blah, fucking blah; but then the truth hits me hard again – that in a few minutes time a massive Rasta called Levi is going to ring on the doorbell and take me back to live at my Mother's. And if anything is going to make me fucking depressed, it's that.

I've cleaned as best I can, but after speaking with James we agreed that it was probably an idea to get someone round to give the place a proper spruce to get it shifted a bit more quickly. He's also started making noises about possibly dropping the price a few grand, as people aren't beating down his door to see the place. I don't know why, as this is a fucking great flat.

I go from the kitchen back to the living room, and a hundred blurred memories of happier times flit through my brain; of nights spent in debauched mayhem, of a living room full of people after Carnival one year, of dinners, and drugs, and lazy days with the X-Box.

And then I hear the buzzer, and all the memories vanish in an instant. I hit the intercom and tell him to come up.

I met Levi when he was ferrying stuff around on 'Fourteen and Gone', a low budget thriller that went straight to DVD three years ago. I'd been playing a gangster opposite Tom Harrison and Oliver Rowsall; and since then, both of their careers have blossomed. Tom is now the lead at a thing in the National, and Oliver went off to score a tasty role in an HBO series. Levi was the man who would take everything from A to B in his transit van, permanently stoned and happy with it.

When the shoot finished, he told me to give him a call if I ever needed him for anything, and so when I knew that I had to ship everything out of here, he was the first person I thought of. He's a big fucker, Levi, and he'll do whatever I ask him to without much hassle, and perhaps as importantly, he'll be quite happy to puff away as we do it. He managed to help clear a location of all the props in about half an hour after smoking a reefer that would have floored Howard Marks.

I leave the door open and go to run the butt of the spliff under the tap and dunk it in the rubbish. No sense in encouraging too much too soon. Levi strolls in and shoots me the first genuine smile I can remember seeing in about a month.

"Charlie. How you doin', mon?"

"Good Levi," I say. "How's everything with you?"

He nods. "Everyting fine. What we do today?"

"We're clearing the place. Most of the stuff's going into storage, but then some of the rest of it is going up to Willesden Green."

"You're moving?"

He's not the sharpest tool in the box, is old Levi, but his heart is in the right place.

"Unfortunately so, yeah."

"Shame, mon. This a fine place."

I feel the pang again and ignore it.

"Yeah, well. Things happen. What do you want to do first?"

He looks around carefully as he takes in everything that needs to go down, and processes everything to work out the best approach for getting everything in the back of the van. He already looks ripped to the tits, so it's probably good that we're starting earlier. He wanders into both bedrooms.

"Everyting? The couch break down?"

I nod. He sucks his teeth for a moment, thinking.

"Okay. The couch first, then the beds come down."

"Okay."

The next half an hour is spent taking apart the couch in the lounge with a fair amount of swearing on my part, and an almost zen-like ambivalence from Levi, who tells me not to worry, that it will come. I'm sure the fact that he blazes up a spliff the size of a Mini helps with chilling him out. Eventually we break it down and get it downstairs into the van and follow with the beds. The van is looking packed already, but I go with Levi when he says that we can get a little more in there, and so a couple of the boxes come down. This looks like it's going to take a few trips.

When it's looking about as packed as it can get, I climb into the front seat next to him.

"Where first Charlie?"

"Scrubs Lane. Storage."

He nods, and we're away. The other good thing about using Levi is that he lives in the Grove, so there's no need to pay out for congestion charge. I don't drive, as there's very little point owning a fucking car in London, especially when you've got everything on your doorstep. But I have noticed that there seems to be much less traffic ever since they introduced the charge to the area. I'm not that fussed either way, but you can't move in and out of any shop on Portobello without them bleating on about how it's killing their business. But it doesn't seem to do Levi any harm, and from what he's been telling me there seems no end of people who are prepared to sock him some cash (never to be claimed, obviously) to get him to do some transporting in and out of W10. I've wondered if he ever brings in anything heavier for some of the moodier residents in the area, but then if I was moving drugs or guns around the last person I'd go for is a six foot four dreadlock Rasta who pumps out dub from the stereo twenty four seven.

It takes no time to get to the storage, which is another reason I went for it. Left at the end of St. Quintin's, past the North Pole, right onto Scrubs Lane, and you're there. I went to sort out the room the other day and although it's not cheap, I don't plan on it being in there for long. So fuck it. Keeping it in the same postcode is my mental link to the area and means that when I come back and rent (as I plan to very, very soon) then it won't be far for Levi to come and pick it all up again.

We pull through the gates and we're in. The real estate in this place, just up the road from Westfield and overlooking the canal, is probably worth a fortune. Which gives you an idea of just how much this storage racket must be worth. I'm just hoping the small room I've rented is big enough to squeeze all the stuff in. If things start going really tits up staying at Pats, then I might end up moving in here myself.

Everything comes slowly out of the van, onto the trolley, and up in the lift to the first floor. Opening the door to the small room in which I'm supposed to cram nearly everything I own I'm already thinking this may be tight. Very tight. I turn and look at Levi, who just grins at me.

"Plenty big enough, Charlie mon. Plenty."

I'm not convinced, but over the next twenty minutes or so we manage to get the sofa in, followed by both beds, and I'm starting to relax a little. It should all go in, and anything that doesn't will just have to come up with me to Mums. That should go down well.

We swing by Sainsbury's on the way back to the flat and I pick us up some sandwiches, which we then eat perched on boxes, in silence. I don't protest when Levi starts to roll a gigantic reefer, but only take a couple of tokes on it when it's offered. I learnt the hard way long ago to be very wary of anything he's built. He passed me a spliff on the way back from a day on the shoot that made me think I was going to lose my fucking mind.

After that's been smoked it seems to take a bit longer to get everything downstairs, but part of that might just be the sheer amount of crap that needs to go in the van. Boxes of pans from the kitchen, books, CDs; my whole life broken down into tiny pieces and all off to be packed away in a cold cupboard. By four o'clock the flat is empty, bar a suitcase full of clothes that's coming with me up to Willesden Green, another holdall containing my computer, toiletries and some other bits and pieces, and a cardboard box containing my small telly along with the Xbox. There's no way that I'm going to endure life at Pat's without some form of digital entertainment.

Levi seems to read my mood and says nothing all the way back to the unit, and the silence continues as everything comes up in the lift and slowly gets squeezed away into the room. When we're done I just stand there for a moment staring at what, up until this morning, was the furniture of my life, and is now just stuff, piled high in a cupboard. I'll just have to come and reclaim it all soon.

I was going to ask Levi to drop me up to Willesden Green, but it's as easy for me to get a cab. Besides, I don't want to run the risk of him bumping into Pat. That would just be a barrel of laughs. So instead, he drops me off outside the flat.

I slide out of the van onto the street. The 'For Sale' sign tilts listlessly to one side in what passes for the front garden, amidst the rubbish that always seems to dance about the bins.

"Thanks Levi. I appreciate your help. Like I say, I'll sort you out next week. Soon as."

He nods at me. We've barely spoken since lunchtime, and I think he can tell just what a wrench this has been for me. He's not asked me what's going on, but then I wouldn't have told him anyway. One of the many reasons Levi was perfect to help out on a day like today is that he will never feel the need to fill a silence with idle chatter and is totally comfortable with saying absolutely nothing. But then being semi-permanently stoned is always going to help with that. That, and the fact that he's probably completely uninterested.

I watch the van pull away, then let myself into the house, conscious that this is the last time I'll be coming in here. There's music from behind the door of the bedsit on the ground floor, some fucking terrible rock noise that sounds like it's taxing the speakers on a crappy laptop to breaking point. Whoever's been living there must have been there for at least six months, but our paths have never crossed. So it is in London – it's not just that you don't know your neighbours, but that you wouldn't want to know them either.

I open the door to the flat. The suitcase, holdall and box sit there by the door. The place looks smaller without any of my stuff in it. It's just gone half five, and the traffic will be shit for at least another hour and a half. I send Pat a text to let her know I'll be there around half 7, and I won't need feeding, just to make sure there's no misunderstanding. I wander in and out of the empty rooms, just looking at the space. I can remember the day I moved in here as clear as yesterday; it was shortly after the release of 'The Trampoline', and I was full of myself, convinced that I was on the verge of something big, that before too long I'd be picking up a whole house round the corner. But it wasn't to be.

I fish my tin of dope out of the holdall, and skin up a fat reefer for myself on the kitchen counter. I open the window in the sitting room, and crouch down to smoke outside it. There's no point in stinking out the flat with the smell of puff when I'm trying to sell it. There's not much going on in the street. A car drives past, and I follow that until I see a man walking a dog the other way. I follow him all the way up to the corner of St. Marks, and he turns up there and I lose him. A quiet street. That's one of the many reasons I love – loved – this road. Because for all the hustle and bluster that West London has to offer, St. Quintin's had a quietness, a dignity that some of the other streets just can't match.

It's beginning to get dark, but in about a week or so the clocks will go forward (or back, I can never remember which), and it will stay light until gone 7, and that's when this area really begins to come into its own. The Grove thrives on sunshine, and although you could say that of practically anywhere, I think it's especially true of round here. There's an energy that summer brings that seems to get under the skin of Portobello, and gently bubble away from May through to August, until it reaches a climax with Carnival. Then the whole place sighs, and by the time the hangovers have worn off its September, and the long slow descent into winter begins again.

I flick the spliff butt out of the window and make a silent promise to myself, that I'll be back here and renting by July at the latest. Once the flat is sold, and my finances sorted out, then things will be able to change pretty fucking rapidly. I hope.

But right now, I've got some time to kill before I call a cab to take me up to Willesden Green, so I may as well go crazy. A can of Stella and a bag of chips should be a good last supper.

It's dark when the cab arrives, and beeps twice from the road to let me know it's here. Like every other minicab driver I've encountered in the last five years, he seems to have lost the power of his legs to get out of his car and come and ring the bell like a fucking normal person.

I walk down with the box with the TV in it and tell him I'll be a couple of minutes, then walk back up. Even though I've walked through every room at least ten times in the last hour, I do a final tour just to check that I haven't left anything behind. Picking up the bags, I flick the lights off for the last time, and double lock the door behind me.

The bags go in the boot, and I go on the back seat. The smooth sound of the Carpenters plays incredibly quietly, and it's good to see that this driver isn't trying anything too maverick like tuning his radio to something other than Magic FM.

"Do you know Churchill Road?" I ask him.

He turns round to look at me like he's never heard of the fucking place, and then leans forward to start tapping at his Satnav.

"It's alright. I know where it is," I tell him. "Just head for Willesden Green and I'll direct you."

He nods and pulls away. Satnav has changed things a little, in that at least catching a minicab isn't so much an exercise in brushing up your map reading skills while paying for the privilege. It always amazed me just how quickly drivers would reach for the A to Z from the glovebox and dump it expectantly in your lap. Surely if you're driving a cab knowing where you're going is kind of the whole point. The moment you take directions from someone, then it's less of a cab journey and more an expensive lift.

As we cross Harrow Road my heart sinks with the realisation that there's really no way out of this, that it's really happening. I'm 37, and I'm moving back in with my mother. Rain starts to spot the window.

I direct him down the route the 52 goes and can't even be bothered to debate the small national debt he wants for ferrying me the few miles up here. There's just enough left of the sixty quid that Mum gave me to sort him out, so I put it in his greedy hands, and he drives off, leaving me with two bags and a box on the pavement of Churchill Road.

I open the front door quickly and carry the box in, and then drag the suitcases in behind me. There's a small side light on in the hall that does nothing to improve the overall mood of dank gloom that cloaks the house like a wet towel. I drag everything in. There's the sound of Eastenders coming from the living room, so I stick my head round the door.

Pat watches silently in the almost dark, another sidelight casting a small glow on the table to her right. She waits a moment before turning her head to look at me.

"You're here then." She turns her attention back to the screen.

"Looks like it. I'm going to make a cup of tea. Do you want one?"

"If you're making one." She waits until I've left the room, then calls out after me. "Charlie, can you put everything upstairs first? I don't want to trip over it."

"No problem," I reply. Anything for a quiet life. I nip into the kitchen to stick the kettle on, then lift the box up first. The room's even smaller than I remember it, and I look down at the single bed and tell myself that it's only for a little while, and the moment the flat is sold I'll be able to get out and rent somewhere. There's a small table at the end of the bed, so I stick the telly on it straight away.

Once the two bags are up, there's barely any room to breathe. The tiny cupboard that pre-dates the existence of Ikea will be packed in no time, and it looks like I'm going to have to live out of my case for the foreseeable future.

I delve into the holdall to fish out my tin and proceed to skin up an extremely strong reefer.

I bring Pat out her cup of tea, and she's already fixated on some gardening programme on BBC2.

"I'm just going to have a fag in the garden," I tell her.

She takes the tea. "Still got enough money for tobacco, then."

I bite my tongue. I'm not going to get into this now.

"I only have the occasional cigarette. Usually when I'm stressed."

She shrugs, and I leave her to it. It's just gone half 8, so I reckon I've got at least twenty-five minutes out there before I'm disturbed. It's still spitting outside, so I need to pull my hood up and cower underneath the limited shelter that the tiny porch over the back doorway has to offer. I light the spliff and drag on it deeply, trying to anaesthetize the blue funk I can feel myself slipping into.

There's a point for most people at which the feeling of returning to a parent's house ceases to feel like coming home. For most people that's probably when they leave and go to university, but for me it was about halfway through the run of 'The Mocking Half'. You could feel the tension here every time you walked through the door, and I was becoming increasingly aware that I just didn't want to be here. The semi-permanent anxiety that I felt during the filming of 'The Twelfth of Never' was never relieved by coming back to this house, and I would cry myself to sleep because I honestly thought that no-one gave a shit. Molly had already left home by that stage, in her first year of Brighton University, and not in any rush to come back and visit the hell that was life in London. And so, it was just me, muddling through adolescence, film sets and school that each seemed to hold their own particular horrors.

School became almost unbearable for my final GCSE year. 'The Twelfth of Never' was released in September, and I paid for it right through until June. Any thoughts that the intense attention that the film rewarded me outside the school might translate to popularity inside quickly vanished, and instead just ramped up any perceptible difference between me and everyone else. As I'd been away for a large part of the final term filming and had been slaving away on a drama series for the BBC over the summer, all the friendships that I had thought solid proved in fact to be all too brittle and fragile. I returned to a cold hostility, with the entire school clearly convinced that I now thought I was hot shit and needed taking down a peg or two. The fact that I was playing an emotional wreck for most of 'The Twelfth of Never' didn't help, and only intensified the bullying.

Things improved when I went to St. Charles sixth form down in the Grove, but it was still hard going. I jacked it in halfway through the second year, never bothering to sit my A-levels, when I nailed a tasty role as a young soldier in a thirteen-part series around the First World War. Shooting lasted nine months, and by then it was summer again. I was loaded, and rented with Casper Hough, one of the other actors in a pit on Elgin Crescent and stayed in the Grove ever since.

Until now. Where I find myself smoking puff in a rain-soaked garden in Willesden Green. Back living with my mother for the first time in about twenty years, with the levels of hostility between us still as gently masked as ever.

The rain is beginning to fall a little heavier now, and I'm nearly at the roach. I hold it out to the sky for a moment, giving up when no drop falls directly on the end. But it's out anyway. I feel a little light-headed, as I did pack that pretty heavily, and so let myself back into the kitchen and spoon another load of sugar into my now lukewarm tea.

Churchill Road.

Fucking brilliant.

I wake up as I hear someone coming up the stairs, and even with the lights on full I still wonder where the fuck I am for a second. And then it all comes flooding back as I take in my surroundings, lying back on a single bed with my suitcase on the floor.

I came straight up a couple of hours ago with the excuse that I had to unpack, but the truth was I'd rather be anywhere else than watching telly with Pat in an atmosphere of barely concealed contempt. I managed to get as far as opening the case and looking at my clothes when the events of the day caught up with me and I lay back on the bed and fell fast asleep. That, and the knockout reefer probably helped.

I check my phone to see what the time is, and it's just gone 11.15. That means Pat's likely to have been in bed for about forty-five minutes, and whoever's creeping up the stairs is only too aware of this and is also aware just how much grief will ensue if she is woken up. It must be Sofia, the tenant, and from the too careful creeping going on, I would guess that she's probably had a skinful. She reaches the landing, and creeps past the door, pausing for a second as she's no doubt registering that the light is on, and that I've now moved into the spare room. I'm sure she probably has an idea of who I am, and if you're from the arse end of Eastern fucking Europe then even a hapless twat like me is going to seem like a major fucking celebrity. I hear her open the door and close it quietly.

I'm awake now, so swing my feet off the bed and dive into the cardboard box to set up my telly and Xbox at the end of the bed. It's not like I've got a lot else going on, so I might as well go for a tour round Liberty City to while away the hours.

It's gone eleven when I finally wake up, the headphones I was wearing next to me on the pillow. I'm not sure what time I eventually crashed, but it must have been late. I know this is going to cause no end of disapproval from Pat, but I don't really give a shit. Rehearsals start next week, and I can't wait to be out and doing something again.

I yawn and look at the ceiling, listening for noise from downstairs before I get up. I can't hear anything, so maybe Pat has ventured on one of her rare forays outside the house. If she has, I hope she remembers to get me some fucking cash.

I swing my legs out of bed and try to find a spare piece of floor that I can plant them on, somewhere that isn't covered with the clothes I began to sort out last night. This room really is fucking tiny, and if there's one thing that's more emasculating than going back to live at a parent's, it's sleeping in a fucking single bed. And then it's not actually the sleeping, but rather the waking and the realisation that your life seems to be heading very fast in reverse. I stay there for a moment longer, listening for any signs of life. I can't hear anything, so I guess the coast is clear.

I pull on my sweatpants and make my way downstairs. The kitchen is empty, Pat's laptop in its usual spot with the lid down tight. It reminds me to check my email to see if the rehearsal schedule has come through from Carol yet, but I'll do that in a while once I've broken in the day with some much-needed coffee.

I stare vacantly out of the kitchen window at the garden while the kettle boils, then fill up a cafetiere. I know that there will be some sulking pretty soon if I don't offer to sort out some money for everything that I use in here, on top of all the cash that I'm borrowing.

I take my coffee through into the living room, thinking I'll sit on my arse and catch some shit daytime telly. I've just flicked on the TV when a groan from the couch behind me nearly makes me jump and spill my coffee all over the carpet.

There's a bedraggled mess on the sofa, curled up and nursing what is clearly a crippling hangover.

"Fuck, you scared me! You're Sofia, right?"

She nods, looking blearily at me.

"Shouldn't you be at college or something?"

"You are Charlie, yes?"

I nod. She's wrapped in a dressing gown and looks like she's just woken up. A mug of cold tea is next to her on the side table, and even though I can smell the booze on her from here, she's more attractive than she appears in the photo I saw upstairs. Maybe she just looks ten times better without the pus-filled tit draping his arm around her shoulder.

"Good night, was it?" She groans again, burying her head in her hands. "I thought you sounded pissed the way you were coming up the stairs last night."

She looks shocked. "You hear me? No. I try to be quiet. To not make noise."

The poor girl looks petrified. And I doubt that it's me that she's worrying about disturbing coming in late at night.

"Don't worry," I tell her. "You were quiet. I don't think you woke up my mother."

She nods and looks relieved if not entirely convinced. "What time is it?" she asks.

"Gone eleven, I think."

"You are right, then. I should be."

"What?"

"I should be at college. But I just do not feel well enough. So I stay."

"Where's Pat?"

"Is Friday. Is her day for going into office in Mayfair for translation. She leave early."

"Okay," I say. "She never told me."

Sofia shrugs.

"So how are you getting on with her?" I ask. But I think I already know the answer. She looks nervous, like she feels uncomfortable talking to me about this.

"It's okay, I know I'm her son, but I think she's as big a pain in the arse as anyone."

She smiles at this, then winces.

"I drank too much last night. I saw friends from college. We drank in pub in Covent Garden."

Of course you did, I think, but don't say. But then if I was a foreign language student, I'd probably drink somewhere pretty and touristy too. I look at her curled up on the couch, and I try and put myself in her shoes. It must take guts to leave home to move to one of the biggest and meanest cities in Europe and try and make a life for yourself. Not least when the odds are stacked against you by lodging with the Wicked Witch of North-West London. If it was me in her position, I might well have fucked it all off and gone straight to Victoria for the first coach back.

"Do you like living in London?" I ask.

She shrugs. "Is okay. Very expensive."

Tell me about it. "I know. Do you work?"

"At a bar in High Street Kensington," she says, nodding. "Riley's."

If it's the one I'm thinking of it's a fucking shithole, but then fair play to the girl; she's clearly grafting.

"You are actor, yes?"

"Yes."

"I see the film, 'The Twelfth of Never'. A long time ago, at home. It was a beautiful film, I think."

"Thanks."

"It made me feel like you know great sadness."

"Thanks," I say. Part of me is thinking that that's acting for you, but then what she's said echoes in my brain. That I know great sadness. Perhaps I did then. Perhaps I still do. Perhaps that's what's wrong with my fucking life.

"You didn't tell me how you're getting on with Pat."

She shifts uncomfortably.

"The only reason I ask," I say, "is because you've been here nearly four months, right? And most of her tenants only last six."

"She is very intelligent woman," says Sofia, clearly digging deep to reach for something to say.

"She's rude," I say. "And manipulative. And mean."

"What is manipulative?"

"Like she tries to get you to do what she wants."

"Ah. Yes, I see." She looks at me, suspicious. "But you are her son?"

"By blood, yes. But she's not really into the whole love and affection thing."

"That is shame." She pauses. "I thought everyone in London like her."

I laugh. "Yeah, I guess sometimes it must seem that way. But no, not everyone. At least, not all the time. Where's college?"

"Tottenham Court Road. The London School of Languages."

Which I'm guessing is one of those places above the doughnut shops and noodle bars that litter that end of the street, ever since people stopped buying records and the Virgin Megastore died.

"Your English is pretty good."

"Thank you. I try."

"So, what are you going to do when you finish?"

She shrugs. "I may stay here. Try to find job. But is not easy."

Try acting, I think. "You might get something. What do you want to do?"

"I don't know. Maybe some kind of teaching. I like children."

"That could be good," I say.

But there's no way I'd step foot inside a school in London. At least not without some heavy-duty Kevlar and a black belt in some kind of Martial Art. A junior school might be okay, as they're still small enough not to do any real or lasting damage, but all you have to do is get on a bus anywhere in London around 4 in the afternoon, and you know that stepping foot inside a school could be a one-way ticket to either the morgue or the mental hospital.

Sofia nods. "I like drawing and painting. I could teach the little children."

"Yeah," I say. But suddenly I'm distracted. She looks fucking rough and everything, what with being hung over, but all the conversation we've just been having has sent a load of blood surging to my penis. I'm developing a serious hard on. I haven't even got a dressing gown on to try and disguise it. If I get up it's going to be dead obvious, so I curl my feet up into the chair I'm sitting in. All I can do right now is hope that it goes away.

There's some shit on the TV about people who dress their pets up as members of the emergency services, so we both watch that in silence for a while. Then my silent prayers are answered.

Sofia yawns and stretches. "You need to use bathroom?"

"Nah, I'm okay," I tell her. "You go ahead."

I watch her leave the room, and she hasn't got a bad set of legs on her, even though it's impossible to check out her arse with the towelling robe she's got on.

I wait until I hear the lock slide across on the bathroom door, then go upstairs as fast as I can. I pick one of yesterday's socks off the bedroom floor and lie back on the bed.

Wanking over a Serbian language student. That it's come to this.

Two hours later. Sofia went out about half an hour ago, and I'm trying to sort out my bedroom so I can walk in and out without tripping over everything I own, when the mobile rings. You could knock me down with a feather when I see the name that comes up on the display. It's Dad. This is too much of a coincidence that he should be calling just after I've moved back here. Pat must have been on to him to let him know I'm here, and not out of any concern that I could be in trouble, but rather that it's a deep fucking inconvenience to her. I look at my phone for a second, and then answer.

"Hi Dad."

"Charlie! How you doing son?" He sounds overly jolly, as he usually does after the six month or so gap that usually passes between phone calls. It's as if an exuberant telephone manner in some way disguises the fact that otherwise he's fucking useless at staying in touch.

"Just peachy. I take it Mum's been in touch?"

"Why d'you say that?"

My fucking parents. Jesus.

"I haven't heard from you in God knows how long, and the day after I move back in with Pat you decide to call me? You tell me, what are the chances?"

There's an uncomfortable pause at the other end of the line.

"Well, she did email me. I have to say, I don't know what was more of a surprise. The email from her, or the fact that you're selling your flat. Are things that bad?"

You have no fucking idea, I think.

"I've just had a bad run. I've got a job. A feature. Starts next week. Low budget, but I'm the lead."

"That's great, Charlie. Just great. Why don't we get together? It's been ages since I've seen you. And I'm sure the twins would like to see their big brother."

"Half-brother," I say. "What have you got in mind?"

"Iolanthe has got a yoga course this weekend, so I'm looking after the twins. I thought I'd take them around Portobello Market. You could show us around."

Bonus, I think. At least Iolanthe won't be there, so there's a chance that we might actually be able to talk about something else rather than what's hot in Elle Decoration this month. I wouldn't be in the least surprised if the yoga course that she's doing is one to enable her to become a teacher. She's deluded enough to think the world needs more of those.

"You sure that you want to take them round Portobello? It can get a little hectic."

"I'm sure it'll be fine. So how about it? Outside Ladbroke Grove tube? Half ten?"

"Okay. Sure. I'll see you then." I hang up, figuring why not? It's not like it's going to be interfering with my busy social schedule.

I'm sitting in front of the TV downstairs with the sound on mute, and the script of 'Finding Jessica' on my lap when the mobile rings. It's Carol. I pick up.

"Hey babe."

I wince at the blast of coughing. She should really quit.

"Charlie, darling," she says, and there's a pause as I hear the click of her lighter being put to a fresh B&H. "I need to thank you."

"Really?" I have no idea what she's on about.

"For Elijah, darling. Elijah. What a find! Remarkable."

Of course. It's Friday. Just gone 5. He went in to see her about an hour ago. And if he's only just left it must have gone well.

"You liked him?"

"Darling, honestly. A diamond in the rough. Such raw talent. I have to say, well done on giving him the reading from Taxi Driver. I didn't think it would work, but it did. And he hasn't even seen the film!"

"So, you think he's good?"

"I do, darling. I really do. And there's a part coming up in a St. Anthony's that I think he'd be perfect for, so I'm going to send him out for that next week."

"You don't think he's too rough around the edges?"

The sound of a huge drag on the other end of the line. "Darling, he's frightfully street, but it gives him an edge that any one of your RADA boys would kill for. And he was nothing but charming with me. He listened; he took direction. I think he could be something special. I really do."

"I'm pleased you like him. Just don't go forgetting your old clients now, will you babe?"

She chuckles throatily down the phone. "Of course I won't my love. Are you all set for next week?"

"Absolutely. I've got the script on my lap right here."

"Good boy. I know you'll never let me down Charlie."

I smile at this. Carol's too kind. "Unless it's a drama for Salt and Acre, right?"

"Their loss, darling. Their loss. You've got the schedule for next week?"

"Yup. All fine."

I was quite surprised to see that the week of rehearsals we've got are all taking place upstairs in a pub in Chalk Farm, but I guess that's how low a budget we're working too. It's good that Donovan managed to get any rehearsal time at all.

"When do I get paid, babe?"

"It's the usual story darling. First day of photography. I tried to wangle it so that you'd get the money through for the rehearsal time, but they can't do it. That okay with you?"

Right now, the difference is simultaneously fucking enormous and non-existent. Enormous because the sooner I receive any kind of money then I cease to have to rely on going cap in hand to my mother; and non-existent because right now I've got nothing else to do anyway – it's not like rehearsing for this job is going to take me away from any other work, and the way I'm feeling right now I'd pay them good money just to have somewhere to escape from that isn't this house.

"That's fine," I say. "Not a problem. I'm glad you like Elijah though, babe. That's great news. So what did you tell him?"

"What I've told you. That I like him, and that I think he's got real talent."

"It's all down to my coaching, you know."

"Of course it is, darling," she says, soothingly. "Of course it is. Have a good weekend, Charlie."

"You too Carol. I'll speak to you next week."

She hangs up. I flick through my phone and find Elijah's number, and dial. This time it goes straight through, and it only rings four times before he picks up.

"Hollywood. You alright, blad?"

"So tell me. How did it go?"

"Nang, man." He's trying to be cool, but I can hear the excitement in his voice. "The woman want to represent me, innit."

"So I hear. She was really impressed, you know. And she doesn't impress easily."

"Serious?"

"Serious. And she told me that she's going to send you out for an audition next week. For St Anthony's, right?"

"That program's fucking gay, blad."

"Listen, Elijah. I don't know if you want to take my advice or anything. But the one thing I've learnt is that a job is a job. Don't turn anything down, get there on time and be polite, and you'd be amazed how far you could go."

There's a pause. I'm guessing that no-one's ever offered Elijah any kind of career advice that he's even considered listening to before.

"Yeah, alright Hollywood. Safe."

"I start rehearsals for my own film next week, but you can call me if you want to ask me anything. Right?"

"You is definitely batty, man."

This kid's even got his comic timing down pat. "Oh fuck off," I tell him, and I'm about to hang up when he says something else.

"Hollywood?"

"Yeah?"

"Thanks fam. You're alright." The line goes dead, and for a moment I sit there, genuinely touched.

I get off the 52 outside the Estate Agents shortly before 10, and toy with the idea of going in to hassle James and see if there's any news about whether anyone has shown any interest in buying the flat. Taking a peek through the window, there's no sign of him. That could be a good sign; maybe he's already showing someone round this very second.

The weather's been pretty good all week and has managed to hold today. The sun beats down out of a bright blue sky, and the first warm flush of spring has coaxed all the girls out of their winter wear and back into miniskirts. Tons of gorgeous little minxes flood out of the tube and straight across the Grove to head straight under the Westway and into the Market, and I've got a great vantage point to check them out from the spot I've taken up just under the bridge. There are already enough people lurking directly outside the tube, and the last thing I want to do is look too much like a tourist. So, I'll stay here – I can still see everyone coming out, and it means that I'm not going to look too much like a desperate saddo. Besides, most of the rest of the people waiting there must be around fifteen years old, and I'll probably be taken for a paedo if I linger there too long.

It's gone half 10 when I see a familiar face emerge from the station, only it's not Dad; rather the sight of my nieces skittering out onto the pavement, followed by my sister as she tries to get the pair of them under control before they run out into the road. For a split second I think that that's strange, but then the realisation hits me that it's no coincidence. Molly chastises the girls briefly, then begins to look around to see if she can locate a familiar face. I raise my hand for a second, and then she spots me and smiles. Even from here I can see that she's looking knackered, but then I guess you would if you're raising two girls single handed while holding down a full-time job.

Molly has been working for the council ever since Duncan left her five years ago. Up until then she'd had a pretty kushti existence swanning around looking after the girls, hanging out with her friends and drinking coffee, but then Duncan decided he'd had enough and left, pretty much out of the blue, to move in with a twenty-eight-year-old model. Despite earning a small fortune running his market research agency, he wasn't exactly forthcoming with the child support, and so Molly had to go out and find work for the first time in about seven years. She had a clerical background and so managed to land something in the Environment department at Hammersmith and Fulham council, which as far as I can make out involves arguing with a lot of people about their recycling responsibilities. She only just manages to stay sane because she's able to work part-time and still look after the girls; so now as they're getting older it seems increasingly most days like she's moving from one argument at work to another at home.

The girls are already fighting as they're crossing the road, but then they're at that age. Sky is ten, and Flower is eight; with both going on for seventeen. I've worked with a few kids over the years, and I've always seemed to get on with them okay – child actors seem on the whole to try and behave well as their parents have drummed into them that they are highly replaceable. Sky and Flower don't have that neediness, and although I'm highly aware that they're blood relations, that doesn't prevent me thinking that they're both capable of being a massive pain in the arse.

Sky reaches the other side of the road first. She's chewing, which she probably thinks makes her look older and cooler. It doesn't.

"Hi Charlie," she says.

"Hi Sky," I say. "Hi Flower," I say to her sister who's joined us. I reach out to give Molly a hug. "Hey Moll."

"Say hello to your uncle," says Molly.

"Hello," says Flower, clearly already incredibly bored.

"I didn't know you were coming," I say. But I'm not that surprised. This is Dad all over; prime James Reed behaviour. He hasn't seen either of us in about six months, and despite the fact that it might be nice to talk to him about everything that's going on in my life, he's clearly thinking that he might as well try and get us both out of the way at the same time rather than organise separate visits. It's not that it isn't good to see Molly; it's just that it might have been good to be treated a little less like a package.

"He rang me last night," says Moll. "I thought it would be nice for the girls. They haven't seen the twins since before

Christmas. How's things with you?" Her brow furrows as she asks, so I guess she's heard all about it.

"Dads told you then."

"He mentioned something. You're back living with Mum, right? Sky, stop it! We need to wait here for Granddad."

"Yeah. Back at Churchill Road. In your old room."

"Jesus. You poor sod. How is she?"

"Same as ever."

"That must be fun."

"You have no idea."

"Girls, please. It's not for much longer." The pair of them are pulling at Moll's hands, trying to drag her up the Grove in the direction of the market. "So, what happened with the flat?"

"I've just had a bad run. I took out a little too much on credit, and it all got away from me. I had no choice. But things are looking up."

"Yeah?"

"I'm the lead in a feature. Got a week of rehearsals on Monday, and then we shoot."

"That's great, Charlie."

"How about you? You look good," I lie. Fucking exhausted is what she looks like, and there are lines on her forehead that make her look older than me.

"Bullshit. But thanks anyway. I'm okay."

"Heads up. Look who's coming."

Dad emerges from the tube and looks around for a good thirty seconds or so before he sees us waving over the road. He waves back then pushes the double buggy across towards us. Anyone would think that he's taking his grandkids for a day out.

He reaches us, and grabs us both in a hug, kissing us each on the forehead in turn. "It's good to see you," he says, then crouches down to speak to the twins in the buggy. "You remember Charlie and Molly, don't you guys?"

The pair of them look up at us, non-plussed. I'm guessing that's a 'no'.

Molly calls out to the girls, who are talking to each other in hushes whispers. "Sky, Flower. Come and say hello to Grandad. And to Sam and Emma."

"Hi girls!" he says, a little too happy, and leans down to kiss them both on the forehead. The four children all look at one another blankly in silence, and then the girls resume what they were doing while the twins stare off into space again.

"So where shall we go first? Shall we grab a coffee?" he asks. "Come on Charlie. You're the native. Where's best?"

Not anymore, I'm not, I think but don't say. "This way," I say, and lead them down towards Lancaster Road in the vague direction of Starbucks. Normally I'd be tempted to try one of the smaller cooler ones on Portobello, but it's going to be a fucking nightmare with this many of us.

Sky and Flower kick off momentarily, and Dad and I walk ahead slowly as Molly reads them the riot act and assures them that we'll be coming back up this way so that they can see the market.

"How you doing, Charlie?" asks Dad, in a tone that expresses a deep concern which we both know really isn't there. It's all well and good to sound like you give a shit, but it takes more than a slightly protruding bottom lip and a raised eyebrow. It takes an occasional phone call, and the possibility of meeting just for fun, and not when his ex-wife tells him that my collapsing life is impacting on hers.

I shrug. "You know. Okay."

"Really?"

I'm going to start getting riled if this continues much longer, so I change the subject. "How are these two?"

"Oh, you know," he says. "Keeping me busy. I didn't think I'd be able to do this all again at this time in my life, but I'm finding that I'm actually quite enjoying it."

Second time lucky, I think. I bite my lip.

"How's Iolanthe?"

"She's okay," he says. But there's a flicker there that tells me that perhaps this isn't the full truth, and that maybe the penny is beginning to drop with him that in fact she's a high maintenance, self-obsessed pain in the arse.

"She's doing a yoga course?" I ask.

"Yeah," he nods. "It's very good for her. Helps her stay grounded."

Fat fucking chance of that happening, I think. I've met a lot of people who are up themselves over the years; almost every actor is. But only a few have come close to the total self-absorption that personifies Iolanthe. I'm gobsmacked that she actually went ahead and had children, but perhaps it's to have more people to worship at her feet. Dads not exactly had a great run at relationships, and my guess is that it's only the kids who are keeping this one together. And if it all goes tits up, I'm pretty sure that Dad will be the one who's left looking after them, even when Iolanthe's 'career' as an interior designer keeps her doing, well, fuck all.

One of the principal qualities of being a successful designer is to be able to listen to what other people want, in addition to having great taste – and unfortunately Iolanthe fails spectacularly on both counts. Rather than take any inspiration from other people she'll talk loudly over them and try and vomit some horrible Moroccan décor all over their walls. And she wonders why she's not doing very well.

So, it's left for Dad to support them, and working as a freelance copywriter is never going to keep them in the manner to which Iolanthe has become accustomed. That, and the fact that he's the one who seems to end up looking after the kids all day while she's out making 'contacts', which as far as I can gather involves prancing around shops, talking over people and drinking the occasional coffee.

I wonder what ever happened to his drive. He was taken on by one of the biggest ad agencies in London at just seventeen, after striding in there and charming one of the receptionists to let him up and speak to the creative director. He pitched a couple of ad ideas to this guy, who must have been in a good mood as he paired him up with another creative straight away and paid him a small fortune. Dad nearly created a couple of key campaigns, but they always seemed to go with some other guys' ideas; and when Jeff, his creative partner keeled over from a coke-induced heart attack in his early forties, Dad left and set up his own 'consultancy'. He must do some work to be able to afford the house and Iolanthe, but I know he struggles.

We wait at the corner of Lancaster Road as Molly manages to persuade the girls to head in the right direction, and they run on ahead of us with Molly trying to keep them in her eyeline.

"It's lovely to see you both," says Dad.

"It's good to see you too, Dad," says Molly, shooting me a glance that tells me it's not just me who thinks he's crap at staying in touch. "The girls have been very excited about seeing their Granddad and their cousins."

I'm pretty sure this isn't exactly true, as the girls are currently running ahead of us up the road, fairly oblivious to anyone else's existence. The twins stare ahead, mute, and the pair of them have barely moved since Dad got here, apart from perhaps to blink occasionally. Perhaps Iolanthe is drugging them.

"They okay, Dad?" I ask of the twins. "They seem a little quiet."

"They're fine," he says. "They just had a late night. Trust me, they get a lot more perky than this."

We wander along Lancaster Road towards the noise of Portobello, and Molly shouts at the girls to slow down and not run off into the crowds, as they'll never be found again. They don't seem very impressed with this part of the market; all fruit and veg, and open-air olives with plastic sneeze-guards, as if that's going to suddenly improve the inherent questionable hygiene of having your produce dribbled on by a flock of coughing tourists.

"I love olives," says Dad as he passes. They look revolting to me, but he can knock himself out.

"Coffee first," I say.

The queue at Starbucks is already fifteen deep despite it only approaching eleven, so we join the back.

"There's nowhere to sit," says Dad, as if it's a massive shock that there isn't a table for eight available in one of the busiest tourist traps in London. Sky and Flower are already whining about the wait, and demanding croissants as well as sparkly fruity waters. There's already clearly some kind of system developing among the canny tourists, some of whom are lining up for their coffee, leaving their mates to lurk around tables with a view to poaching them as soon as any become available. This is making the already tiny space in here even more cramped, and the combination of family and increasing claustrophobia is already beginning to wind me up. I'll just have to ride it out and begin breathing deeply looking at the ceiling. The ten minutes it takes to reach the front of the queue and place our order seems like an eternity and isn't made any shorter when one of the twins starts crying, shortly to be joined by the other one. Dad juggles trying to get their biscuits with talking to the young Polish girl behind the counter, and then makes a big show about paying. There still aren't any seats available, so I hustle everyone back out onto the street while I wait at the station for the coffees to arrive.

Finally, I'm out, and we walk back up Portobello towards the covered market. The twins have stopped crying now they have something to eat, and Sky and Flower seem placated with their bottles of fashionable water and the fact that there seems to be a lot more of interest on either side of the street.

"They're behaving very well," says Dad as they have a look at what's on a stall.

"I reminded them that this is where Kate Moss and Lily Allen shop," says Molly. "And that they could bump into them, so it's probably a good idea to try and be grown-up."

"Let's find somewhere to sit down," I say. It's only been half an hour and I'm already feeling fucking exhausted. It's a nice enough day, so I lead them up past the market on the left-hand side and take a left along Cambridge Gardens so we can go and sit on the grass in Portobello Green for a bit. The girls aren't having a bar of it, and so we tell Molly that we'll see her later, and she disappears into the throng underneath the canopy. I just can't face it, and from the look of it, neither can Dad, and so we truck along Cambridge in silence until we flop on a section of grass that's been carefully screened for dogshit. The twins come out of the buggy, and toddle around quite happily in the sunshine.

"You okay, Charlie? Really?" asks Dad.

"Yeah," I say.

I honestly don't know where to start. And I'm sure he doesn't really want to hear any of it anyway. He's got enough of his own shit to deal with without me dumping on him.

"I just wish I could help a bit more, you know? But it's difficult when I've got these two."

"I know, Dad. I know."

The twins look sweet chasing around after each other. I still can't quite get to grips with the fact that Dad has managed to have another set of kids before I've even attempted it. Looking at them now as they play around on the grass, it makes me think that I'm missing something. I would like to have kids, but then it helps if you at least have a girlfriend, and that seems like a long way off right now. I get a sharp pang of Callie once again. Life's full of moments, and you only realise the significant ones when they've long drifted past you.

"So what did Mum say to you?" I ask.

He grins ruefully. "You know your mother. She wrote to me telling me that you'd moved back into the house, because you were selling your flat. She seemed to think I might be able to help in some way."

"And clearly it's a massive fucking inconvenience having me around. Thank God she doesn't show it."

Dad laughs at this. "She's not changed then?"

"Not in the slightest. If anything, she's worse. You know that no tenant of hers has ever lasted past six months? That's got to tell her something."

He raises his eyebrows. "If she was a little more self-aware, she might. So, tell me about this feature. And you've got the lead? That's fantastic."

"Yeah, I'm pleased. It's a great script, and the director is pretty smart. His last short was short listed for a BAFTA last year, so he clearly knows what he's doing. Even more so if he's casting me for the lead."

"What's it about?"

"A guy who falls for a big woman despite his prejudices. They're good characters. And you'll never guess who's exec producing the film." Dad looks non-plussed. "Only James Laurenson."

He still looks confused, but then this is him all over. He's never been that into film, and only has a passing knowledge of who everyone is in the business; he's very much a passive observer rather than an active fan.

"Come on, Dad. James Laurenson? Massive film director? His debut film was 'The Twelfth of Never'? In which I acted about twenty years ago?"

"Oh him. He's a shit, isn't he."

"You could say that, yeah."

He calls out to the twins who are veering a little too far away from us. "Sam! Emma! Back over here please. No, I remember how unhappy you were during the filming of that. It did turn out to be a great film though." He turns to me. "Mostly down to your performance of course."

I smile. "Naturally."

"No, but he sounded like a complete shit. And of course, I never agreed with your mother about what he asked her to do."

My blood runs cold. "What?"

"Shit. I was always sworn to secrecy. Still, I guess its all a long time ago. And if you've not got a right to know now, then when?"

"What are you talking about?"

He sighs. "You remember that you came back from the shoot one night, and you were upset? That you said you weren't going to go back? James Laurenson told your mother that some of what he was doing was going to be difficult for you, but that it was essential for the film. Your mum said that was fine. She basically said that he could treat you how he liked if it was going to get a good performance out of you. Hang on a minute, I'd better go and get them."

He gets up off the grass and chases after the twins, who are veering towards the back of the stalls that the Green leads on to. I sit there, in silence, trying to take on board what he's just told me. Pat Reed, my own mother, was complicit in making me the unhappiest I think I've ever been. She effectively gave Laurenson a blessing to treat me like total fucking shit for his film. Any normal mother may have offered something in the way of reassurance – that what he said didn't matter, that he was being mean for a reason, but not Pat. All I received in turn was silence, and the lasting impression that it was me who was responsible for her every unhappiness. I look at Dad, now effectively dragging the twins back towards our little patch of grass. Sam is crying. You carry on son, I think. Life's shit. Get used to it. You'll need to with a father like yours.

"If you can't stay here, you'll have to stay in the buggy," he's telling them.

"Don't want to," says Sam. I'm surprised, as I didn't even know they could talk. But then, any normal parent might have mentioned this little tidbit.

"He's talking?" Dad lets go of Emma's hand, who promptly runs off in the direction of the market again.

"They both are. Charlie, can you grab her?"

I get up, and chase after my half-sister, who is giggling away as she makes her way across the grass. I scoop her up and she starts wriggling, and then looks at me and starts crying.

"Hey Emma. It's okay," I say as soothingly as I can muster. "I'm your big brother, Charlie."

This doesn't seem to make a blind bit of difference to her, and as I bring her back to Dad she's now screaming. He takes her and puts her in the buggy next to her brother, and now the pair of them are howling.

"I'd better walk them round the block. Try and calm them down."

"Right," I say. "I'll stay here and wait for Molly."

"See you in a bit."

I nod, and he walks off. I sit there, staring into space. The truth is I'm fucking angry. It wasn't just Mum who was responsible for Laurenson bullying me on the film; it was him too. His weakness and inability to do anything or want to do anything about it was just as much permission as Pat ever handed the director. I was clearly just a commodity, something to be bartered over and played with, rather than a living human being with actual fucking feelings.

I'm still fuming when I hear Flower screaming her way along Cambridge Gardens, with Molly yelling at her. Flower is marched into the Green by Moll, closely followed by Sky who has a look on her face like butter wouldn't melt. Flower is hysterical, screaming her little head off, and Moll is furious and seemingly oblivious to the fact that everyone is now looking at us.

"If you ever – ever – behave like that again, you will never ever see any pocket money again for as long as either of us lives!"

I don't think I've ever seen Molly this angry. The vein on her temple is literally throbbing with rage, and she looks like she could pop at any moment.

"Jesus, Moll. What's going on?" I ask, quietly, hoping that she'll follow my lead and dial down the volume a little.

"Flower, has, and I can't believe I'm actually having to tell you this, but Flower..."

"I didn't mean to," sobs Flower, interrupting. "It was an accident!"

"Don't lie to me, young lady!" shouts Molly. "Don't you dare! It was not an accident!"

"What is going on?" I ask. I'm trying my hardest not to swear in front of the girls, although I'm sorely fucking tempted.

"Flower has tried to walk off with a necklace without paying for it. And the first I know about it is when the girl on the stall grabs her wrist. So naturally I challenge her. You know, 'what do you think you're doing putting your hands on my daughter?' "She's stolen one of my necklaces. It's in her pocket," she says. "Nonsense," I say. "You must be mistaken. My daughter doesn't steal." Only I'm looking at her face as I say it, and she's not only looking petrified, but fucking guilty!"

Molly really screams this last bit, and some of the surrounding people on the grass are clearly beginning to enjoy the show.

"I didn't steal it. It was an accident," says Flower.

"Then what the hell was it doing in your pocket, Flower? Try and tell me that. You can't, can you? And there's no reason for you to look so pleased with yourself either," she says, turning to Sky.

"What have I done?" whines Sky, the smirk promptly falling from her face.

"I'm willing to bet good money that you put her up to it. It wouldn't be the first time, would it?"

"Oh, fuck off," says Sky, almost, but not quite, under her breath.

"What did you say?" screams Molly. She really does look like she's about to have an aneurysm.

"Nothing," says Sky.

"Right. That's it. We're going home. And there'll be no TV tonight, or for the rest of the week. And no pocket money for the rest of the month."

"But that's not fair!" whines Sky again, as Flower bursts into a fresh set of sobs.

"Fair doesn't come into it," says Moll. "We're going. Now." She turns to me. "Sorry, Charlie. And apologise to Dad. I'll speak to you soon. Right, you two," she says, dragging them both away by the arms. "We're leaving. And wait until your father hears about this."

I can still hear Flower's sobs as they disappear out of sight back onto Cambridge Gardens. The show now over, all the people sat on the Green slowly begin to look back at each other and no doubt dissect what's just happened. I look up at the sky and try to wish myself out of existence.

Fifteen minutes later, and I realise that Dad hasn't come back, and I fish out my phone to see that there's a missed call from him. I ring the voicemail.

"Hi Charlie. Sorry to have to run, but the twins are screaming their heads off, and I realise I've come out without Sam's favourite toy. Now he's realised, he's never going to settle, so I'm just going to call it a day. Sorry. Give my love to Moll. Let's catch up soon."

It's just gone 11.20. We couldn't even last an hour together. Jesus. My fucking family.

I get up with as much dignity as I can muster and walk across the Green towards the Westway. The moment I hear someone call out my name I wish that I'd gone back out onto Cambridge Gardens.

"Charlie! Over here!"

I look to my right, and its Sally, a production assistant from the last BBC thing I worked on. She's sat there with a guy who's looking at me with no small amount of amusement, so I'm guessing they caught the whole show. Plus, they've seen me sat around doing fuck all for fifteen minutes, so I can't fake being too busy to talk. I wander over.

"Hi Sally. How's it going?"

"Yeah, not bad. This is Bill."

We nod and shake hands.

"So, you busy?" she asks.

"Not bad. Just about to start work on a feature with Donovan Taft."

"Nice," she says.

"Funny. I could have sworn you were just workshopping some open-air play for us just then," says Bill.

I smile tightly. Comedian, I think. "You caught that. My family," I say.

"Nice," he says, and Sally nudges him to shush.

He's a prissy little camp cunt and no mistake. I can feel myself getting wound up, and for a split-second think about kicking him right in the kisser, again and again until his fucking head explodes. He looks up at my face, and the smirk disappears from his smug cunt face, so I guess what I'm thinking is written large all over my chops.

"I should be off. Nice to see you Sally," I say, blanking Bill but making a mental note that if I ever see him again, I'll fucking do him properly. He looks more than a little nervous as I turn and leave the Green, and this gives me a little warm glow inside.

After the morning I've had so far, any kind of victory is a bonus.

APRIL

How's everyone feeling today?

Excellent.

We're making a film, people.

Making a fucking film.

Best fucking job in the world.

Monday morning, and I'm at the room above the pub at half 10 on the dot. Punctuality is something I learnt very early on in this game, and I've stuck to ever since. I've been on a couple of sets when some twat actor has played the big star card, turning up late, or lingering in his trailer when he should be hitting his marks on the studio floor. And no-one ever thinks, that's okay, they deserve special treatment because they're incredibly talented. No, what the crew are in fact thinking is 'fucking hurry up and do your job, you big headed, self-important, time wasting cunt.' People need no excuse to hate you if you're an actor; they see an overpaid tit with the emotional needs of a hungry toddler, so why give them any additional reason for loathing? Turn up on time. It's the least you can do.

I ring the bell on the door, and I get buzzed up. A small blonde creature greets me at the door and introduces herself as Charlie ("another one!") and ushers me through, offering to get me a coffee. I tell her that would be lovely and walk in behind her. Donovan gets up from his chair where he's poring over a copy of the script and comes to greet me.

"Charlie. How's it going?"

"Not bad, Donovan. All right, mate."

"Let me introduce you to everyone, at least those who are here. You've met Charlie, she's going to be helping me out this week and on the shoot. Do you know John?" He points out a big guy wearing expensive yet functional clothes who can only be the DoP. So much for Roger, I think. I walk over to shake his hand.

"Hi mate," I say. "Charlie."

"John," he says.

"I think you know Arthur?" says Donovan. "He's our production designer."

Arthur looks up from a sketchpad and grins at me. I recognise him from Nicholas Nickleby, when he was working as part of the set-building crew. Funny guy, I remember, and liked a smoke if memory serves.

"Hello mate! Long time!" I say.

"Alright Charlie? Good to see you." He's showing some sketches to a woman who Donovan introduces as Rebecca.

"She's my co-producer," he says. "These guys are here for this morning's read through, then they're off to do some pre-prod down in Sussex."

"Hi," I say.

"Hi," says Rebecca, and immediately her phone rings. "Sorry," she says, and picks it up, wandering out of the room as she speaks on it.

"It's a bit like that at the moment. She's doubling up as the line producer. And first AD. Such is low budget. I'm sure you've met Oliver? Duncan? And this is Holly."

Oliver and Holly are familiar faces who I've seen in various things over the years, but not worked with; but I know Duncan, and he's a terrible old Queen. A real bitch, and not half as good as he thinks he is. He played the travelling theatre manager in Nicholas Nickleby, and although he could be highly entertaining, his constant need to be the centre of attention whenever the camera stopped rolling eventually got on my tits. And I'm pretty sure he noticed. I've not worked with him since, and he's filled out and lost some hair in the intervening years. If he winds me up, I'll have no qualms in pointing that out sharpish, as I'm betting that will hurt.

"Hi," I say to all of them and go to hug Duncan. "How are you darling?" I ask him.

"Fabulous," he says.

"Let me guess. You're playing Timothy?" Timothy is Jessica's gay confidante in the script, clearly written as an ageing and emotionally bruised poof. He'll barely have to act.

He smiles at me, but it doesn't quite reach his eyes. "How terribly astute of you, Charlie darling."

I'm already thinking it could turn into one of those shoots.

Then other Charlie brings Izzy Myers into the room. She's already a little out of breath coming up the stairs and has to sit down to catch her breath.

I go over to say hello, and she greets me in that broad East End accent of hers. "Hello, Charlie. How are ya, babe?"

"Good, Izzy. Lovely to meet you."

"You too darling."

Everyone's already stacking up behind me to greet the undisputed star of the film, so I move out of the way to let everyone else pay tribute and go over to the table where there's a coffee machine on the go and fill up one of the Styrofoam cups. It's weak and lukewarm, which is only to be expected. I sneak a look back at Izzy sitting in the chair, and I'm already thinking that it's a fucking good job that I'm a half-decent actor, as to play out falling in love with her is going to be no picnic. Her arse is spilling out over either side of the plastic chair she's slumped in, and her tummy has concertinaed up as she leans forward to say hello to everyone. I just hope the chair she's sitting in holds up.

Other Charlie gathers the chairs round in a circle, and we begin the read-through. I've been here a hundred times before and it's always the same, an energy in the room that feels like the start of a rollercoaster; only you never know just how much it's going to thrill you, or, for that matter, whether it's going to go completely off the rails. Everyone reads his or her part just so, careful not to come across too actorly while still respecting the text. Of course, Duncan still overdoes it a bit today, coming across perhaps overly Queeny in his desperation to get a laugh. Izzy sounds great, and clearly knows what she's doing, and I think I acquit myself sufficiently. Donovan is clearly enjoying himself and reads out all the directions as well as some of the lesser character's lines. By around one we're all done, and everyone lapses into small conversations amongst themselves while Donovan talks to John the DoP, Rebecca, and Arthur. I'm thoroughly unsurprised to see Duncan attach himself to Izzy with indecent haste. As the star of the film, and a genuine gay icon, I'm surprised he waited until after the read-through to make her his new best friend. I talk with Oliver, who's in his early twenties and is playing the lovelorn son of a farmer who in love with Holly's character, the student daughter of new people to the village in the film. He's just come off a play at the National, and we talk about mutual acquaintances, having a good bitch in the way that only actors can.

Other Charlie comes back with some sandwiches from M&S for lunch, and we all fall on them with indecent haste as by now all the biscuits have gone and we're absolutely starving. I notice that Izzy is careful to only take two sandwiches and seems to make a great show of eating them very slowly.

It can't be easy being that size, and I'm betting that part of her natural exuberance is a show. People expect fat people to be jolly, and so she lives up to that. I know from experience that its weird enough having people stare at you in public, and she's got the double whammy of not only being famous but being huge with it. Even if she wanted to lose weight it would be tricky, as her size is now what she's known for, and how she gets work. She wouldn't have got this role if she was half the woman she is now.

We say goodbye to Rebecca, John and Arthur, who are off to the South Downs to check out the locations, and then we start again. We go back and read through the scenes with all of us in them, and Donovan talks through what he wants from the characters, and why they are all doing what they're doing. He's a smart director; shrewd enough to know not to go too hard right now, but just put us in the right head space about who and where the characters are so that when we come to the shoot, he's already pushed a lot of our buttons. By the end of the day, we're all feeling pretty good, and as I walk out with Izzy we're both looking forward to coming back tomorrow.

"He's good, innee?" says Izzy, just before she climbs into her car.

"Very," I say. "This could be a good one."

"I think so too babe. Plus, I get to do a love scene with you, eh? Lucky me."

"You're right there, Izzy. Normally I charge good money for that, you know."

She gives a throaty laugh and closes her car door. She drives off with a wave, and I walk back to the tube. For the first time this year I finally feel like things might be finally turning around.

The rest of the week passes quickly, as Donovan takes us through our paces, leaving the last two days to properly explore Roy and Jessica's relationship. By Friday afternoon we're buzzing, as I've finally got under the skin of Roy, and am living and breathing the character in a way I've not found myself doing for some time. Izzy has clearly got Jessica too, and she's got the vulnerability of the character underneath her mask of confidence perfectly.

We're just breaking for some coffee around 3 when other Charlie hands Donovan her mobile.

"Fuck off. Are you serious? Can't we get another one? …What do you mean that one's been trained?"

"What's going on?" I ask Charlie.

"It's the cat. Some scheduling issue."

The cat. John and his crew have already started shooting the cat over the past couple of days, in order to save time. The cat acts as a kind of judge on the relationship, and whenever Roy and Izzy get together it appears to check them out from a distance, purring. Then when they eventually get together, it jumps through the window and sprawls all over the duvet, bestowing its approval like some kind of furry Cupid. It's the one thing in the script that I'm not overly keen on, but Donovan seems set on it, and he clearly knows what he's doing, so I'll go along with it.

But right now, he does not seem happy.

"Fuck them! We had the cunt booked first!... But I don't want to shoot that first… Only if we fucking have to. But I want you to try and find another way. Fuck!"

He throws the phone to the floor, and it shatters. Other Charlie picks up the pieces.

"Sorry Charlie," he says.

"That's okay." It doesn't look too bad, and she's already piecing the phone back together.

"Everything okay?" I ask.

"That fucking cat! John has spent the past two days getting some fucking great footage of the little cunt – sorry Izzy.."

"Don't worry about it babe."

"…and now the trainer says that it's been booked for a fucking cat food commercial for a full week the week after next. When we've scheduled in the bedroom scene. So that means that not only has John now got to work the entire fucking weekend to try and get all the shots I want with the money grabbing cunt trainer – sorry Izzy…"

"Honestly darlin', don't worry. He sounds like a cunt," she says.

"Yeah. Cunt," I add.

Donovan can't help smiling. "Anyway, it's going to fuck up the schedule. And I hope you two are ready, because it looks like we've got to move the bedroom scene forward to Monday now. Because of the fucking cunt's cunting cat!"

There's a second's silence, and then Izzy chimes in with perfect comic timing.

"Cunt!"

Sunday night and I arrive down at the location. I've got the train to Brighton, and it's not a moment too soon. The weekend has been spent trying to stay sane in Churchill Road, which has involved smoking the last of the Charas that I got from Bob and holing up in my tiny room living Empire of Blood and shooting the crap out of passers-by. I had a massive standoff with the cops and died in a hail of gunfire. Now that's living.

I tried to get hold of Bob to try and score some more puff to take down to the shoot, as I'm bound to get a bit clucky without any, but no joy. So far, he hasn't returned my calls, and though I'm sure he will, I'm now in the fucking countryside and it's a little late, so I'll just have to hope that one of the other cast or crew is holding.

Other Charlie picks me up in her mini, and its brand new. It's exactly the car that I would have expected she'd be driving, and although we haven't discussed it, I'm betting that Daddy bought it for her while she finds her way in the film business. I'm pretty sure that he'll be paying her rent too.

She drives me to the bed and breakfast where I'm being put up for the duration of the shoot. The woman running it greets me as if I'm Tom Cruise or something, and I would imagine she's just going to burst when she meets Izzy. I'm shown up to my room, which although is a bit floral and twee for my tastes is at least tidy and clean – an improvement on some of the places I've stayed in my time. I unpack my suitcase and shove everything in drawers, and I'm just running a bath when my mobile rings. It's Donovan.

I pick up. "Hey."

"Charlie, mate. You okay? Trip down alright?"

"Fine."

"The place okay? Charlie found it. I know it's not the Ritz, but you know our budget."

"I've stayed in worse," I say. And that's true. I remember doing a shoot about seven years ago on a small Israeli picture and ended up staying in a fucking tent in the middle of the desert for a couple of nights. It might have been kind of romantic under the right circumstances, but all I could think about at the time was that there was nowhere decent to take a shit. And that's not much to ask when you're working on a movie.

"Good to hear," he says, then after a pause. "So, I was hoping we'd be able to get together for a light dinner before tomorrow night, but I've got a lot of stuff to sort out before tomorrow. I'm going to have to blow you out. I'm sure you'll be able to grab a sandwich or something. I'm sorry."

"It's okay, Donovan. Don't worry about it." And I'm not that fussed. I'm sure the old bat downstairs will be able to sort something out. But he does sound stressed on the other end of the phone, and that's the first time I've heard any kind of stress in his voice at all – normally he's just one cool customer and doesn't seem to let anything ruffle his feathers. That said, he is shooting his debut feature tomorrow, and that's enough to put anyone on edge.

"Cheers, Charlie. I appreciate it," he says. "I'll see you tomorrow."

"Sure. See you then."

And he's gone. I go to turn off the water in the bathroom, and strip off and climb in. I don't envy Donovan. I've never been tempted to direct. There's more than enough that can go wrong when you're in front of the camera; the thought of even trying to manage that many people and make that many decisions on a minute-by-minute basis is enough to make my head spin.

My alarm goes off at 6 sharp and I climb out of bed and haul on my clothes and am waiting outside when other Charlie comes to pick me up twenty minutes later.

"We not picking up Izzy?" I ask.

Charlie shakes her head. "She's staying at another place. She's getting picked up by one of Arthur's crew."

I nod, thinking that that's a bit of a relief. It would have been slightly fucking ambitious to think that Izzy would fit in this Mini.

It only takes fifteen minutes to get us through the winding country lanes to the cottage that acts as the location for Jessica's place. Catering is up and running outside already and so I saunter over and grab a coffee and a bacon roll. Other Charlie ushers me into the front room that looks like it's going to act as an impromptu trailer, given that there seems to be nowhere else to go, and so I sit down and polish off my breakfast.

Donovan comes in, and he's looking fucking stressed. "Hey Charlie. You alright?"

"Yeah. How are you doing?"

He nods. "Yeah, okay. Okay. Not bad."

Fuck me, I'm thinking, if this is you not bad, then we're in trouble if anything goes south. His brow is furrowed, and it looks like he's carrying the weight of the world on his shoulders.

"You got breakfast? Good. Good. Izzy's on her way. We're just getting set up for the first shot now. I'll get Diana in here to do some make-up."

He marches out again. I sip my coffee and follow him out of the door. There's a kitchen off the hall and looking in I can see Donovan and Rebecca having an urgent, whispered conversation. Neither of them sees me, so I turn back to the lounge. I sip my coffee, wondering what the fuck is going on. A couple of minutes later a woman with short dark hair arrives and introduces herself as Diana. She sits me down in front of a mirror in the corner and starts tending to my face.

"Is there something going on?" I ask her.

"I don't know babe," she says.

"Donovan and Rebecca seem a little stressed."

She shrugs, and I get the impression that I'm asking the wrong person. From the couple of minutes that I've known Diana I've kind of got the impression that there's not a whole lot going on besides her undeniably excellent hair.

"Have you seen Izzy yet?" I ask her.

"Here in a minute, apparently," she says, and rubs her thumb over my cheek. "That'll do you for the moment."

There's the sound of a car outside, and a minute later in walks Izzy. It's the first time I've seen her without make-up, and she's even rougher without any. And we're in bed for our first scene together. I could kill that fucking cat.

She slumps in the chair opposite me. "Hello babe. How you doing?"

"Good sweetheart," I say. "I hope you're ready for me."

"I'll always be ready for you big boy," she says. "Fucking nice house, innit?"

Other Charlie appears with a coffee for Izzy and hands it to her. "Where'd they turn this place up then?" asks Izzy.

"It was Donovan's Granny's. I think he's spent a lot of time sweet-talking everyone in the village to let him film here. He's been telling them all that he always loved coming here as a little boy. Isn't that sweet?"

Sweet it may be, but that would explain how come the place is already looking like a bomb hit it, and yet there's no-one here offering any complaints. It must be handy having relatives who have picturesque treasures like this to play with. Up until last night this place was probably perfect – the idyllic countryside cottage. But march a grip up the stairs in dirty work boots with his arse hanging out and it all starts to fall to pieces very quickly.

"You've both brought a robe, haven't you?" asks Charlie.

Izzy nods. I don't.

"Fuck it!" I say. "Fuck!"

"You're kidding!" says Izzy.

I shake my head.

"Oh, I'm sorry Charlie, I should have reminded you when I collected you this morning," says other Charlie.

Yeah, you fucking well should, I think. "Is there one here I could use?" I ask.

"Leave it with me," says other Charlie. "I'll have a look round and see what I can come up with."

Ten minutes later and she reappears while Diana is doing Izzy's make-up, and I'm listening to the pair of them bitch about another actress that they both know.

"It's all I could find, Charlie," she says, and hands over a faded tartan dressing gown. It looks ancient. "I think it was Donovan's Granddad's."

"No kidding," I say. "It smells like he fucking died in it."

Izzy turns and looks at it. "I think it might quite suit you babe."

"Oh fuck off," I say, grinning. "Thanks, Charlie. But I think I'll leave it. It looks like I'll just have to go up in my vest and pants."

And I do. Twenty minutes later and I'm climbing under the sheets, and taking off my T-shirt in front of John, Donovan, Henry who's doing the sound, and a strange little man called Tony who I've only just met. Tony is the cat wrangler, and the cat, Bob, is currently sat on his lap checking everything out. It's a semi-closed set, and I'd love to think that it's because they want to preserve the modesty of Izzy and me, but the truth of it is they've got to keep it low key or otherwise the fucking cat will freak out. Izzy came up before me, and is currently underneath the sheets, looking across at me. "Come on lover boy," she says.

I do my best smile and slide over towards her. She presses her body against me, and it feels like I'm being smothered by a warm jelly. We look over at Donovan, who's still looking like a man on death row.

"What do you want us to do, Donovan?" I ask him.

He nods. "Okay, so this is the morning after the night before, right? And Roy is realising that he's really into Jessica. And it starts with a gentle wind up, some kissing, then I want you to kiss her breasts and make your way down her stomach. And just as you're about to move down to give her head, the cat's going to jump on you."

"So, you're going to see my tits?" asks Izzy.

"That's okay, right? Like we discussed."

"No problem. Just no fanny shots," she says.

"I promise," says Donovan.

I'm not sure if I've missed something, but I'm pretty sure that this scene has changed pretty fucking spectacularly since I read the script. When we talked in rehearsal Donovan was planning to shoot the entire thing much more PG, and now it seems like he's aiming higher. Or lower.

"I thought we were going to shoot all of this waist up, covered by the sheets?" I ask.

Donovan shakes his head. "I think it's going to have much more impact if we see the cat jump while they're naked. Three reasons – we see that there's real intimacy there, it confronts the audience's prejudices about larger people…"

As he says this Izzy is nodding like it's all fucking fine with her.

…"and also, it's going to ramp up the comedy of the moment when they're interrupted by the cat so much more."

"Right," I say.

"Come on lover," says Izzy, winking at me. "Don't tell me you've never fucked a fat bird."

I throw her my best confident smile, but inside my stomach is churning. It's not that I've got a problem with chubby people especially, it's just that I don't really fancy them. Sure, I've been joining in all the earnest bullshit all week about this being a worthy issue to confront, and how it will explode the phallocentric myth that all men want to fuck skinny supermodels; that this story has the potential to re-examine modern sexual politics in the way that no film has before, and blah, blah, fucking blah. All that may well be true, but big girls just don't do it for me, and if anything, the idea of getting physical with Izzy is making me feel more than a little bit sick. She's great and everything, and we get on, but it's not like I'd be queuing up to take her on a fucking date.

"So, we're good?" asks Donovan.

"Sure," I say. Like I've got any kind of fucking choice. It's the first shot on day one of the first bit of work I've had in months, and the last thing I'm going to do is start acting like a prima donna. No, it looks like I'll just have to knuckle down and get smoochy all over Izzy's plentiful torso.

"We ready, Tony?" asks Donovan. "Bob knows what to do?"

Tony nods. "Don't worry," he says in his reedy little bank manager voice. "Bob knows exactly what to do."

I look at the cat that's currently sat on Tony's knee, and I swear the furry little twat is eyeballing me. That's the other thing that I never mentioned to anyone prior to today (I thought it might affect my chances of landing the role), but the truth is that I really, really fucking hate cats. There's no discernible reason for it, but they just freak me out. Always have, and always will. It's the way they look at you like they know what you're thinking, and just kind of stare you out with an air of malevolent superiority. And I'm sure they can sense when you don't like them, and just go out of their way to make your life even more difficult as a result.

Which is what I'm getting right now from Bob. He's a tabby, and his eyes have been fixated on me since I climbed into the bed. Tony has him on his lap and is running his hand across his back like a low-rent Blofeld, but I swear the cat has got his own fucking plans about how this is going to play.

"Okay," says Donovan. "Do you want to run the lines, or are you happy to go?"

Izzy and I look at each other.

"I'm happy if you're happy," she says.

"Sure," I say. "Let's go."

"OK," says Donovan. "Rolling John? Levels okay Henry. I'll do the slate." He puts the clapperboard in front of the lens. "Finding Jessica, scene thirty-four, take one. Action."

I roll on top of Izzy and kiss her on the lips. We've both been careful to chew some gum beforehand, so at least neither of us is going to be inflicting fag breath on the other. She's got her tongue in my mouth, and I can only hope that I look like I'm enjoying it.

"OK Charlie," calls out Donovan. "Now move down, kissing as you go."

I do as instructed, and move my face down Izzy's body, kissing her on her neck, and then I uncover the biggest tits I've ever seen. I've come across some huge knockers in my time, but these are phenomenal. They probably each come with their own postcode.

"Great Charlie," says Donovan, as I run my tongue down into Izzy's cleavage. "Now, can you get a nipple in your mouth?"

Make it fucking easy for me, I think. You try even finding the nipple on tits this big. I reach round with my hand to find it, and then stick it in my mouth. There's a faint taste of lavenderish soap on Izzy's skin.

"Great," says Donovan. "Now I want you to kiss her stomach on the way down. Okay, Tony, you ready?"

I shuffle down the bed, kissing Izzy's stomach as I go. It's riding up in folds of flesh as I do so, and I blank it out, trying to imagine firm, young, tight skin as I go, but it's not easy. It feels like I've been doing this for several minutes, and I'm acutely aware that so far there is no sign of the fucking cat. I can hear Tony issuing encouraging soothing whispers to Bob behind me, but so far, the little shit is refusing to hit his marks.

"And cut," says Donovan. "Is there a problem Tony?"

"Bob doesn't seem to want to go just yet," he says.

"Bob does understand we've got quite a lot to do today, doesn't he?" says Donovan, a touch acidly.

"He'll be fine. It usually takes him a couple of takes to get into the swing of things." Bob is still staring at me, immobile on Tony's lap as his back gets stroked. A couple of takes? Any more than that and from the look on Donovan's face, it won't live 'til lunchtime.

"Okay, we'll go again," says Donovan. He looks up to see Rebecca put her head round the door very carefully, and I can feel Izzy clock their exchange as well as me. Rebecca shakes her head very gently, and I swear he turns a deeper shade of green as she does. I don't know what that is about, but I know I'm not the only one keen to find out.

"Okay. John, rolling? Speed? And action."

I start again. Izzy and I kiss. I try to cram her enormous tits into my mouth. I run my mouth over the not inconsiderable folds of her belly flesh.

And the fucking cat stays exactly where it is.

"Cut!" says Donovan. "Look Tony, we've got quite a lot to do here, you know. It's not like your fucking Hugga Chunks ad, or whatever starring fucking role you've lined Bob up for next week, where we can hang around all cunting day until he decides he feels like doing what we want. We need him to jump on Roy's back, and we need him to do it sometime this fucking Millennium. Okay?"

Donovan looks like a man on the edge, like he might seriously pop a blood vessel at any point. The hushed tones in which he's just been threatening Tony have clearly hit home, and he's staring wide-eyed at Donovan, nodding and gulping like a dying goldfish. Bob, meanwhile, still has his lazy, malevolent glare fixed on me.

I've seen some director wig outs in my time, but they usually come a bit later down the line of production, when there's more than just one scene in the can. This must have something to do with whatever else is going on. That, or Donovan fucking hates cats even more than I do.

"Okay," says Donovan. "Let's try again. You two?" He says to me and Izzy, "Perfect. Keep doing what you're doing. John, you ready? Turning? Henry? Okay. Finding Jessica, scene thirty-four, take three.

"Action."

Later, when the bleeding has finally stopped, I find out exactly what happened.

I'd just put my face in the folds of Izzy's stomach when I became acutely aware of a yowling sound behind me, followed by the sensation of having my back flayed alive. Terry had clearly been more than a little rattled by Donovan's little pep talk, and rather than let Bob do what he was encouraged to do in his own time, took matters into his own hands, and effectively flung the fucking beast on to my naked back.

I'd love to think I acted manfully, but I remember screaming, and jumping backwards trying to grab Bob, who by this point is sinking his claws deep into my shoulders. He can sense that I'm trying to grab hold of him and decided to make a break for it in the only sensible direction available; away from the crowd of people and the person who is throwing him across the room – and this happened to be over the top of my head and out of the door. I can only be grateful that he didn't go the other way and take my fucking nuts with him on the way out.

John offered to show me the footage, as he said he'd never seen anything like it. The only thing that came close, he said, was when a cartoon character went off a cliff and its limbs start wind-milling underneath it. The last thing I ever want to do is relive that moment. The pain alone is enough of a souvenir.

After what seemed like an eternity of scrabbling over the top of my head with every claw drawn, Bob finally shot out of the room, leaving me bleeding all over the sheets.

I'm currently 'relaxing' on the sofa downstairs, and there's no sign of the little bastard. With any luck he's been run over. I've yet to look in a mirror, but from the looks I keep getting from anyone who drifts into the room, I'm guessing I'm not looking so pretty. I swear my left ear is still pissing claret. I've never known throbbing like it.

I can still hear Tony faintly calling out 'Bob?' out in the garden. He'd better pray he sees that fucking cat before I do, as if it comes near me, I swear I'm going to rip its fucking head off. It's already tried to do the same to me.

Izzy is taking a break with me down here, and we keep looking at each other with deep concern. There's definitely something going on, because there's nothing going on. Nobody is doing any set ups, there's no lights being rigged, or cables being laid, and there just seems to be a complete lack of activity of any kind. For a film set, this is unheard of. People keep moving around in hushed whispers, as Rebecca, Donovan and John have all been in an urgent conference for the last half hour or so since Bob went psycho.

It's getting to near eleven when Donovan finally comes into the room, followed by Rebecca, and slumps on the couch next to me. Izzy looks up from the magazine she's reading.

"How you doing Charlie?" Donovan asks.

"I'm fucking sore," I say.

"I'm really sorry," he says. "Terry gave me the impression he had half a fucking clue. Who knew?"

Both him and Rebecca are staring at the floor, and I'm getting the feeling that I'm about to hear someone say 'It's not you, it's me.'

"What's going on, Donovan?" I ask.

"We've been closed down," says Donovan. "Our funding got yanked. We've been spending the entire weekend trying to salvage it, been on the phone to everyone we know, and beyond. Germany, Japan, fucking Finland, you name it. No-one's come through. All the seed money has gone. We were hoping – convinced – that someone would step in this morning once we started shooting. But nothing. We're fucked. We haven't got a choice."

I feel sick. For a moment I think I might actually throw up.

"What a fucking load of old bollocks," says Izzy.

"But you had the money. I thought it was sorted," I say.

"It was," says Rebecca, as she looks at Donovan. "And then it wasn't."

"I honestly don't know what happened," he says. "Laurenson said the money was a lock. And then on Saturday he calls, tells me he can't go through with it. I asked him for his help in trying to find another investor, but he told me he's all tied up with this new project this weekend, and so he's not going to be able to spare the time."

"He's fucking jealous, is what he is," says Rebecca. "He doesn't want you making a film that's any good."

"But there's no money," says Donovan. "We spent the entire weekend slashing the budget. I was going to do it for nothing, so was Rebecca. We were going to see if the crew would work for deferred payments. But we still couldn't get the money."

"You tried the bank?" asks Izzy.

Rebecca snorts. "The bank don't want to touch us with a fucking bargepole. It's difficult enough to get them to lend money on things they might see a return on, but they're convinced they won't get their money back from film. Not when our exec producer has done a runner."

I look at Izzy, and she's just looking at Donovan and Rebecca like they're both a piece of shit; and in that split-second I realise just how good an actress she really is. She can play the tragic overweight cockney with a heart of gold until the cows come home, but up until this point it's been clear that she's been putting on a brave face, and now she knows she's not getting paid any attempt at being a team player is flying straight out the window.

"So, it ain't fucking happening?" she asks. "This is fucking unbelievable."

She turns and looks straight at Rebecca, and the venom in her voice could easily kill. "And none of us are getting fucking paid?"

Rebecca looks at the floor and shakes her head. "We've done everything we can. The only other option is for it is for the money to come out of our own pockets. And they're just not that deep."

Izzy shakes her head, and murmurs something that sounds like "fucking shower of shite," then she stands up.

"Can someone take me back to my hotel?" she asks. She comes over and stands in front of me. I look at her, and for a second, I think she's going to punch me in the mouth.

Her face turns, and she sneers at me, aggressive. "You haven't ever fucked a fat bird, have you Charlie? I can fucking tell." She shakes her head. "You've got no idea how to touch a fucking woman, you useless cunt."

I stare at her, open-mouthed.

"You think I don't know what a fucking chore it was for you to fake wanting to get it on with me, lover?" She spits out this word, quite literally, and a tiny fleck of spit rests on her bottom lip making her appear even more rabid. "You're a fucking joke, you know that, Charlie? You've put in one good performance in your entire career, and I don't know how much of that was a fluke of puberty. At least I don't have to play opposite you anymore, you useless, hack, cunt."

I'm so astonished by her outburst that I'm left speechless. I'm fighting for some kind of comeback, but my mouth is just hanging open in disbelief.

Donovan and Rebecca watch as Izzy leaves in silence, then Donovan turns to me. "That should help should we ever get another shoot date sorted."

I laugh. "You're fucking kidding, aren't you? It's over Donovan. Can't you fucking see that? It's fucking over. And you know why? Because of James fucking cunting Laurenson, that's why. You made the mistake of getting involved with him, didn't you? The man is a total, evil cunt. And you were fucking stupid enough to fall for all his fucking patter. You know why he recommended me for this role, don't you? So he got to fuck me all over again twenty years after the last time. He buried you, Donovan. Rebecca's probably right. He saw how good you were, and just thought 'fuck it.' I can do without that kind of threat to my position as the UK's number one director. And so he fucked you."

Rant over, I become aware that the whole set has fallen from quiet into total silence to listen to the outburst that's floating through the open windows. Donovan looks like he's about to burst into tears.

"Fucking cry all you want," I tell him. "But it's not going to make the slightest bit of difference. It's done."

I manage to persuade other Charlie to give me a lift back to the Bed and Breakfast and pack up all my gear in about five minutes flat. She's already gone by the time I've come back down, and I just hand my key over to the simpering mare who runs the place without a word, ignoring every single one of her questions; especially the one about who's going to settle the bill. I know Donovan's going to end up forking out a shit load of cash out of his own pockets, but that's the very least he can do. And he should learn a very valuable lesson about ever getting involved with James Laurenson again.

I set off in the direction of the train station. It's probably around a five-mile walk, but right now that suits me just fine; I'm in no hurry to rush back to Churchill Road. I'd been counting on three fucking weeks away, and now I'm on the first train back. And without a fucking pot to piss in. That's just perfect.

I fish out my phone to try to ring Carol, as I'm guessing by now, she's heard what's happened and is trying to get hold of me. There's no signal, so I plough on ahead under slate grey skies.

Fucking Laurenson. The one job that's come my way in the last six months, and he's fucked it for me again. I'm beginning to wonder now if it was a deliberate attempt to fuck with me directly. Donovan said that it was his idea for me to play Roy. Perhaps it was always his intention to pull the funding for the film, and this was just one more way of fucking me over.

The more I think about it, the more sense it begins to make. James Laurenson has clearly made it his mission in life to fucking ruin mine. I bet that little bitch Lucy Fontaine told him what I said about him at the Studios a while back, and he's now taking his revenge. And he's not doing badly; so far today I've had the world's chubbiest tits in my gob and been savaged by an insane cat. Rounded off with not getting paid.

I look up at the gathering clouds and blink out the first drop of rain as it hits me square in the right eye. The air smells of electricity, and I know that in less than five minutes I'm going to be totally fucking soaked.

Perfect.

I finally get back to Churchill Road gone eight o'clock, still damp from the downpour earlier that afternoon. The journey back was about as much fun as protracted dental work, as I ended up waiting for a very slow train for around an hour and a half. It was tiny four-carriage seventies antique that didn't even have a buffet trolley; not that it would have made much difference if it did as I wasn't counting on needing any cash for a while and am totally fucking skint. One thing goes in my favour – the tiny rural service means that there's no guard at any point to check my non-existent ticket, and I manage to slide through the barriers at Victoria by bunching up behind someone else.

I've got three pound coins in my pocket, which is just enough to pick up a packet of crisps which only marginally takes an edge off the chronic hunger that's been causing my stomach to wail since I got on the train, and also covers the cost of catching the 52 to Willesden Green.

It's cold as I get off the bus, and since I've not managed to get my trousers properly dry all day, I'm starting to feel like shit, and all I want to do as I get in is climb in the bath and pretend that today never happened.

As I let myself in, Pat leans back from her vantage point at the kitchen table to see who it is, and I swear that I see the tiny curl of a smile flicker at the corner of her mouth as she sees me come in.

"Oh, it's you," she says. "I wasn't expecting you back so soon."

I leave my case by the door and walk through to the kitchen. "Is there anything to eat? I'm starving."

"There's some ham in the fridge. And some new potatoes."

I'm aware that she's watching me as I grab the food from the fridge.

"Can I have a glass of this wine?" I ask, fishing out half a bottle of white from the door.

"I suppose so," she says. I pour a glass, and take the plate over to the kitchen table, and place it down opposite where she sits with her laptop.

"So?" she says. I could swear she looks like she's actually fucking enjoying this.

"They lost the funding. It all fell through," I say.

She looks at the top of my head, and to my right ear. I've been getting looks like this all day, so I can only imagine Bob did a pretty special number on me. It's still fucking throbbing; that's for sure.

"I got attacked by a cat. A scene went wrong."

"Well, looking at you now, I doubt they would have been able to continue using you anyway. It might be a blessing in disguise."

I stare at her. "How on earth can the film not happening at all ever be a blessing in disguise?"

She shrugs. "All I'm saying is looking like that, they'd probably have to find a replacement. So at least you were spared that small indignity."

Indignity, I think. There's no greater fucking indignity than coming back here, penniless, three weeks early and having to listen to Pat's load of old crap. That's indignity. I place another forkful of ham and potatoes into my mouth, and chew quickly so that I can escape somewhere else.

"They lost the funding?" she asks. I nod. "So does that mean that you didn't get paid?"

"Yeah," I say.

"Well, what are you going to do for money?"

I shrug, and the truth is I have no idea. I've been thinking about this for most of the way back, and I'm just going to have to hope that Carol is able to line up something else for me. I haven't been able to get hold of her yet as my phone died just as I reached the station and managed to get a signal.

"I don't know," I say. "Something will come up."

"Hmmm," she says, unconvinced, and turns back to look at her laptop.

I quickly finish my plate and stand up. I'm not rising to this now, and I don't want to get into a fight. Pat and I are long overdue a big conversation, but I'm not prepared to go there after the day I've had.

"You won't mind if I have a bath?" I ask, and I take my wine upstairs.

I lug my case up and dump it in my room, then take my glass of wine through to the bathroom. I rest it on the side of the bath and flick on the hot tap, then go back to my room to dig out my sweatpants which I'm going to collapse into once I come out. I plug my phone into the wall and switch it on. Immediately I get the beep of voicemail. It's a single message, left at midday. It's Carol.

"Charlie, darling. I've just heard. Absolutely fucking diabolical. I'm going to give them a piece of my mind, my love, don't you worry. Keep your chin up darling, you'll always be my favourite client. Call me back soon as you can." She hangs up, and I grin. Carol always has the knack of making me feel better.

Fuck them, I think. Fuck them all. Donovan, Rebecca, Bob the evil cat and Terry Fuckwit his incompetent trainer. Fuck Pat downstairs, and that fat cow Izzy; and fuck, first and foremost, the evil cunt overlord that is James Laurenson. Fuck them in the ear with a barbed stick that will leave splinters on the way out. Fuck them in the arse with a fifteen-inch syphilitic dick that spits black pus. Fuck them, fuck them, and fuck them again, once more. Hard. For luck.

I pick my towel from where it hangs on the back of the door and slope off to sink into the bath.

It's around half 9 when I wake up the next morning. I took a trip into Empire of Blood late last night for some gratuitous violence, and it seemed to have had the desired cathartic effect of making me feel better. The one clear priority is to hook up with Bob as soon as is humanly possible, as I could really do with getting severely twatted today.

I know he probably won't be up yet, but I fire off a text anyway, and I can only hope that he'll get back to me sooner rather than later. If I'm going to be living here until the fucking flat is sold, then I'm going to need some heavy anaesthetic. I put a call in to James at the Estate Agents, but he's not in. I wander downstairs to fix myself a coffee, half praying that Pat won't be around, as I really don't feel like talking to her.

She's sat at the table, her laptop open in front of her, and it's almost as if she hasn't moved from the spot all night, like a spider ready to pour venom into anyone unfortunate or stupid enough to wander into her web.

"Morning," I say, filling up the kettle.

"Mmmm," she says, which I take it is halfway between a greeting and a command not to disturb her while she's working. I could antagonise her further, but as I'm going to have to debase myself shortly and effectively beg her for some more money, there's little point in winding her up. Instead, I fix a pot of coffee in silence and pop a couple of slices of bread in the toaster. Everything made, I put a cup of coffee down in front of her, and then take mine through to the living room and flick on the TV.

I munch my toast while watching chavs tear each other apart on Jeremy Kyle, and then hit the mute and dial Carol on the mobile. It rings for a while and then goes through to the answerphone.

I frown. Deeply strange. It's now gone ten, and Carol is always in the office at ten. Always. I dial her mobile, but it goes straight through to voicemail. It's possible that Carol may have gone out, but then she would have left Annette to grab the phones, just in case.

I've just hung up when the mobile rings. It's James the Estate Agent.

"Charlie! How're things? Are you 'on set'?"

Last time we spoke I was bragging about nailing the lead role in the feature and was making a big fucking hoo-ha about how I wasn't going to be around to do anything flat related for the next month. I wish to God now I'd kept my fucking mouth shut.

"Actually, I'm back in London. They've run into some problems on the production, so the start's been put back for a bit. They're pretty sure we'll be up and running in the next fortnight."

I listen to myself as I'm trotting out this utter shite, and if I heard me then I wouldn't believe a word of it.

"Oh, okay," says James, and I can hear the confusion in his voice.

"So, what's the latest? Any biters?"

"There's a couple who are going back to have another look tomorrow. I'm not sure though. They could be time wasters. But it's good that you got in touch, as I needed to get hold of you. I was showing some people round on Saturday, and there was some mail for you. Normally I wouldn't bother you with it, but it looks serious."

Fuck, I think. What now? "Oh, okay," I say. "I'll swing by the office today and pick it up."

"Great. And sorry to hear about the film, Charlie."

He hangs up. I might be wrong, but I'm fairly certain I just heard genuine pity in his voice. And if I'm getting that from an Estate Agent of all people, then my life's in a lot of fucking trouble.

I come downstairs shaved and dressed, and despite doing what I can with some Savlon after the bath, the back of my neck and the top of my forehead still looks like it feels, which is extremely sore. I don't know what was in that cat's claws, but I suspect something radioactive as it hasn't really stopped throbbing since it happened. All I need now is for it to become infected, which is entirely possible given my current run of luck.

Pat's still tapping away at her computer, and as I enter the kitchen, I already know that she's not going to make this easy for me.

"I was wondering…"

She cuts me off before I even get a chance to ask. "Now's really not a good time, Charlie. Can't it wait?"

"Not really, no," I say. "I hate to have to ask, really I do. But the film getting cancelled has screwed my cash flow. If you could see your way to sorting me out with a little bit, maybe fifty quid or something, then I'll get it back to you as soon as I can. It looks like someone's going to make an offer on the flat this week, so it won't be long."

She sits there, tight-lipped and silent for a while, as she works away at her computer. There's nothing I can do apart from stand there while she does, being made to feel even more broke and useless. Then she stops and turns to me with an exaggerated sigh.

"Fifty pounds? This will have to stop, you know. I can't keep bailing you out just because you haven't got any money. You're going to have to find something else. And soon."

I nod, contrite. Only Pat has the magic ability to make me feel even more shit about myself than I already do.

She digs into her purse and comes up with two twenties, and hands them out to me. "It's all I've got. It'll have to do."

I take the money. "Thanks, it means a lot."

"I mean it though, Charlie. I'm not a piggybank. You're going to have to find a job."

"I'll be back tonight," I say. I know I need a job. Tell me something I don't know. That's why I'm trying to get hold of my agent.

I try ringing Carol again while I'm on the 52 on the way down to the Grove, but there's still no answer. I leave a message on the answerphone asking Annette to call me back, and then try Carol's mobile again, but it's still off. Weird.

I get off the bus opposite the tube and walk into the Estate Agents.

"No James?" I ask the blonde at the desk nearest the door.

"He's out on a viewing," she says. "You're Charlie, aren't you? There's some mail here for you."

She hands me a bunch of envelopes. I rifle through them, and it seems like the usual load of credit card statements and bill reminders. But then there's one that seems new. There's a red stamp on the envelope saying 'URGENT', and that's never a good sign. I look up, thank her, and walk out of the office.

I've got that yawning ache in the pit of my stomach, so I slope off down across Lancaster and into the library before I open it. There's plenty of red type all over it demanding my immediate attention and that I respond to them as soon as I possibly can. And as I look at what it says, I wonder just how much worse things could get.

It's a demand from Her Majesty's Revenue and Customs. Apparently, there's quite a significant sum I owe in unpaid back taxes.

£37,476.24, to be exact.

I carefully lean forward and slump my head onto the desk, praying that when I surface again it won't be real, but knowing, of course, that it is. I've got a cold sweat forming just below my neck across my shoulders, and I'm thinking that I might be sick.

This must be overdue from three years ago, when I did a couple of ads for a new range of biscuits. They paid me an absolute fortune, which of course all vanished pretty much immediately, and I've been trying to match it since. It was around this time that I left my accountant, Mr. Rogers, who'd been serving me loyally and (with the benefit of hindsight) extremely well for around fifteen years; largely because I didn't like what he was telling me. Which was that I should be being a lot more careful with my money. He'd always been on top of making sure that I sorted out all the important stuff like tax. I thought I knew better and could sort it all out without him. How hard could it be?

I take another look at the letter. As it turns out, it's a little bit harder than I thought.

I check the rest of the mail from the flat, and it's all my creditors asking me to get in touch with them to let them know when they might expect some of their money. It's a good job that I can make some calls when I get back to Churchill Road, as I suspect that I'm going to be on the phone for a while.

I send Bob a text to see if I can swing by sooner rather than later, but I'm still getting nothing back, so in the meantime I decide to make the most of all this free time, and rifle through the papers on the off chance that Spielberg might be doing some casting in the Guardian.

My phone rings at 4, waking me up from where I've passed out on a table. I get an audible tut from one batty old crone who looks over disapprovingly, and I guess that I'm a shave and a wash away from looking like a proper tramp.

Finally, Carol ringing back, I think, until I see on the caller display that it's Bob.

"Bob, how's tricks?"

"Good Charlie, good. How's the film?"

"Not happening. They lost their funding," I say.

"Bummer."

"So I'm back in the Grove. You around?"

"'Course," he says. "Come on over."

Get in. I may be on the brink of career, financial, and even personal collapse, but while I can get stoned, life really can't be that bad.

I'm out of the library so fast you can almost see the dust fly, and ten minutes later I'm outside Bob's building waiting for him to pick up the intercom.

"Hello?" The sound of bewilderment personified. It's as if Dylan from the Magic Roundabout was brought to life and dropped in a shit council flat in Ladbroke Grove.

"It's Charlie," I say, and there's a buzz.

I get up there and there's already the sound of the kettle boiling. I close the door behind me and walk through to the living room where Bob's already back in his customary position on the mouldy couch, looking dangerously like he might be swallowed by it at any moment.

"Hey," he says.

"Hello mate," I say. "Cup of tea?"

"Lovely," he says, and he's already turned back to the TV. He seems even more lethargic than usual.

I put his tea down in front of him, and he looks shit-faced. I'm not going to ask him what he's been up to all day, because it doesn't take a rocket scientist to see that it's been mostly getting royally fucked up.

"Sharks," he says.

"Yeah," I say, and look at the telly. Unusually he's not watching soft porn on MTV and seems transfixed by the shoreline attacks of a Great White shark on a seal in the surf. It shoots out of the water in slow motion and bites down on the seal like a jelly baby.

He makes a noise next to me. "Huh." It's a kind of stoned cough cum single laugh and is clearly indicative that he's probably been at it since he got up this morning, assuming he ever went to bed last night.

"Unlucky," I say.

He giggles. "Unlucky! Yeah."

"So, what have you got for me, Bob? Can I pick up a quarter?"

He nods, eyes closed. "Of course, Charlie. Of course." His eyes remain closed, and the Rizla remains unrolled in his hands.

"You okay?" I ask after he's remained motionless for about thirty seconds.

"Uh," he grunts. "Ketamine."

Oh good God. No wonder he's in a state. I've only done K a couple of times, and although it can be a lot of fun, it is also the most effective way of leaving the planet for a while. There was one time that Nick and I did it at the flat mixed up with some coke, and four hours passed in a kaleidoscopic haze while we babbled away incoherently to each other. Deep down the K-hole.

"Have you got any more?" I ask.

He nods, eyes still closed. "Mmmm."

"Well, rack 'em out then."

"You might have to do it, I think, if it's all the same with you."

I think that's what he says. It sounds more like yumahavdoehthinallsamyu. I take the half rolled spliff from his hands, and finish building it for him. I fire it up, watching him for a while. He's totally fucking lost it. It's quite flattering in a way, as Bob must really trust me to let me come over while he's in this state. Because anyone could rob him blind while he's like this and he'd be none the wiser.

"Bob?" I say, and push the spliff between his fingers, which are currently splayed on his thigh.

"Mmmm," he says, and manages to raise it to his lips. He drags deeply. He manages to open his eyes and looks over to me.

"There's some in a wrap in that pot," he says carefully, and then slumps back onto the couch again, his eyes closed.

I lift the lid on the pot, and there's a bag containing what must be a couple of grammes of ketamine. I take another look at Bob, wondering if this is really a good idea. Then I remember the letter that I'm going to have to deal with tomorrow. Right now, a short drug holiday from my own head is probably just what I need. I rack out a couple of thick lines, and fish a twenty quid note out of my wallet.

"Cheers," I say, and hoover up a fat one. I drag deep on the reefer and lean back into the couch, and the last effort that my conscious mind makes is to make sure that the spliff rests in the ashtray on my lap.

Time means nothing in the K-hole, and in between bouts of paralysis and crazy fractal dreams I have several insights that I'm sure would make the world a shinier, happier place. I'm sure that when I try and impart all this wisdom to Bob it comes across to him much as he does to me, like a brain damaged farmer trying to gargle yoghurt. As I come down from the repeated hoovering of lines, I know that I've realised something very, very important, but the incredibly frustrating thing is that I'm so fucked up that I can't remember what it is.

As I come round, I tune back into the TV and reach for the remote so that I can put something else on, as I'm not really in the mood for the National Geographic channel. Both of us sit there, fucked, basking in the weird post K feeling you get on returning from an intense psychological and psychedelic head safari.

Bob is silently building another spliff, and we both sit there in silence until it's dead in the ashtray.

"I haven't done that for a while," I say.

"Me neither. I got given some in return for some puff. I thought God was talking to me for a little while."

"Me too. I like the visuals. Like Timothy Leary painting the inside of your eyelids."

Bob nods. "So did you want some puff?"

I pick up a quarter from him and hang around for another reefer and a pizza that he's ravenous for, and which I'm more than happy to help him eat. He's completely forgotten about the forty quid I owe him for the last bit of Charas, and with the state of my finances I'm not about to start reminding him.

It's approaching midnight, and I'm back on the 52 with all the drunks heading back to Willesden Green before it even occurs to me to check my phone. I'm pretty sure that at one point while we were both deeply off our tits, I could hear it ringing, but that could have been anything.

There's a message left for me, and so I dial through to the voicemail. There's a guy noisily making his way through a bag of chips behind me, and so I block my ear to try and hear my phone.

It's Annette. From Carol's office. At first, I think there's something wrong with the phone, as I can barely make out a single fucking word she's saying. I turn up the volume on the handset, and the second time brings some chilling clarity. In between the sobs Annette is trying to tell me that Carol had a colossal heart attack yesterday afternoon, and she's dead.

As I look out of the bus window at Chamberlayne Road drifting past beneath me, the acrid whiff of vinegar from the seat behind me seems to snap me out of my woolly stoned haze, and only seems to bring the tears to my eyes all the faster.

A week later and I'm sitting in a small church in the far reaches of East London, a good hour in the wrong direction on the Hammersmith and City Line. As I made my way over here, I tried to imagine Carol cramming her enormous arse into one of these seats on the way into Soho, and how she managed to last an entire train journey without having a fag.

I got hold of Annette the day after she left the message, and she was still in pieces about what had happened. Apparently, Carol had called Rebecca, the producer on Finding Jessica, to give her a piece of her mind. After shouting colourful insults at her for fifteen minutes she slammed the phone down, lit another fag, and then (according to Annette) leant back in her chair making a strange gurgling sound and then tipped forward abruptly, slamming her head on the desk. Annette took one look at her (and this was when she started crying again), and she knew instantly that she's gone.

An ambulance pronounced her dead at the scene, although I suspect that was partly because they took one look at Carol and thought 'fuck trying to carry that.' Apparently, it was quite an operation, with the police and fire brigade all mucking in to try and get Carol back to ground level. There was some debate about whether to get her out through the window, but in the end, they managed to wrestle her down the stairs. There was an autopsy, and it revealed that she'd died of a massive coronary. But at least, as Annette said, she didn't suffer.

Carol's dad, Joe, called me on Thursday morning, and asked me if I would read a poem at the funeral. As her longest standing (and most recognisable) client he was sure that she would have wanted me to read something. The fact that I was her best client goes to prove just how fucked her life really was. I agreed, of course. Anything for Carol. Initially he suggested that I find a poem to read, but after having a look and finding that everything was by Emily Dickinson and was deeply fucking morose, I told him that I'd write something myself. He seemed more than happy with that.

I've barely been out of my room all week, and even Pat seems to have been keeping her distance since I told her what happened. I looked at myself in the bathroom mirror this morning, and for a second almost didn't recognise myself. An old man looked back at me; grey flecks in his beard and black rings underneath his eyes. I managed to iron most of the creases out of my suit and look marginally better for a shower and a shave; but I suspect I still look like shit to the outside world.

I never would have recognised Carol's dad, so it's fortunate that he spotted me and introduced himself. He's a tiny guy, about five four and nine stone, if that; and anytime that he and Carol were ever out together I suspect that most people thought that he was her breakfast. Poor guys in bits though, losing his only daughter, and you can see the strain that he's been living under all week. Thank fuck Carol had some cousins though, or otherwise I think I might have been roped in to carrying the coffin down the aisle, and that would have been no fun at all.

But right now, I'm sitting in the second pew back, looking over the reading that I'm going to have to do when the service finally starts. Annette sits next to me and I'm aware of a constant stream of tears that trickle down her chubby face, plopping off her two chins into a tissue.

I turn round to have a look who's here, and there's a reasonable turnout. Some familiar faces, although no-one who's going to stop any traffic in the famous stakes. Mostly it's just full of people. Normal people, who all wear black and gentle smiles, and look like they loved and miss Carol. It's good to see.

Then I see Elijah, and I'm pleasantly surprised. He catches my eye, and nods, taking a seat towards the back of the church. I left him a message this week about what had happened and where the funeral was, but had heard nothing back; and so, had assumed that he wasn't coming. I'd clearly underestimated him and feel a little ashamed with the realisation that he may well have more class than I could ever aspire to.

There's a couple of speakers set up at the front which have been playing New Romantic ballads since everyone started filing in. They were clearly a favourite of Carol's, and there's something about Ultravox's 'Vienna' and Spandau's 'True' that really seem to fit the occasion. Then the music is faded down, and as a new track is played six men stagger down the aisle carrying the coffin on their shoulders.

Whether it was on her instruction or not, the fact that Carol enters the church to John Waite's 'Missing You' is a touch of total genius, and one that manages to bring a smile to my face while my eyes fill with tears.

The vicar waits until the track has finished before walking up to the pulpit, and then he looks up. He tells us that Joe thanks us all for coming, and that Carol would have been delighted with all the people that made it out today. That she went too young, too soon, but at least she went as she would have wanted, with a fag in her mouth. Chuckles from the congregation.

He talks about Carol's life, and her work. About how she worked with countless actors, young and old, finding them work and doggedly working on their behalf. How it takes a special kind of determination to become an agent, a unique sensibility, and one that Carol had in abundance. How she made the careers of many a young actor, and that one of those she did will now read.

And he introduces me.

I get up and walk to the front, and as I look out, I tell myself that I'm not going to cry. That I'll read what I've written, but I won't cry. I unfold the piece of paper that I've been clutching in my hands for the past half an hour and look down at it.

I clear my throat. I look out as expectant faces wipe tears from their eyes. And begin.

"Carol came along to see me in a play called 'The Mocking Half' in the West End, in what now seems like a lifetime ago. She came to see me backstage afterwards, and she told me that she really liked the way I played the role, and that, if I would like her to, she would love to represent me. I was only fourteen at the time, so I was over the moon. Here was this woman who wanted to be my agent. Shortly after that she put me in touch with a director who was making his first film..." I pause, for a moment, as a memory of that first meeting with James Laurenson pops into my head. "I got the role, and ended up in a very successful film, 'The Twelfth of Never.' And I never looked back."

This, of course, isn't strictly true, but this isn't about me, it's about Carol. I could go into the details of the frightening unpredictability and crippling poverty of the life of an actor here, but this crowd doesn't want to hear that.

I could go into what's been occupying my almost every waking thought as I've been on the cramped single bed in Churchill Road, either lying back looking at the ceiling or hunched forward indiscriminately running down passers-by in Empire of Blood; that Laurenson is as responsible for her death just as much as her overloaded heart ever was.

I look out at the sea of faces looking up at me, and the silence is broken by a delicate cough from the back; and that's when

I realise that I've not said a word for the past thirty seconds. I'm beginning to get some very strange looks.

"What can I really say about Carol?" I'm asking myself as much as the congregation. "Without her, none of you would ever have an idea who the hell I was. Looking at you now, I can see that most of you still don't. Not that it matters. Carol was always there for me, and never gave up trying to get me work. Even when I was convinced I was the world's worst actor, and that I may as well give up, she was always behind me, telling me that it wouldn't be long before I'd be back working again. I don't know what I'm going to do without Carol."

I look down at the floor. There are tears in my eyes; a heady cocktail of grief spiked with shame and self-pity. I don't know what else to say, and so I quietly walk back to the pew and sit down, where Annette squeezes my arm. I'm aware that I haven't said half the things that I was intending to, but there's not much I can do about that now.

Another song starts to come through the speakers. 'A Place in the Sun' by Stevie Wonder. Tears roll down my face as I listen to it, and it only reinforces how little I really knew Carol. To me she was just a meal ticket, someone I had charmed long ago and thought I could manipulate with little effort, as in all honesty I thought I was the biggest actor on her books by a long shot. And so, I could gently push her around, trying to get her to go the extra mile to find me some work. I had no idea what music she liked, what she did outside work, what her father's name was. That didn't interest me because I'm a selfish, egocentric twat. Totally solipsistic.

Annette squeezes my arm again, all too aware of my tears. It's not just Carol though. It's me. Alex's words to me as she left my flat with Nick just over a month ago echo in my head; that I'm an emotional leech, that I don't give a fuck about anybody but myself. And it's hard to argue. Because although I know I'm going to miss Carol, the grief I'm feeling right now is almost as much for the death of my career.

It's not as if I've got a shit load of agents knocking down my door wanting to represent me. I seem to be the kiss of death to any project that I come anywhere near, and I feel way too old and twice as scared to start knocking on doors. Alex was right. I abuse people's better nature, and only realise what I've done when it's too late.

I'm a fucking no-good piece of shit.

There are soft smiles in my direction, and murmured comments about my "lovely words" on the way out of the church after the service, but I know it's all your standard funereal bullshit. I was given the simple task of saying a few words about Carol, and I even managed to fuck that up.

Elijah is standing outside smoking a cigarette, and I walk straight up to him.

"Can I get one of those?".

He fishes out a pack wordlessly and offers them to me. I light one up and feel myself relax just a little as the smoke fills my lungs.

"Nice one for coming," I say.

He shrugs. "Had to come, blad. She sorted me out, innit."

"You got a job?"

He nods. "Next week. St Anthony's." He draws on his cigarette, drops it on the ground. "I owe you, Hollywood."

"You deserve it, Elijah. I wouldn't worry about getting another agent, either. Someone will snap you up soon enough."

He shrugs again, and it's a gesture that tells me he's only too aware how good he is. That he's going to smash St Anthony's out of the park, and from there he's going to go off and charm someone else into giving him a job. There's a raw charisma about him that will see him right.

Carol's dad disappears into a black car behind the main hearse that is going to take him off to a crematorium somewhere. There was an announcement that there's going to be a wake at his house, and all are welcome, but I just don't think I can face it.

"You got a spliff?" I ask Elijah.

He grins and nods at me. We walk around to the back of the church and sit down on a grave, and he builds a reefer with a shocking amount of skunk, and lights it up. The stink of the grass is overwhelming, and they can probably smell it on the other side of the church. He inhales three times, quickly, and passes it to me. One toke in, and I know that this is a very strong spliff, and it's probably a good idea to leave it alone, so obviously I take another drag and hand it back to him.

"Fuck me, that's strong." I cough a little.

Elijah takes another deep drag and nods sagely. "You didn't think I'd come."

It's a statement, not a question. I shake my head. "Why would you? You'd only seen her once. It's not like you'd been with her for years. Not like some of these guys."

He drags on the spliff again and passes it. "She would have been there for me."

The simple truth of this strikes me. Carol would have. She would have been there for any one of her clients. No questions asked. She would have tracked out to any corner of the capital, or country, to show her respects for someone she'd worked with. I doubt I could say the same about myself. I was struck by how many people there were in the church, how many people Carol knew and loved. Who's going to be there when I go? A family I don't like, Bob if he's not too stoned, maybe

Elijah if I'm lucky. That's it. No wife. No children. I'm a fucking joke.

I take another toke and lie back on the gravestone to look at the sky. Elijah takes the spliff from me.

"You want to go to the wake?" I ask him.

"Nah," he says. I'm relieved, as there's no way I want to turn up there.

"Then let's wait until everyone goes, then head back to the tube."

"Safe."

We're silent for the long journey back, and I'm guessing that until we get back to W10, he's actually a little relieved that I'm on the tube with him. He hasn't said anything about it, but I remembered what a big deal it was for him to come away from the Pleasance down towards St. Quintin's, so God knows how hard it was to get on the tube all trussed up in a suit and come to a church in the East End of London. It makes me respect him all the more.

We get off at Ladbroke Grove, and I walk up to the bus stop.

"What do I do? Next week?" he asks.

I'm still very woolly-headed from the loaded skunk joint from about an hour ago, and so I look at him blankly for a moment.

"St Anthony's. Next week, blad. What do I do?"

I look at him for a second, and behind the fuck you eyes that are his default look, I can see he's nervous.

"You've got the script, right? And a call time?"

He nods.

"Then learn your lines and turn up on time. You'll be fine. There will be a run through, and you'll be rehearsing for a couple of days. Just listen to what the director tells you."

"I ain't never done this before, Hollywood."

"Would you feel better if you ran the lines with me?"

He looks a little relieved at this suggestion, although he's still trying to ride it out a little with the usual bluster.

"You don't need to do that, man," he says.

"I don't mind. Seriously. It's not like you're keeping me from anything else."

Ten minutes later and we're walking through the front door into Elijah's flat. It's on the sixth floor of one of the buildings that lurks near Bob's place and it's nowhere near as fucking horrible as you think it's going to be once you're through the front door. Perhaps it's just the exteriors of these places that are designed to look like big prisons, as Elijah's mum is clearly house proud.

The place is spotless, and as he's been deeply twitchy about anyone seeing him coming in the flat. I'm guessing that he's bunking off school, and the last thing he wants is for his Mum to find out about it. He shows me into the living room, and there's no sign of inner-city decay here, rather just the normal trappings of family life. A flatscreen telly in the corner with an Xbox underneath, and a photo of Elijah with his Mum and sister resting on the mantelpiece. Eiljah's mum is smiling for the camera, and despite her obvious pride in her children, there's a steely strength underneath that you can sense in her photograph.

"This your Mum and sister?" I ask him. He nods, disappearing into the kitchen to put the kettle on. "She know you're out taxing hapless individuals for their wallets and phones?" I call out after him.

He comes back into the living room looking sheepish. "That ain't me, blad. But you don't know what it's like round here."

He ducks back into the kitchen. He's right. I don't.

"So where's the script?" I ask him.

He goes into his bedroom and returns with a dog-eared copy of a screenplay, and hands it to me. I flick through it, and highlighted in orange is the character name 'FELIX'. I take a look. It looks like Felix is a gunshot victim, and the only living witness to the murder of his friend. Nice.

Elijah comes in with a cup of tea for each of us, and hands it to me before sitting down on the couch.

"Felix, right?" I ask.

He nods. "Yeah."

"So tell me about him."

"He's been shot up, innit. His brother's dead, and his girlfriend is trying to get him to tell five oh who shot him up. But he don't want to."

"Okay. So you want to run the lines?"

He nods.

"Okay, so we start on page five. You've just been shot, and Charmaine finds you, and she's screaming."

He knows the words, and he's good. He twists himself up on the couch a little as he delivers the lines, and as he does I'm wondering if he's actually seen someone shot. I wouldn't be surprised, but I'm not going to ask him.

"That's good, Elijah. Nicely done."

He smiles, pleased with the praise. We carry on, running through the rest of his lines in the piece. Finally, Felix agrees to talk to the police, saying that he and Charmaine will run away together – only to suddenly develop complications and snuff it on page 54. He performs it well, and I'm impressed.

"You'll be fine. That was a good reading. Any director will be happy with that."

He smiles uncertainly as I tell him, pleased to receive the praise but now showing all the signs of being a real actor: the bluster of earlier has gone, replaced with an obvious doubt about what he's doing.

"Serious?" he asks.

"Elijah, listen. I was about your age when I started professionally, and I used to shit myself all the time. Acting can be brilliant, but it's the scariest thing in the world. I thought at any minute I'd get found out, that people would suss that I didn't have a fucking clue what I was doing. But you know what? It took me a while to figure it out, but everyone feels like that most of the time. They feel like a fraud. And that's okay. Because it's that feeling that keeps you on your toes, keeps you open to everything around you. Trust me, everyone is shitting themselves most of the time. They're just fronting it out. And I know you can do that."

He nods. "What if they need to find me before next week though? Everything came from Carol, and she's gone."

I shake my head. It's so different for him. He's at the beginning of a career which I'm willing to bet could be long and glorious. He's landed a good role in a respected Beeb drama. He's going to get snapped up in no time.

"Don't worry. I'll speak to Annette, and make sure that they know what's going on, and can get in touch with her if there's any news with the shoot. Remember, all you need to do is listen, be polite, and don't act like a cock. The key thing in this business is being someone who people want to work with. Don't ever get up yourself and start thinking you're some kind of fucking star. That's the quickest way down the toilet."

As I listen to myself talk I'm thinking 'good advice' – just a shame I don't follow it myself. God I can be a prick.

"And I wouldn't worry about getting another agent," I continue. "Keep your nose clean and you'll get snapped up soon enough. You're a good actor, Elijah. Seriously. What does your Mum think? She must be proud."

He looks down at the floor, sheepish. For a moment I'm confused, wondering why he's looking like that.

Then the penny drops. "You've not told her?"

He shakes his head. "You don't know her, blad. She wants me to focus on school before I go off and do anything else. She'd go mad if she thought anything I was doing would get in the way of my GCSEs."

What, like mugging people and smoking puff? I think, but don't say.

"You're not telling her?"

"I need to take time off school, blad."

"What about permission?"

"I faked a letter innit. And the school have sorted it."

"What about your mates? Do they know?"

He shakes his head. "Nah, man. They'd be raw jelly. I tell, next thing I know I get shanked."

"Jelly?"

"Jealous Hollywood."

We've all got it rough in some way. Sounds like we've both got difficult mothers, but at least with him it's only his mates and not his actual flesh and blood who would try and stab him in the back through envy.

"Well, you'd better hope that none of them watch TV, 'coz you're going to be on it soon. Then what will you do?"

"I take my GCSEs in two months blad. Then I can leave. Go college. Learn acting. I just need to get out of fucking school, man."

"Fair enough. The only piece of advice I'm going to give you is don't smoke puff the day before the shoot. You're going to want to keep a clear head, and you'll be better if you're straight. Trust me."

He nods. "Alright. Safe."

I pick up an Xbox controller from besides the television. "So, what games you got?"

We spend a couple of hours dicking around on Mortal Kombat, and although I take him to pieces a couple of times overall he's by far the better player. Hardly a surprise if he's bunking off a lot and playing all day. He kicks me out shortly after half 3 so I'm not here when his sister gets home, and he has to answer any awkward questions about who the hell I am and what I'm doing there.

I've timed the journey back badly, and so the 52 is full of screaming yoot all trying to play the latest grime track to one another on their phones. I keep to myself, my head buried in a copy of the paper that I've nabbed from outside a newsagent – the last thing I want to get into now is a question-and-answer session with a group of teenagers about being 'that guy from that thing.'

Pat is out when I walk through the door. I nip upstairs fast and dump my suit on the bed and change into jeans and a T-shirt and build myself a reefer to smoke in the garden while I'm there. I go back downstairs and stand outside the back door. I've only just lit the fucking thing when I hear the front door close and am about to put it out on the wall when I listen to the footsteps in the hallway, and I can hear that they're not Pat's.

I leave the back door open, looking through, and look as Sofia carefully enters the kitchen; looking as if she expects Pat to jump out and grab her at any moment. She sees me out the back door and smiles cautiously.

"She's not here," I say. "No idea where she is."

She nods. "Would you like a cup of tea?" she asks.

"Lovely," I say, and continue puffing away as I watch her through the kitchen window. "Where've you been?" I ask. "I've barely seen you this week."

And I haven't. Part of this is because I've been locked away in my room pissing about on the Xbox, but she's barely been around anyway. She leaves first thing, and comes back late at night, creeping up the stairs as delicately as possible.

She looks out at me. "I look for somewhere else to live."

Only to be expected. Pat drives away another one. The woman is impossible to live with.

"Lucky you," I say.

She brings me out a cup of tea. I offer her the spliff, but she turns her nose up, frowning a little as she shakes her head no.

"I look with two other girls from college. We look for flat up in Kingsbury but is still expensive."

Everywhere is expensive. This is London. "I'm sure you'll find something," I say. "You've had enough here then?"

"Your mother is kind woman but is time to move I think." She frowns, looks at me. "You had funeral today, yes?"

I nod. "Yes. Carol. My agent."

"You know her long time?"

"Over twenty years. I had to do a reading. It was hard."

"I'm sorry," she says, and she reaches out to put her arm on mine. I lean into her body, and she envelops me in a hug. I nuzzle her neck a little. This could be just what I need. I pull back and bring my face round to kiss her on the mouth.

And she pulls back, looking at me.

"What are you doing?"

"I thought…" I begin; and stop. Because from the look on her face, I've judged this horribly, horribly wrong.

"No, Charlie. I give you hug because you lose someone. I don't want sex with you. I have boyfriend in Belgrade."

I nod, looking at the floor. I'm a no-good, selfish, piece of shit sex pest. My eyes fill with tears again. I don't even fancy her, and I still get knocked back.

"I'm sorry," I mumble.

"Is okay. You are nice man, Charlie. But I think this is not good for your brain."

I look down at the end of the spliff in my hand, and it's dead. I drop it on the ground. I nod. I can't even look at her.

"I think you are in bad place at the moment," she says. "But it will get better."

I nod, and a tear runs down my cheek.

"I go out tonight," she says. "Please do not tell your mother about me leaving. I would like to do it."

I nod again, still looking at the floor. I don't have to look up to feel her pitying smile as she leaves, and I sit down on the bench in the garden. It's still slightly wet from last night's rain, and I can feel my arse getting damp, but I don't care.

I really don't care anymore.

I'm back in my room, driving aimlessly around in 'Empire when the front door closes. I've been hiding back up here since Sofia got ready and went out around an hour ago, and so the only person who that can be coming through the door is Pat.

I've barely seen her over this past week. Most of it has been spent in my room, occasionally going downstairs to forage for food; and we've barely spoken. There's still so much still unsaid between us that I scarcely know where to start. I've already taken the opportunity to go down and stuff myself with toast, so at least I'm safe for this evening. But I know I'll have to go down at some stage.

But not tonight. Tonight is for Empire of Blood, and I spy a Bugatti coming down Fifth Avenue. I wrench the driver out of the seat, kicking him in the head, and climb in and speed off; leaning out the window to take out a row of nuns with the Tommy gun for good measure.

It's late when I wake up the next morning. I feel like shit, and I'm painfully aware that the nothingness that the day holds stretches out in front of me like a yawning chasm. I'm an unemployed actor without an agent; about as desirable in the job market as a primary school teacher with an erection and a meat cleaver.

I can hear Pat scuttling around in the kitchen downstairs and try as I might there's no putting off seeing her. I need a cup of coffee and some toast, and that means going into the kitchen. Her lair.

I pull on my sweatpants and slope downstairs. I don't say anything until I've put the kettle on, then turn round to her.

"Morning", I say.

"How was the funeral?" she asks.

"Busy. Sad. Your usual funeral really."

She nods, tapping away on her laptop.

"You did a reading, didn't you?"

I nod. "Yeah. Well, more like a few words about Carol, from someone who knew her. That kind of thing."

She nods. "Right."

There's silence for a minute while the kettle boils, and I make some coffee. I take two cups over and put one in front of her, taking the seat opposite hers.

"Sofia is moving out," she says.

"Really?"

"She told me this morning. So that means I've got to get someone else in. And soon. Especially since you're living here rent free."

And you just couldn't resist reminding me of that, could you, I think.

"I was hoping I might be able to at least have my own room back," I say. "At least until I move out."

"And when might that be?" she asks, pointedly, her attention still firmly on the screen in front of her.

I sip my coffee. I don't know when it might be, and the last thing I want to get into now is a recap of my ever-worsening financial situation. James the Estate Agent says that there still haven't been any offers, which is unusual, but suggests dropping the price if I want a quick sale. It's not like I want to do that, but I'm rapidly running out of options. I'm now getting the occasional 'follow-up call' from both my mortgage lenders not so gently nudging me as to when they might expect their fucking money, and now I've got all the money I owe the Inland Revenue thrown into the mix. I need to clear my debts, and soon. But if I drop the price much more then I'm barely going to walk away with any money at all.

I really need to get out of this fucking place.

"I don't know," I answer. I bite my tongue to prevent myself saying that I really don't want to be here anymore than she doesn't. "I'd like to think soon, but I don't know. I'm not having much luck selling the flat."

"Right," she nods. There's a thick pause while I sip my coffee.

The clock on the kitchen wall ticks loudly. We both sit there, waiting to see who speaks first. Pat breaks the silence.

"What are you going to do for work? I take it there's no jobs on the horizon?"

"It doesn't look like it."

"Then you're going to have to get a job. I'm sorry, Charlie, but I'm not a bottomless pit that you can keep dipping into whenever you need cash. If you want to live here rent free, then the least you're going to have to do is earn your own spending money." She looks up from her screen to stare directly into my eyes. "Especially if you're going to carry on smoking that stuff in the garden."

There's no point denying it. I could go into one about it being something of a necessity if I'm living with her, but it's probably not the best idea.

"There are several places around here." She looks down to her screen again. "I suggest you try and find bar work or something. You can't afford to be proud."

I stifle a hollow laugh. Any sense of pride that I once had is quickly vanishing as my ego is stripped naked and beaten in Pat's emotional version of an extraordinary rendition. Pride. Jesus. My life is disappearing down the toilet with almost superhuman speed.

I grit my teeth and clench my fists until my knuckles turn white.

"I stopped being proud a long time ago. You know I saw Dad a while back?"

She raises her eyebrows. "Really?"

"Yeah, you know. You sent him that email saying that I'd come back here, and it was obviously highly inconvenient for you. Well, I went to see him. And he told me something interesting, that was supposed to be a secret."

She doesn't look up at me as I'm talking, but I can see her jaw get a little tighter, so I know I'm getting through.

"What did James Laurenson say to you during 'The Twelfth of Never'?"

"I don't remember Charlie."

"Oh, I think you do. You must remember. I came home that night in floods of tears, saying I wasn't going back. And you told me not to be ridiculous, that I had to go back. It was fine with you; you didn't really care how I was feeling. Fuck it. Send him back on the film. Only Laurenson told you he was going to tear me to shreds, didn't he? He effectively asked for your permission to go ahead and fuck me up, and you went ahead and said, 'that's fine.' No problems there, not for you. I was the most miserable I've ever been in my life – apart from now, which is running a close fucking second, by the way – and you said to Laurenson to do whatever he wanted to me. You could have said something, told me that was what happened, not to worry. But you didn't, did you? You never said a word."

She looks at me, and her eyes seem more dead than ever. "Have you finished?"

I say nothing and wait for her to speak.

"How dare you, Charlie. How dare you. Of course I didn't say anything. You had a role most people would have killed for, and you were giving the performance of a lifetime. That's what I was hearing from people on the set, and I saw it myself on more than one occasion. You were unhappy? Boo-hoo. You wanted reassurance? I wasn't going to do that. Not when it would have taken you out of a place where you were giving such a good performance."

I can't believe I'm hearing this. "But I was just a teenage boy! I was your son! Didn't you realise how important any kind of comfort was?"

She looks back down at her screen. She seems totally unmoved. "That's just not me, Charlie."

There it is. That's the crux of it, right there. It isn't her. Why am I even bothering with this conversation, I wonder?

"It wasn't always like this, was it? I can remember you being happy, once. When I was small. That's partly why I liked acting. Because it made you happy. And I'd go along for auditions and try out for things, so long as it made you happy. What the hell happened? I get some success, and rather than be pleased for me, it's been like you've been making me pay for it ever since."

"What should I be apologising for? Tell me that."

There's a tiny flare of anger in her voice now, like I'm finally hitting a nerve.

"Raising you and Molly single handed while your father decides to go off with another woman? Encouraging you to pursue something you loved, and develop a very successful career? And for what? For you to squander everything you worked so hard for, and come back here to live with me again? You want me to apologise for that?"

I stare at her, gobsmacked. She really thinks that she's the one with a grievance here. Like twenty years of emotional abuse is just to be expected.

She looks over at me. "If you didn't spend quite so much time flitting between feeling sorry for yourself, and that the world owed you a living, you might achieve a great deal."

I stand up. "And if you didn't withhold affection with such obvious relish, then maybe I wouldn't be such a gigantic fuck-up."

I storm out of the kitchen and stamp back upstairs.

Four hours later and I'm trawling the bars around Willesden Green, abasing myself horribly in the search for some bar work. The Aussie contingent seems to have it all sewn up round here, and there's nothing going in the first three pubs I try. But then I enter a bar with delusions of grandeur; it thinks it belongs in Notting Hill but is clearly punching above its weight. Even as I walk in, I can feel my hackles rise with the ambient music in the background, and the one bored oaf in the corner sipping at an overpriced coffee. There's a lot of brushed chrome and overconfidence here, but then I haven't got a lot of choice.

The only other guy in here, a muppet in his early thirties with fashionable glasses and a stupid triangular fuzzy patch of hair on his chin grins at me as I walk up to the bar.

"G'day mate, how's it going?"

Fucking Australian. Quelle surprise. I slap my best, warmest smile on my face.

"Hi. I was wondering if you're looking for any bar staff?"

The grin never leaves his face. "You're in luck, mate. Sam handed in her notice only last night. She's off round Europe. So I'm looking for someone to take her place. You've got experience?"

"Yeah," I lie. Jesus. It's bar work, not rocket science. How hard can it be?

"Great. I'll start you off with a trial shift tomorrow night. That okay?"

I grin back at him. "Fine. I'm Charlie," I tell him, offering my hand.

"Greg," he says, shaking it. "Good on you, Charlie. I'll see you tomorrow. Six thirty."

I walk out. That was easy. As I'm at the corner of Churchill Road I realise that I didn't even ask what they pay, but it doesn't really matter. It's never going to make me a fortune, and so long as it gets me out of the house and earning a bit of pocket money then that's fine with me.

But the sooner I sell the fucking flat, the better.

I have a cheeky little one-skin spliff the next evening before heading out to the bar, just to take the edge off the prospect of doing some hard physical labour.

Friday night, and it's still quiet at twenty past six. Greg is behind the bar and grins as I enter. "Charlie. How are ya? Come behind." He opens the hatch at the back, and I follow him in, and he begins showing me round the bar. The till takes me a couple of goes to get my head round, and he hands me a little swipe-card on a chain so I can use it properly. Even though I've been an enthusiastic drinker my whole life, I'm still none the wiser about what half the drinks behind here are – but then I'm guessing I'm not the only one. If this is an Aussie crowd, they'll all only be drinking fucking lager anyway.

"Here's the draft," says Greg, pointing out the taps behind the bar. "The barrels are in the basement. Don't worry about changing them, I'll do that if it needs it."

Good job, as I wouldn't have a clue how to do it anyway. "Prices are all here. Have a look and see if you can remember a few. It'll help when we get busy later."

"What time it that?" I ask him.

"Depends. We've got a DJ tonight 'coz it's Friday. He starts at half nine, and it doesn't usually get busy 'til gone ten. It really picks up after the pubs shut, and then it's hectic until close."

"What time's closing?" I thought it would be normal bar hours, and now I'm feeling like even more of a dick for not asking before.

"One. Don't worry mate, you'll have fun. Honest."

I grin, but inside my stomach is churning. I sincerely fucking doubt this will be fun. I already need a drink.

Greg looks like he's reading my mind. "Oh, and sorry mate, but there's no drinking while you're working. We like you to keep a clear head."

"No problem," I say, still trying to keep the grin on my face, but it's getting harder by the second.

"Cheer up, mate. You might even enjoy it. I'll buy you a drink at the end of the night. How's that?"

"Great," I say. "Don't worry. I always look like this."

A couple of after work punters come in and order two pints, so Greg stands back to watch me as I pour them out. Neither of them seems to recognise me, and I do alright pouring out the beers, and by seven I'm beginning to think that this might not be so bad after all.

And then Danny comes in. I clock him as he saunters in, and before he's even come up to the bar I've marked him out as a media wannabe dick of some description. He's in his mid-twenties and looks like he's got far too much energy. Floppy blond hair and expensive jeans. I'm praying that the black shirt he's wearing doesn't mean that he's working behind the bar, and therefore I'm going to have to talk to him all night, but my heart sinks when he walks up behind Greg and slaps him on the back.

"How you doing Greg?" he says.

"Alright Danny. This is Charlie."

He looks behind the bar and clocks me, and I see the recognition in his eyes as he says hello. He comes behind the bar and shakes my hand.

"Hello mate," he says. "Danny."

"Charlie," I say, thinking, but you already know that, don't you?

A couple more punters come in, and I serve them, and then Danny serves a couple, so what with all the activity it must be at least five minutes before Danny gives in playing it cool and turns to me.

"You're Charlie Reed, aren't you?"

I'm sorely tempted to try and bluff it. To tell him that this happens all the time; that I'm always being mistaken for the guy. That having the same name doesn't help. So much that I'm thinking of changing it. But I don't.

"Yeah," I say.

"Shit!" he says. "What are you doing here?"

This guy's a genius. What the fuck does he think I'm doing?

"Sorry, stupid question," he says. It must have showed in my face. "I'm just surprised to see you working here, that's all."

"Can you keep a secret?" I say quietly.

Immediately he leans forward. "Of course." His brow is all furrowed as I talk to him, like suddenly we're the best of friends.

"It's not like I don't have a problem with bar work. I don't." He's nodding now, listening as I'm talking. "But I probably wouldn't be here unless it was for a very, very important reason."

"Yeah?"

"Look, I can't really talk about it," I continue. "But all I'm going to say is that I thought it would be a good idea to work a couple of bar shifts as research for something I've got coming up."

He nods like I've just imparted some great wisdom.

"Right, of course. Because I was wondering what you'd be doing working here. You know, I've got to tell you, that performance in 'The Twelfth of Never' was one of the best things I've ever seen."

"Thanks," I say.

"What was it like working with Laurenson? He's got to be absolutely the best director working in film today. No question."

Great. Suddenly the evening stretches out in front of me like a marathon that I'm going to have to run in barbed wire slippers. It gets worse as Danny proceeds to tell me about the couple of shorts that he's made, as well as the music promo that he's shot for a friend's band; and it dawns on me that I could quite possibly be stuck in my own personal hell. I'm working a bar shift in Willesden Green with a director ten years my junior who's convinced he's the heir to Orson fucking Welles.

In between serving, Danny continues to prod me as to what the experience of working with Laurenson was like, and I tell him that I can barely remember as it was so long ago. He bangs on at me about his favourite moments from all the Laurenson movies he's seen, and I try to look like this isn't the worst evening of my life. I check my watch, and it's only eight. I'm now hoping it's going to get busier simply so that the DJ's music might drown out Danny's cineaste wittering and that he gets too busy to talk.

"So, you going to Cannes?" Danny asks. "You know Laurenson's got his new one in competition this year?"

That doesn't surprise me. The cunt will probably win the Palme D'Or.

"No, not this year," I say. "You?"

He nods. "Yeah. First time. Going out there to pitch a couple of projects."

I swear I have to grip the bar taps to prevent me from punching him in the face.

"I've been meaning to ask you Charlie," he says. My heart sinks. With the witless and seemingly unmonitored jabbering that I've been subjected to so far, the way that he approaches this means that he's going to want something.

"What's that?" I ask.

"Do you remember the script I sent you? I'm sure you get a lot, but I sent it through to your agent in February."

Oh Jesus, I think. Kill me now.

"I get a lot of scripts," I say. "Sorry, Danny. Which one was yours?"

At least he has the decency to look embarrassed.

"It was the one with the Fireman and his son. They go on a road trip?"

I remember. It wasn't as shockingly awful as some of the stuff that I've read, but it wasn't great. The main problem being that he has these two people in a car for most of the film, stopping off and staying at a host of different places. As a debut director he has fuck all hope of raising the financing for this, as I'm sure he'll find out on the Croisette of Broken Dreams.

"I'm sorry," I lie. "I never got it. Things have been a bit rough recently. My agent just died."

Danny looks shocked. "Oh God, I'm sorry." He pauses for all of about ten seconds before continuing, "So, could I get you a copy of the script? It's just that if you were interested it could be good for both of us."

He turns to serve someone who's just been waiting at the bar, which is fortunate, as it gives me the chance to turn away and open my mouth in a silent scream. I don't go as far as hitting myself in the face, despite being sorely tempted. He finishes serving and turns back to me, looking expectantly for an answer.

"Sure," I say. "I'd love to read it. Get me a copy for when I'm next back in here."

"Thanks, Charlie. Wow. That would be awesome."

"No problem."

Two women approach the bar and go over to speak to Greg who grins at them. He points out the two tables along the far wall which have had 'Reserved' signs on them all night. I can't help but double take as they go over and take their seats. One of them looks very familiar, but I just can't place her. She comes up to the bar, and I dodge serving her to take a sudden interest in the fridges, and so Danny serves her drinks. She takes a round back to the table which is already beginning to fill up with a group of friends. A guy joins them who also looks familiar, but I can't place him either.

Just as this is starting to bug me, the answer walks through the door. Callie. My ex, the one who got away, is looking more perfect than ever. The table all greet her like the unbridled goddess she clearly is, and she must sense that I'm staring at her from the bar, as she turns to look at me.

There's a flicker of confusion as she recognises me; clearly wondering what the hell I'm doing here. She turns to the table to see if anyone wants a drink, and then comes to the bar. My heart leaps a little higher in my chest as she approaches.

"Hi Charlie."

She looks as good as she ever did, and still smells amazing; a mix of summer and a future I'll never see.

"Hey Callie. How are you?"

"I'm good. Here for Angie's birthday. You remember Angie?"

She turns to point her out. I don't, but Angie is looking over here, so I give a little wave, and she waves back; then turns back to the group, probably to continue telling them what an enormous shit-bag I was to Callie while we were going out together.

"What are you up to? You got married, right? And babies?"

She grins, and nods. "Twins. You want to see a picture?"

"Of course."

She gets her phone out and shows me two gorgeous toddlers as they're standing up next to a couch. The smile on my face is genuine, as they're beautiful kids, and she's obviously an amazing mum; but a little piece of my heart is breaking as I think what could have been.

"They're beautiful," I say. She takes one look at my face and must be able to read me like a book, as she smiles and quietly puts the phone away.

"How's things, Charlie? What you up to? Still in the Grove?"

I could try and lie, but Callie's one of the few people who could sniff me out without even trying. I shrug and look around.

"This is my first night," I lean forward to whisper to her. "I'm pretending it's for research."

"And really?"

"I've had a bad run, Callie. Lost some work, got in some debt. My agent just died, and I'm back living with my mother. And now you catch me on my first night working behind the bar. Just when I thought things couldn't get any worse."

She smiles at me, eyebrows arched in sympathy. Not from her, I think. I don't think I can take pity. Not from her.

"You'll bounce back," she says.

I'm suddenly all too aware that Greg is checking me out, as I've been leaning over the bar in conversation while Danny is serving all the drinks beside me. Not that I really give much of a shit, but there's no way I'm going to get paid if I carry on like this.

I lean back, away from her.

"So, what can I get you to drink?"

"Right," she says, and I think she's a little shocked that I'm suddenly all business. "You know me, Charlie. A vodka tonic."

"No problem."

I fix her drink, and she offers me a tenner. I can feel Greg's eyes on me, so I take it.

"Sorry, Cal. I'd do you a free one, but it's my first night."

"Don't worry, Charlie. All fine."

I run it through the till, only when I turn to give her her change, I see that she's walked back to the table and is already trying to play down the encounter with a very curious Angie. I look at the three pound coins in my hand.

A tip. Charity from my ex-girlfriend.

The rest of the evening drags out slowly with Danny and I serving out drinks for the largely (as to be expected) Australian, and drunk clientele that fills up the bar. The one positive side to this is that as the floor gets busier Callie's table gets obscured from view so I don't have to see her as I work. The DJ sets up in a booth by the opposite corner, which does us a favour as it means that the drunks have got another focus besides the bar. He plays a lot of shit, but the crowd seem to like it. I get one or two looks from some of the people as I serve them and become aware of a few nudges and whispers as the evening wears on, but I grin and bear it. I've not got a choice.

Callie drops by the bar to say goodbye around half 11, but it's packed, and I barely get a chance to speak to her. The last I see of her is the back of her exquisite head as it disappears onto Willesden High Street and out of my life for good.

It all starts to go horribly wrong after midnight. The place fills up as the more sensible establishments turf everyone out and they all seem to decide to come here for one last, drunken drink. Try as fast as we can, Danny and I can't keep up with the tsunami of people at the bar all clamouring for drinks, and it's two deep at every point. At this point, if I was pissed and on the other end of the bar, I'd be getting wound up – especially if one of the bar staff clearly didn't have a fucking clue what he was doing.

Which is very much the case with me. The busier we get, the harder it gets to keep up, and I'm getting increasingly flustered the more and more people come to the bar. I'm forgetting what people have asked for, I've no idea what the prices are, and now it's packed the place is fucking roasting.

I'm drowning. There's no sign of Greg, and if there was, I'm sure that he'd step in and end this madness.

The natives are getting restless. I've just served one girl a couple of Gin and Tonics, and I hand her back her change of a pound.

"Oi," she says. "I gave you a twenty."

I don't know for sure what she gave me, but I'm certain it was a tenner.

"It was a tenner," I say, deciding to try and front it out.

"It was fucking twenty quid," says her mate, slurring slightly.

Danny's clocked what's going on and comes over to my side of the bar.

"Everything okay?" he asks me.

"I gave him twenty quid and he's only given me change for a tenner." The girl is pissed, and she's talking to Danny like he's in fucking charge, even though the little twat is at least ten years my junior.

"She gave me a tenner," I tell him.

"Okay. Charlie, can you use my till for a moment? Thanks."

He goes to where the phone on the bar is, and quickly punches in some numbers. I'm half-way through serving someone else when Greg appears from the office in the basement.

"What's going on?" he asks me.

I nod to the two girls who are now watching me like store detectives and seeing which one of them can bad mouth me better to the other one.

"The girl over there says she gave me a twenty quid note. I'm sure it was a tenner."

Greg looks a little fucked off but tries to hide it. He must really be short for staff, as he kind of fake grins at me.

"Don't worry, mate. It happens all the time."

He goes over to speak to the two girls. Everyone at the bar is now watching the sideshow develop with increasing interest as Greg goes over to speak to them. I haven't got a choice but hear what they have to say as I serve the guy next to them who looks at me with a degree of sympathy I could honestly do without.

"He's trying to fucking rob us," says the first girl.

"I'm going to give you the benefit of the doubt," says Greg to the drunker of the two. He goes to the till and fishes out a tenner and hands it over to them under my nose.

"You shouldn't employ fucking thieves," says the girl.

My jaw tightens.

"You'd think he earned enough money doing those fucking commercials," chips in her friend.

Something snaps. I'm about to hand over a glass of tap water to the guy I'm serving when I hear this, and so I throw it in the girl's face.

"Fuck off!" I scream.

Everyone at the bar turns and stares at me, like they can't quite believe what's just happened. The drunk girl then throws her glass at me, and I duck. It goes crashing into the row of bottles behind me, and several smash to the floor of the bar. The big fucker who's been working security on the door quite happily for the past three hours is jolted into action as he hears breaking glass over the sound of Blondie and elbows his way through the crowd to the bar.

"These two," says Greg, pointing out the two girls, and the guy marches them away to the front door, kicking and screaming as they go.

Danny, and the rest of the punters all lining up to buy drinks all look at me open-mouthed.

Greg turns to me. "Charlie, why don't you take five minutes? I'll take over for you."

I slink away, my cheeks burning, and go and sit on the stairs. I can hear glass being swept up and dumped in a cardboard box and kicked to the side.

Two minutes later, and the rush at the bar is over, having been dealt with quickly by someone who knows what they're doing, and Greg pokes his head round the top of the stairs. I've seen this look before as he fixes his gaze on me, and it's largely from tired directors who are coming to the end of a long day that's not gone their way at all.

"Charlie, thanks for coming, but I don't think it's going to work out. You can leave now."

The look on his face tells me that's not a request so much as an order. I don't bother asking him about the money.

I grab the jumper I came with, and leave without another word, making my way to the door with as much pride as I can muster. I'm not sure, but I think I can feel Angie's gaze follow me out of the door as I leave, so no doubt Callie will get to hear all about my sacking in the morning.

I feel sick. I'm half-way down the road back to Pat's when I realise that at least this means that I'm not going to have to see

Danny again and refuse his attempts to get me into his shitty film.

Although I'm down over the evening, I've still got to look at that as a tiny bonus.

MAY

This is the key scene, Charlie. What we've been building to.

So no fear. Don't hold back.

I want you to let loose.

Surprise me, Charlie.

Surprise me.

It's been over a week since I left the bar, and I've given up. Fuck trying to find a shitty job. I don't care if I can't get any cash. I'm quite prepared to hole up in the room upstairs at Churchill Road, smoking puff and indulging myself in contract killings and an orgy of violence on the bloody streets of prohibition era Manhattan. Normally I wouldn't smoke in the house, but I don't fucking care what she thinks anymore. We don't even see each other. I don't come downstairs if she's around, and she doesn't bother trying to speak to me. It seems to suit us both fine. I wait until she goes out and then bolt downstairs to sort stuff out, and I've been making sandwiches late at night to smuggle back to the room. She's got wise to that however and has now stopped buying bread. Either that, or she's hiding it. It doesn't make much difference to me. I've taken the tin opener and have taken a load of tins of beans up there, so I'll be just tickety-fucking-boo.

I don't want to go out unless she's out too just in case she changes the locks. Then I'll be really fucked. So, it's safer to stay indoors, even if we never speak.

James the Estate Agent rang last week. I'm not sure what day it was, but he's finally had an offer for the flat. It's considerably less than I'd hoped for, but he seems to think it's worth taking. I don't have the energy to fight anymore. After all my debts have been paid, I'm going to end up with about eight grand, which isn't a lot. I might be able to find somewhere to live that isn't fucking Churchill Road, but beyond that it's not giving me many options. I should really start trying to find another agent or trying to find some more work. But I just don't care anymore. All I want to do is sit in front of the screen in my room, killing and smoking, and killing and smoking.

I've no idea how long I've been holed up, and I'm not sure what day it is when I walk into the empty kitchen; until the open newspaper on the table tells me it's Wednesday. I doubt it's accidental that Pat's left it open on the double page spread, but I sit down and look at it anyway.

It's yet another profile of James Laurenson. The Guardian's G2 section is just as full of hysterical crap as any other article I've ever read about him, but this time the focus is much more on his new film, and how honoured he is to be entering it into competition at Cannes.

His fat, grinning face leers out from some poolside chair in the Hollywood Hills. There's an inset photograph of Lucy Fontaine in a killer dress looking over her shoulder at some premiere or other, with a caption underneath saying 'Romance?'

I don't know how long I'm staring at the article for, but I suddenly snap out of it as a sudden realisation hits me like a train; one that I thought I'd lost while deep in the K-hole with Bob.

I know exactly what I have to do.

I laugh out loud. I feel like a lead weight has just been lifted from my shoulders, and I'm almost light-headed. Giddy.

I listen to the kettle boil, and a plan starts to form in my head. The paper says that the Festival starts next Monday. Laurenson's film plays on the Friday.

By the time I've made coffee and two slices of toast, I've got the beginnings of a solid plan.

I bound back upstairs two at a time.

A shower and a shave later, and I'm looking almost human again. The first person I call is Bob. For the first time in a long time, I'm not thinking about dope, so much as a safe floor to kip on if everything goes tits up at Churchill Road and Pat does change the locks.

I'm on the bus when I call Elijah. I get his voicemail and ask him to give me a call. The other key part of the plan involves Jimmy D, and so I'm just hoping he's going to be in his office so I can try and see if I can charm him in the way I'm hoping.

It's a beautiful day as I get off the bus and make my way to the Kensal Rise offices.

The building is nice and cool inside, and there's the usual crowd of media nobs and beautiful women swanning around without any obvious purpose. I follow a guy wearing shorts and sandals who looks like he's heading back to an office through the doors, and my luck's in. He holds open the door for me and I walk through.

He's going for the lift, and I'd rather not get stuck in any kind of small talk and so turn left and take the stairs up to the second floor where Jimmy's office is. I knock, and someone tells me to come in.

A sharp looking guy is yapping away on the phone as I come in, and he cups his hand over the phone and raises his eyebrows at me.

"Is Jimmy around?" I ask.

He raises his finger for me to wait for a second, and then spends another minute rapping up his call.

"Sorry mate," he says, putting the phone down. "You're after Jimmy?"

"Yeah. I need to speak to him."

"He's probably at the lock up checking on the equipment for next week. Are you after blagging one of the Cannes parties?"

"You got me," I say, grinning. "You going?"

"I wish," he says, shaking his head. "Got far too much on here. You got his mobile, right?"

I nod. "I'll call him on that. Thanks."

His phone rings again. "Sorry," he says, and answers.

I mouth 'see you later' and leave the office. Excellent. Jimmy, as I suspected, is going to be doing a couple of parties at Cannes, and that's my ticket down there. I fish out my phone and call him as I'm on the way back down the stairs.

"Jimmy D. Charlie Reed. I need to ask you a favour, and it's probably not what you think. Can you give me a call? Cheers pal."

I hang up. I've never been to Jimmy's lock up, but it's where he keeps all his mobile bar equipment; whenever he caters a party he brings an entire set-up with him, from the actual front down to the booze and cocktail shakers. The whole thing goes up in around a couple of hours, and it looks pretty slick.

It's around two, and my stomach's grumbling as I leave the studios. In my excitement to get things rolling I forgot that I'd be needing some food later, and I haven't brought a sandwich with me, so I'll just have to wait until I hear from either Elijah or Bob before I get anything to eat. I've got fuck all money on me, but now I have a purpose it doesn't seem so bad.

In a fortnight everything will be different.

I'm in the library, beginning to get quite hungry when the phone rings. It's Elijah. I pick up, already walking outside into the sunshine.

"Elijah. How's it going?"

"Alright, Hollywood. Everything nang, blad."

"You done the filming?"

"Yeah. It was heavy."

"I'd like to hear about it. You at home?"

There's a split second of hesitation, then: "In five, yeah."

Ten minutes later and I'm sat in Elijah's spotless front room with a cup of tea in my hands, halfway through a jam sandwich that I cadged off him the moment I walked in. He's telling me about the shoot for St Anthony's, and how everyone seemed really pleased with what he'd done as Felix.

"Serious, Hollywood. It was amazing, man. The director, Johnny, the man says he's going to fix me up with an agent next week. He says big things. Big things."

"That's great, Elijah. Well done."

And it's weird, because I don't even feel jealous. Normally I might feel a touch of the green-eyed monster on hearing about how well someone else is doing, but not this time. I just feel removed from the whole thing, and despite the madness of the course I'm about to embark on, strangely calm if quietly excited. "Did your Mum find out? Or school?"

He shakes his head. "Nah, blad. Everyting cool. I just get my head down, get my exams done, innit."

"Yeah. You'll be fine. Just try and cut back on the skunk while you're doing them. That stuff will give you brain damage."

"Cha. You're a pussy, blad."

You think so? I think. We'll see.

And then I ask him what I need to.

He laughs, at first.

I don't.

And he stops. His face drops.

"No way, Hollywood. No way, man."

"You owe me, Elijah. You owe me. And this is what I want."

He's shaking his head. "No way."

"Find a way," I tell him quietly. "I'm serious. Find a way. I don't want to be a cunt, but I can make your life very fucking difficult if I have to. Find a way, and we're square. OK?"

He's looking at me now, and he's shitting himself. I can almost smell the fear on him. He's not quite the big man he thinks he is.

I stand up. "Call me tomorrow. Yeah?"

He looks up at me, nods. I put my tea down on the kitchen surface as I leave.

Bob's is just round the corner, and so I drop round to see if he's in, but no joy. I'm just thinking that I really need to speak to Jimmy D when the phone rings and his name comes up on the caller display. I grin to myself. It's a sign.

"Jimmy D. How's tricks?"

"Not bad, Charlie. Not bad. How's things with you? Not seen you around for a while."

"I've been keeping my head down," I say. There's no need to go into the specifics with Jimmy. He doesn't need to know what a fucking car crash my life has been over the past three months, and if anything, it's better that he doesn't. "You know, just bumbling along. You still seeing that girl?"

"Poppy? Nope. Sweet girl and everything, but she's not in the running to be Mrs. D. You seeing anyone?"

I bet he heard about the night that never was with Chloe, but I'm not going to go there.

"Not right now. Always looking though."

"Tell me about it. You said there was a favour you were going to ask me?"

"You're doing a couple of parties in Cannes next week, right?"

"Yeah. A party for Fox, and then one on Friday."

My spine tingles. This could be too good to be true.

"Is that the new Laurenson movie?"

"Could be," he says. "You know me, Charlie. I don't know what these things are half the time. So, you after a ticket?"

"Not quite," I tell him. "Can we meet?"

Mercifully he says he's going to be at the lock-up for the next hour, so I head over there. This at least saves me the embarrassment of failing to buy him a drink through poverty.

The lock-up turns out to be a largish room at, of all places, the Big Yellow on Scrubs Lane. I call him when I'm outside and five minutes later he's come down and we're shaking hands.

"Charlie. You alright?"

I give him my best grin. "All good, Jimmy."

"Come up."

I follow him in. He leads me up to the room, which we both just about manage to squeeze into along with all his stuff. I watch him as he sorts out boxes of booze. There's an open flight case that the bar unpacks from; crates of glasses and bar equipment stacked against the walls.

Jimmy is looking at me. "You okay?"

I must be giving something away, as he's got a look on his face like there's something wrong with mine.

I nod. "Yeah, fine. This is just a weird one, Jimmy. We've known each other for a while. I really need a job."

He looks surprised. "Yeah?"

"Yeah. My agent died a couple of weeks ago, and I need to try and nab another one. The best place to do that is at the Festival, but I'm brassic. Totally skint. Which is why I thought of you. I guessed you might be doing a couple of the parties. If there's anything I can do there then at least I'd get the passage paid for, right? And you'll have somewhere to stay for a couple of nights."

Jimmy grins. "Shit, Charlie. I could lend you the money if it's that bad. You don't have to work for me."

I shake my head. "No. I'd rather pay my way. I'm not that up on the cocktails, but perhaps there's something I could do in the background. You know, ice, cut limes or something?"

"Sure. Of course. It's not great pay. You know that, right?"

I nod. "Right now, anything's a bonus. Seriously."

"Okay, Charlie. No worries. I'll find something for you to do. You want to come in the van with me? We leave on Sunday."

"Thanks Jimmy. That's great. I'll see you then."

I leave with a spring in my step and decide to check on my stuff before I leave. I open up the cupboard and begin to rifle through the boxes until I find the one I'm looking for: one that contains various things that I've had in my bedroom for a while. I grab a bin bag full of clothes and tip them out and put in what I've found. A digital camera, a video camera, a chunky silver bracelet I'd forgotten I even had and a couple of other expensive nick-nacks that I'll never miss all go in the bag, and then I shut the door on the life I used to have in St. Quintin's, confident that there's nothing in there I'll need to see again.

It's gone nine by the time I get back, and I can't help but feel a tiny flicker of relief to find that my key still lets me into the house.

The kitchen door is open, and Pat is sat in her usual spot in front of the laptop. She doesn't look over as I let the front door close and walk into the kitchen.

"You're up I see." Her attention never wavers from the screen.

"It looks like it." I cross to the fridge and open it. There's a small piece of cheese and a couple of tired looking tomatoes.

"You shouldn't be surprised that there isn't any food if you never buy any," she says.

I'm going to take the lead on this little contretemps, and not let her inject her usual poison too early.

"Good news about the flat," I say. "I've accepted an offer, so it shouldn't be too long before I get some money and I'm out of here."

She nods, silent. Pat doesn't really do good news. Much better thriving on pain, misery and silent resentment.

"And I know how troubling it is for you to see me hanging around here without working, so I'm off to Cannes. I've managed to get some work out there with a friend, so it's not going to cost me anything. But at least it means I should be able to try and get another agent."

She nods. "It's about time."

Jesus, she can't even concede to say that that sounds like a good idea.

"I'll be off on Sunday. With any luck that should be it, and you won't see me here again."

She nods again. "Fine."

I feel like telling her, screaming in her face, everything that I've got planned. I wonder if it would make the slightest bit of difference, whether anything I do could cause any kind of reaction at all. Somehow, I fucking doubt it. She just sits there, staring at her screen so she doesn't have to acknowledge me. Maybe that will be different in a week's time. Maybe she'll realise that perhaps she has a morsel of responsibility for what's about to happen. Fuck her, I think. Every second longer I spend in this kitchen is another moment that robs me of the last salvages of my dignity.

I don't really care anymore, and with the venture I'm embarking on it doesn't really seem to make a difference, so I ask her.

"Is there a chance of borrowing a bit more money until the sale goes through?"

She sighs. "I thought you were working out there. I thought that would mean that you wouldn't need any more money."

"Kind of," I say. "But I still need to survive here until Sunday. And I thought I could pick up some shopping for here", I lie. Whatever she gives me, there's no way it's going to end up behind the till of a supermarket. I've got far bigger plans for that money.

She turns to look at me for the first time. "I will get some out for you tomorrow. On the condition you pick up some food. But I want you to know, Charlie. That this is absolutely, positively, the last time."

I look at the floor, nodding. I try and disguise a smile. You have no idea, I think.

You have no fucking idea.

I wait until I hear the door slam the next morning before springing into action. I've been packing all my stuff in a suitcase, carefully, with newspaper to make sure it doesn't get damaged, and I take it gently down the stairs and over to the bus stop that will take me to Kilburn. Even with the hundred quid or thereabouts that I'm going to get from Pat, that's still not going to be enough.

The bus takes no time at all, and it's a short walk along the High Road, dodging the tramps who have started early before I end up walking through the doors of Cash Converters.

The guy doesn't bat an eyelid as I open the case to reveal a stack of electrical pieces. He's probably seen it all before. The whole process takes far longer than I thought it would, as they go through everything meticulously, testing to make sure that it all works. I know I'm on the right course, as I feel no wrench at all as I hand over my all my electricals. The games don't get as much as I'd hoped, but his eyes light up at the bracelet - and all together the bits that I've got at Churchill Road, combined with everything I got from Big Yellow adds up to deliver me a small windfall; one that I'm certain should get me what I'm after.

I'm about to hand over the video camera as part of the haul when I have a last-minute change of heart and decide to hang onto it. The guy behind the counter was only going to give me forty quid for it, and I think that I might be able to put it to some very good use.

A while later, and we're done. They've got a copy of my passport along with ID saying that I still live at St Quintin's, but no matter. I walk out with six hundred quid more than I woke up with this morning, and I know exactly where it's going.

I know that Elijah is going to be at school until at least half three, so there's no way I can get hold of him until then. So I get the bus back to Churchill Road.

Pat is still out, which is perfect, so I pack a small bag to take to Cannes with me, even though we're not going anywhere for a couple of days. But I'm getting excited now, and I can't help myself. I go through the mental checklist of who I need to see, what I need to get, and what I'm going to do; and I think I'm set. The key thing now is to keep a clear head and pray that Elijah delivers the goods.

I've only got a tiny bit of puff left, and so I go outside to the garden and polish it off. I'm sorely tempted to try and get some more off Bob, but I know it's a bad idea. I need to keep a clear head for what I've got planned.

I prepare a sandwich with the loaf of bread that I picked up on the way back, and the time on the radio tells me that it's lunchtime, and I've got at least a couple of hours to kill before I hear back from Elijah. I go back up to the bedroom and lie back on the bed. The room looks slightly larger without the TV and X-box at the end of the bed, but I've now got nothing to do. I could read something but I'm not in the mood. So I lie back with my head on the pillow and stare at the ceiling, and allow myself a wry smile as I think that this could well be a view I might have to get used to.

My phone snaps me awake, and I sit up quickly. It's Elijah, and I answer.
"Elijah."
"Hollywood." There's a pause as both of us are silent on the line.
"And?" I ask him.
"Tomorrow." There's another pause. "But I'm going to need the money tonight."
I knew that he'd want this. "No. I'll bring the money tomorrow."
"He won't deal with you, Hollywood. It was hard enough trying to get him to deal with me. Dem heavy, heavy bad men, blad."

Elijah sounds scared. He's trying to front it out as much as he can, but there's a tremor in his voice. He's a good actor, but he can't front that he's not shitting himself. So much of his day-to-day existence is playing the hard man that these must be some serious fucking dudes he's dealing with. But then, given what I'm asking him to do, that's hardly a surprise.

"Okay, you make the meet. But I can't get the money to you until tomorrow. So, I'll see you at four. Okay?"
"You sure you want to do this Hollywood? Serious, blad. This ain't a good idea."
"I don't want your advice, Elijah. I just need your help. Okay? Like I said before. Do this one thing for me, and we're square. Alright?"
There's another pause on the other end of the line.
"Okay."
"I'll see you at your place. Four o'clock."

He hangs up. And I lie back on the bed.
It's all starting to come together.

It's ten to four, and I'm sitting in Horniman's Pleasance waiting for Elijah to get out of school. Pat came back last night with a hundred quid in cash, so altogether I've got just about enough. I'm not quite sure how I'm going to pick up any food from the supermarket like I promised, but then I'm thinking it might be a good idea to move out of Churchill Road a couple of days early. The only other place I can think of staying is on Bob's couch, and although it's not exactly going to be good for my head, at least it means that I'll no longer have to live with Pat.

The money sits heavy in my pocket, and the last thing I'd need now is for someone to come along and try and tax me. But the way I'm feeling right now I'd be amazed if anyone would even try. I can feel it; this aura of invincibility draped around my shoulders like Superman's cape. No-one would even try and cross me. They wouldn't fucking dare.

I check the time on my phone, and it's getting close to four. Elijah will be going back to change first, so I get up off the bench I'm sitting on and make my way out to the front of his block. I can see him coming down the road from a way off, and he's scuttling towards the building at some pace, only to slow down a little when he clocks me standing there.

I nod to him as he approaches. He looks sick.

"You sure you wanna do this, Hollywood?" he asks.

I nod. "Totally."

He swallows, and nods again. "Let me get changed blad. Stay here. I need to be quick before my sister gets back and starts asking questions."

"Hurry up," I tell him.

He nods and vanishes upstairs. I stifle a small smile as I remember back to how we met about three months ago, and how the tables have turned since. I never thought I'd be here then, but then I'm guessing neither did he.

I pull my phone out and have a pretend conversation with no-one while pacing up and down a distance of about ten yards, trying to look less like a man who's waiting to organise a distinctly illegal activity. I'm not even sure why I'm doing it, beyond an awareness that for anyone watching, any kind of exchange between a white guy in his late thirties and a black teenager is probably not going to be exactly kosher.

This sticks in my mind when Elijah emerges a few minutes later and asks, "Have you got the money?"

"I'll come with you," I tell him.

He shakes his head. "Hollywood, I told you man. You don't know these people. They don't fuck about. Serious men."

"I'm not going to give you the money here Elijah. Walk round the corner with me, and I'll give it you then. How long you going to be?"

"I don't know, blad. Five minutes? Half an hour? I'm done when I'm done."

I nod. As we turn the corner I check back discreetly and the coast is clear, and then pass Elijah the envelope that's been burning a hole in my pocket all day.

"Six fifty. Right?"

He nods. "Safe. Where you gonna be?"

"I'll be around. Just call me when you're done."

He nods and disappears in the direction of Golborne Road. I walk up to Kensal Road and into Canalot Studios and order a coffee at the bar. I take it to a table where there's a copy of today's paper, and I flick through, not taking in a single word as I do so. I keep reminding myself that I've got nothing to worry about, that I just need to relax, but then I'm aware that my right foot is auditioning for Riverdance of its own accord, and I grab it to stop it jiggling.

I check the time on my phone. Ten minutes. Elijah said five. Maybe something's gone wrong. Maybe he's been pinched. Maybe he's given them my name, and they're trying to find me right now, as I sit here drinking coffee and failing to read the paper.

I need to relax. I take another sip and reflect momentarily that perhaps coffee wasn't the best choice of drink. I look back at the paper, but try as I might, I can't seem to process a single word that's in front of me.

My phone rings. It's Elijah. I wait for it to ring twice, and answer.

"Are we good?"

He pauses a second, then says, "Yeah. We're good."

"OK. I'll pick up from yours. See you there in five."

I hang up. I walk out of the bar across Kensal Road and down towards his block. He's walking towards me carrying an Adidas boot bag, looking shifty.

"That it?" I ask.

He nods and passes it over to me. I take it quickly, praying that no-one is watching. I turn and walk away. I hear footsteps following me, but don't turn as Elijah catches up to my side.

"You know what you're doing?" he asks.

"How hard can it be?"

"Not that," he says. "It's just... This ain't you, Hollywood. You only play bad men. This is different."

The bag feels light in my hands. "I know. I know it's different. Don't worry about me, Elijah. I'll be fine."

"We're good though, right?"

I turn to him and smile. "We're fine. Now do me a favour and fuck off. Let me know when your St Anthony's is on."

I walk on along Southern Row towards the Grove, swinging the boot bag as I go.

I wait until I'm back in the room at Churchill Road before I open the bag, and gently pull out what's inside and lay it on the bed. It's a lot smaller than I expected, but I sit there for a while just staring at it. I keep getting this weird adrenalin rush that I last had when I was at school, and had smuggled home some porn, or when I first started smoking weed and was walking around with that in my pockets. I look at it, and I know. I know I've crossed a fucking great big line today, and things are never going to be the same again.

I'm staring at my purchase when my phone rings and I nearly shit myself. I check the screen and see that it's Bob, calling me back after I left a message earlier for him on the bus.

"Bob. How's it going?"

"Alright, Charlie. Not bad. How are you?" He sounds ripped to the tits already, but then it is approaching six o'clock.

"Good. Listen, I need to ask you a favour. You know that I've been staying at my Mum's house?"

"Yeah. Bummer."

You have no idea. "Thing is, I'm off to Cannes on Sunday. Going to try to get another agent. I was wondering if I could come and crash at yours for a couple of nights?"

"Um…" This sounds like it might be a bit much, even for Bob. And he's seriously easy going.

"I could crash on the couch. You'll never know I'm there."

A pause. "Okay, Charlie. Sure."

"Bob, you're a fucking star. You in tonight? I'll see you later."

I hang up and start packing my small bag full of clothes. The boot bag goes firmly at the bottom, and the little stuff that I'm going to need for the week ahead goes lightly on the top. I chuck my toothbrush in and take another look around the room to make sure that I'm not going to need anything else, as this is the last fucking time I intend ever setting foot in this room.

The house is still empty when I leave, and that's fine with me. It doesn't feel any livelier when Pat is in her lair downstairs, and at least I don't have to say goodbye.

I get myself into the role of being just a normal fucking guy as I get off the bus and make my way towards Bob's flat; but not so much that I look like I'm trying to look normal. I'm not going to start fucking whistling or anything. But I can't help the buzz of adrenalin that sits in the pit of my stomach.

I hit the buzzer, and as usual it's a good thirty seconds before Bob wrestles himself free from the couch and bumbles down the hall to answer the door.

"Hello?"

"It's Charlie."

I push the door and come up in the piss stinking lift to come out and walk down the few doors to Bob's. I walk in and he's collapsed back on the couch and is already skinning up. My mouth starts watering at the prospect of a spliff, and by the time I've sat down next to him my previous resolution to keep off it for a couple of days has flown out of the window. He fires it up, drags deeply and passes it to me, and I lean back into the couch and inhale.

Bob always does get quality gear.

"Thanks for this mate," I say. "I really needed to get out of the house. She was doing my head in."

Bob coughs slightly, his attention not wavering from the fine array of bikini clad black women all jiggling their arses at the camera in the hip hop promo that's playing on MTV.

"No problem, Charlie."

He sounds a lot more relaxed about it than he did on the phone. I guess it might be a source of concern having somebody crashing on your couch if your primary source of income is selling narcotics. But then we have known each other for some time, and I get the feeling that Bob trusts me, the poor misguided lump. Obviously, he doesn't know about the contents of the boot bag, and nor am I going to tell him; but obviously in the event that the flat gets raided before I leave for France, I've got a crucial element of deniability about the whole thing. Who are they going to believe? The unemployed actor on the couch, or the drug dealer with a shit load of cannabis?

Plus of course, I get to smoke puff for nothing, and it's more than likely that he'll sort my meals out as well, so I win all round.

I don't leave the flat for the next three days. In the meantime, I sit on the couch in a stoned stupor; Bob leaves occasionally to do fuck knows what and return with more munchies, while I sit on his sticky couch caning his weed and pissing about on his X-box.

The worst part of staying here is, without a doubt, having to talk to all manner of insufferable cunts who turn up to buy weed in the evening, most of whom will recognise me and then want to have a big fucking chat about what I'm up to now, and how great it must have been to work with James fucking Laurenson. I grin vacuously at them and tell myself that they're going to have a whole new story to dine out on in a week's time.

Bob seems happy enough to buy all the food and doesn't once ask me for any cash. It's a good job for him that this is a one-bedroom flat or else I probably would have moved in months ago. It's the closest thing I've had to a holiday in living memory. We're very similar in that although neither of us is probably agoraphobic in the strictest sense of the word, we both enjoy our puff way too much and so get too lazy to venture out into the wider world. Especially when I don't have to do anything but wake up and skin up. I'm going to miss this, but I can't deviate from my plans. I'm committed.

Sunday morning arrives, and since I'm going Bob cooks us both a huge fried breakfast that goes down exceptionally well. I'm due to meet Jimmy D at Big Yellow at 11, so make sure that everything is in my bag before that.

I give Bob a manhug as I leave.

"You couldn't lend us twenty quid, could you?" I ask him. "I'll sort you out as soon as I get back."

He smiles awkwardly. I think Bob's major problem is that he's just unable to say 'no' to anything, and so I pocket the note he hands me with a grin and lie that I'll see him in a couple of weeks.

I walk to Big Yellow, taking in some of the Spring sunshine. It's a perfect morning; the sun already high in the sky at half ten, and it's guaranteed that by lunchtime Portobello will be turning into a lazy meat market, with people eyeing each other up over pints of cider with ice and stolen cigarettes. That's certainly what I'd be doing if I didn't have plans, but I do.

I call Jimmy D once I get outside the Big Yellow, and he comes down to let me in. He's already looking a bit sweaty with shifting things about, so I get stuck in straight away and start piling the boxes onto a trolley to come down to his van. It's all business for the next hour as he makes sure that everything he needs comes down; from the ready to assemble bar through to the cocktail making equipment, and some of the harder to find booze that he doesn't want to risk not being able to source in France. It's different seeing him in this environment – the laconic host is very much on the back burner, replaced by a guy who's clearly got his shit together. By midday we're all sorted, and the van is stacked high and half full at the back. We climb in the front, and we're away.

"I never realised it was quite such an operation," I say.

He grins. "No-one ever does."

We lapse into a kind of easy silence as we make our way out of London onto the M25, and down towards the Dover ferry. I begin to get a little nervous as we queue up for our place, with the bootbag in the bottom of my bag seemingly screaming out its existence to every official that we pass, but Jimmy is his customary cool and we sail on in no time.

We park the van and go to grab a seat in one of the many lounges. What I'd really like to do is get out on deck to get some air, but for some reason the ferry we're on is hermetically sealed, and there's no way you can even open a window. So, we sit there looking at the white cliffs as they slowly recede into the distance.

Two hours pass in no time, as we eat overpriced sandwiches and read the papers. There are lots of features on highlights of this year's festival, most picking out Friday's screening of Laurenson's new film as a hot pick, and a serious contender for the Palme D'Or. I grin to myself. He'll definitely be making some serious headlines come Saturday morning.

We're back in the van and being waved off onto French soil in no time. I hold my breath as we drive past the Customs, but then we're home free and cruising down the motorway towards the South of France.

Jimmy wakes me up a couple of hours later and tells me it's my turn to drive. We grab a quick coffee and top up the tank with petrol, and then we're off again. He curls up against the window, and for the next three hours I zone out as I head south; running over the plan again and again in my head, working out the variables that could throw me off course, making sure that I get the outcome that the world and I want.

We eventually reach Nice around two o'clock in the morning, and both of us stretch for England as we emerge from the van. Jimmy has managed to blag a flat for the next week or so from one of his wealthy mates, which is a minor miracle when the festival is on.

We're both knackered, and so after a brief recce to sort out which is the bigger of the two bedrooms and therefore his, we collapse, exhausted. I grab the toothbrush out of the top of my bag, and I can't resist taking out the bootbag just to check on the contents one more time.

I fall back in bed. I'm knackered, but I can't sleep. I'm telling myself it's the coffee I had three hours ago, but deep down I know it's more than that.

It's the plan.

We wake up late. It's gone midday when I hear Jimmy banging about in the kitchen, and so I pull myself out of bed and go in to see if he's got any coffee on.

"Hey," I say, rubbing my eyes.

"I've got to go in for a meeting about the party tomorrow," he says. "Do you want to come with?"

I shake my head. "Not unless you need me. Think I'll chill today. Get some sun."

He nods. "Okay. I might stick around. See what happens. Give me a shout if you're coming in."

"Sure. Will do."

He's out of the door with a grin. I walk out to the balcony of the third-floor apartment we're in and look out over the city. It's far, far better for me we're not actually in Cannes, as it means that I'm less likely to be spotted. The last thing I need now is anyone clocking that I'm anywhere near the festival, and I'm already thinking that I'd better try and pull something spectacular out of the bag before tomorrow so that I can avoid hitting the Croisette until Friday. It would be a total fucking disaster if anyone spots me before then.

I kind of feel bad about letting Jimmy down, seeing as he's brought me out here to work. But then the last twenty-four hours have been illuminating in the sense that we were both almost completely silent for the drive down; and that beyond going out and getting fucked it appears that the pair of us have little in common. We barely talked at all, and I'm sure that that's because outside of the context of leaning over a fat line of coke, there's not much for us to talk about. He's probably as relieved as I am that I'm not coming into Cannes today.

I'm not at all gutted to be missing it. It's a fucking dreadful place, piled high with the worst kind of cunts imaginable. It's bad enough being there when everyone wants a piece of you. I was out here fourteen years ago doing the premiere for an emotional family drama that everyone had high hopes for, and which ended up dying on its arse here and barely even seeing a cinema release in the UK. There's a press officer who plonks you down on a table on the Terrace of the Ritz Carlton, and all manner of witless shitbags come along and ask you banal questions that you try and answer to the best of your abilities. Then you're whisked back to your hotel room where they stick you in a monkey suit and put you in a car that drives two hundred metres to the entrance of the Palais, where you get out to a flash of bulbs on the red carpet. You grin like an idiot for a while, then watch the film with everyone around you dressed like a hostile waiter, only to try and hide in your seat as people begin leaving around you and the ones who remain decide to boo at the end.

But if you're not there for a reason, I can only imagine it's a hundred times worse. As far as the eye can see there are overpaid yanks braying into their mobiles up and down the Croisette, marching from one self-important meeting to the next. Then there are the wannabes who you can spot a mile off; young, clueless and impressionable, walking around in packs clutching their free handbags not knowing quite what to do with themselves.

Then at the end of the night there's a huge fight about which is the hot party to go to, and who's got tickets – everyone queuing up as the perfectly rude French security guys all look like they couldn't give a fuck whether you've got a ticket or not. The party will always, always be shit, and then at the end of the night everyone will end up drunkenly shouting at each other while drinking overpriced beers from tiny plastic cups outside the Petit Majestic or Gutter Bar.

It's a fucking terrible place.

Perhaps my Cannes experience has been permanently scarred from the disastrous screening of 'Benjamin's Blessings' (with a title like that, it was bound to be doomed), but it wasn't much better the second time I came here. That was a mistake; coming out as part of some Arts Council drive to promote the new wave of 'unique British talent.' It was supposed to get us a load of press and try and introduce us to a bunch of producers. The major problem for me, as far as I could work out, was that of the entire group I stuck out like a sore thumb for being neither new, nor, as some no doubt pointed out, talented. I had at least five years on everyone else in the group, and as the fiasco of 'Benjamin's Blessings' was still relatively fresh in the mind, most people avoided me like a soiled nappy on a beach. Lucy Fontaine was also part of that group, and it didn't do her any harm; but then she's one of those actors who can play the schmoozing game like a pro. I'm not the worst, that's for sure, and I've seen some actors who just collapse on meeting someone who could potentially affect their career for the better, but Lucy can work a room like a politician. With better tits.

She's bound to be out here, especially if the rumours about her and Laurenson are true. Lucy thrives in an environment like this. Press everywhere, combined with a thousand sweaty producers and studio execs who she can prick-tease into offering her a job. And there will be agents down there, hundreds of them, all bartering and haggling and striking deals. Bigging up their latest up-their-own-arse twenty something client, most of whom will be broken on the fickle rocks of fame within six months. I've had a career, made films, and if I went down there there's more than a chance that I'd be able to get myself an agent, perhaps try and carve myself out a living picking up scraps here and there; nameless characters who crop up towards the end of the crawl once everyone's left the cinema. Dentist. Window cleaner. Hood number 3.

Not this year.

This year I'll be getting top fucking billing.

Friday morning comes, and I'm trying to recover from the non-existent illness that had me confined to my bed and that meant that I couldn't work Jimmy's first party on the Wednesday night. I woke up on the Wednesday morning and making sure that he was within earshot shoved my fingers down my throat and heaved my guts up into the tiny toilet.

I came out and told him that I was feeling fucking diabolical, and that I was going back to bed. I've obviously still got some talent as Jimmy bought it immediately and told me that there was no way I could work that evening if I was sick. People vomiting and serving drinks don't go together. I nodded weakly, and immediately took to my bed again; the only downside being that I had to stay there moaning occasionally and returning to the bathroom for more theatrics until he went out.

He eventually left at half four, at which point I went back out to the balcony to catch the late afternoon sun and read my book. The view from the balcony is nothing much, overlooking the backs of some other flats, but it still catches the sun and is only a five-minute walk from the beach. It beats London any day of the week.

He got back in the not so early hours of Thursday morning and then slept for most of the rest of the day and that gave me even more free time to myself, so I went down and sat on the beach with my sunglasses on just in case anyone might spot me.

I was back at the flat when Jimmy eventually surfaced in the mid-afternoon. I apologised profusely, and he told me not to worry – with the three bartenders who had arrived in the afternoon he was probably a little overstaffed anyway, and they'd coped just fine. It was a good party, he said. I would have enjoyed it.

He'd managed to blag a couple of tickets for the 'Hindenburg' after-party that night and wanted to know if I wanted to come down. A big studio picture, so no doubt an even more ridiculous party that usual. But I told him no. I wanted to make sure that I was one hundred percent for Friday's party, as I didn't want to let him down again. I'd be there to do my duty.

He ended up leaving around seven as he was going to meet up with a couple of London people about some more work, and so left me to it. I sat on the balcony for a while until the sun dipped behind the flats opposite, then fixed myself a bowl of pasta and concentrated on what tomorrow had in store.

It was hard to sleep last night, and although I must have dropped off at some point, I still feel knackered. The irony is that having faked an illness that got me out of working at the first party, I genuinely am starting to feel a bit sick; but then that's hardly surprising. I don't think I've ever been this nervous.

Jimmy looks at me as I come out of the bedroom and his brow furrows.

"You sure you're going to be alright tonight, Charlie? You still look rough."

I nod. "Don't worry. I'll be fine. Just had a bad night's sleep. I'm raring to go. How was last night?"

His face breaks into a broad grin, and he starts telling me about the stupid amount of booze that was flying around the party and how he managed to lead everyone in a round of sambucas until it felt like the whole place was filled with people "saluting the balloon." Something to do with the party being for the Hindenburg, which apparently everyone who saw it said that the reviews would write themselves as the film was a wingless turkey and likely to go the way of the zeppelin itself.

"And there were a couple of honeys that I got talking to later on," he says. "Shame you weren't there. But I've sorted them out with a couple of tickets for tonight, so we may well see them later."

"Wicked," I say. Hooking up with women is the last thing on my mind. "So, what time do we need to get down there?"

"We won't be able to start setting up until early evening, when all the daytime bollocks wraps up. We'll need to get sorted sharpish and get the bar set up quickly. Shouldn't be too hard. But by all accounts, this will be the party of the festival. It fucking should be if we're doing it."

"So, we've got some time to kill?"

He nods. "The rest of the day is all yours. You could get into the festival and try and schmooze some agents."

"I've sent some emails letting them know I'm in town," I lie. "And I'm waiting to hear back about a couple of potential meetings in the next couple of days."

Jimmy nods. "Cool. So shall we hit the beach?"

"Sure. I just need to get something done first. I'll see you down there."

An hour later and I'm walking up to Jimmy on the beach, and I can't help but smile when he clearly doesn't recognise me until I'm right upon him, when his face drops.

"Fucking hell, Charlie. That's a bit severe."

I rub my hand over my scalp, still getting used to the bristly feel of my new number one crop. I've had the same hair for pretty much the last ten years; every role I've had has always seemed to require no change, and I'm too lazy to do anything to it; the average length, non-descript cut has become as much a part of me as the nose on my face. Even I couldn't imagine looking in any way different.

Until now. My new skinhead cut is unrecognisably me unless you looked twice, and that's exactly what I need. Plus, it also makes me look a little crazed, and a little bit hard, and that only adds to the effect I'm going for.

"You like it?" I ask him.

"It's definitely different."

"Yeah, well. I needed a change."

I drop my sun-cream and book on top of my towel and stretch out in the sun. The warmth feels good on my face, and I dig my feet into the sand, getting just down deep enough so the temperature changes. It feels good, and I focus on the feeling, suddenly conscious that I don't know when, or if, I'll ever feel this again. There's a man walking a tiny dog along the shoreline, and I watch him as he tries to cruise a couple of disinterested teenage boys who should no doubt be in school.

I flick through my book for a while, but I'm too hyped to read. I check my watch. It's getting close to 2, and I'm hungry.

"You want a sandwich?" I ask Jimmy. "My treat."

"Nice one Charlie. That'd be great."

I haul myself up and walk off the beach towards a little café, and I keep my head down as I clock a couple of people with festival bags drinking coffee outside, but they're too wrapped up wanking on at each other about film to pay me any attention. I grab a couple of cheese baguettes and head back down to the beach.

Jimmy thanks me as I hand him his lunch. It's the least I can do for him given what's going down later.

It's around five as we head back to the flat, and the sun is still warm. I'm first in the shower, and I stand there for some time watching the last clippings from my haircut disappear down the plughole. I shave carefully, looking at myself in the mirror and trying out a couple of faces. I haul on the black trousers and T-shirt that Jimmy wants me to wear and check myself out in the mirror. I'm good to go.

While he's in the shower, I grab the keys to the van and grab the Adidas boot bag from its hiding place on top of the cupboard in my room. The sun is starting to dip in the sky as I open up the back of the van and secrete the bootbag in the top flight case, making sure that I know exactly where it is.

I'm back upstairs in no time and the keys are back in their position on the kitchen counter before Jimmy gets out of the shower. By the time he's ready I'm sitting on a chair on the small balcony catching the last rays of the sun.

"You ready?" he asks.

I've not got butterflies in my stomach so much as a nest of kestrels, and my palms are beginning to feel a little sweaty, but I'm ready.

"Let's go," I say.

The drive along the sea front towards the Majestic takes a fair while, as there's the usual load of slack jawed yokels gawping at everything film related, and this slows our progress down. The Palais des Festivals is within spitting distance as we park the van on the side of the Croisette. All Jimmy's patience and good humour are immediately put to the test as several policeman pounce on the van and try and get him to move, but one of the party organisers spots him trying to explain what's going on and comes out to smooth things over. She immediately grabs a couple of security guys to help haul in the flight cases from the van and my heart goes in my mouth as they disappear down the staircase and onto the beach.

All the commotion works in my favour as everything is so hectic that there's only time to grab one of the smaller boxes full of the cocktail equipment and make my way down onto the beach itself. The security guys come back up to make sure that everything comes down, and then Jimmy leaves in the van to try and find a parking place.

The party organiser comes along and introduces herself to me as Jenny but is too flustered to ask me for my name, which is just fine with me. She points out where she wants our particular cocktail section set up, and it's a great spot, under a small tent just near the start of the long jetty; and one that affords you a great view of the stairs so you can see whoever's coming into the party.

I open the flight cases quickly, and with little fuss take out the bootbag and stick it between two cases of limes underneath the small table at the back that I'm going to be working from, and then pull out the sections of the bar from the cases and begin putting them together. I'm already quite far ahead when Jimmy turns up twenty minutes later.

"Fuck me. That was painful."

I look up. "Did you find somewhere?"

He nods. "I might as well have taken it back to the fucking flat. It's fucking miles away. How you getting on?"

"You tell me," I say.

We knuckle down and get the bar built. Jimmy's two cocktail bartenders arrive as we're finishing putting it together, and we're introduced. I've met Francisco before at one of Jimmy's parties, although he doesn't recognise me with my new haircut, which I take as a good sign. The other guy, Max, clearly fancies himself even though he's a fucking midget compared to the three of us.

"Where's all the booze?" asks Francisco.

"It'll be around," says Jimmy. "I'll check with Jenny. Charlie, can you start prepping the fruit? I'm guessing plenty of

Margaritas tonight, so as many limes as you can. In fact, Max, can you give him a hand?"

Shit. I don't want anyone poking around the fruit.

"Don't worry Max," I say. "I've got this. Why don't you have a wonder? Chill for a minute. It would be great if you can find out where I'm going to need to go for ice."

"Okay. Thanks Charlie."

I check on the boot-bag once more as I pull out a case of limes and begin chopping. It's close, and I know that I can grab it in a few seconds. If I can make sure that there are always enough limes cut and ready, and that Francisco and Max have everything they need, then it should all be plain sailing.

It's a relief to have something to do, as it focuses me and stops my head from whirring as it has been doing for the past week. I zoom in on the board, just making sure that everything gets cut and stored, making myself invisible to the rest of the world.

The next two hours pass slowly, as the four of us begin to prepare a bar full of cocktails that people will be able to lift off the side as they come down the stairs. Jimmy, Francisco and Max stay very much the face of the operation, all three facing the party, while I keep working in the background.

The film finishes, and the noise picks up outside the Palais as the black tied audience spills out and the gawpers jostle for a view of the great and the good. Almost immediately there is a melee at the top of the stairs as people brandish their party invitations at the security. Jimmy, Francisco and Max all spring into action, and start filling the front bar with cocktails which begin vanishing immediately from the counter as the first guests arrive.

The studio has clearly spent a small fortune on this party, and it shows. On the other side of the jetty is a huge open marquee that covers a large dancefloor with another bar at the end of it. Waiters dressed in black are already beginning to mill around the growing throng handing out canapés. The jetty itself stretches out into the sea and is lined with intricate lanterns all the way to the edge. A small shiver of excitement goes all the way down my spine as I notice that there is a circular spotlight moving around at the end of the jetty, almost like the police search lights from a helicopter. It really couldn't be any more perfect.

I'm not surprised to see that people are already beginning to make their way along the jetty, as looking back from out there gives you an amazing view of the rest of Cannes; the floodlit Palais, the boats out at sea, the hotels gleaming on the other side of the Croisette, and of course all the no-marks desperate to get into the party, but never will.

I keep my head down and stay alert, feeding Jimmy and the other two with everything they need – diving into the back freezer for more ice, fetching more bottles from the cases that are lined up at the back of the tent, and ensuring that they have fresh glasses on hand whenever they need them. My initial nerves about being spotted quickly evaporate. At the back, beyond the bar, I may as well be invisible. I am below pond life to the partygoers, all far too into making their opinions heard. The buzz on the film is audible, and my resolve only strengthens as I hear that Laurenson has done it again; the wunderkind of British cinema has delivered another sure-fire hit, and one that's so quirky, yet heartfelt, that it could even be in the running for a major award. Maybe even the Big One.

This is good, as it means that he's far more likely to turn up to the party if he knows that everyone is going to be lining up to blow smoke up his arse. Plus, it ensures that when he does, I'm going to steal all tomorrow's headlines.

The party begins to fill up. Jimmy's cocktails are proving to be extremely popular, and I have to focus to make sure I keep on it, providing them with everything they need. But it's hard, as I've continually got an eye on the stairs to see who's coming down at every moment. The last thing I want to do is miss the royal entrance of the Grand Master.

I check my watch. It's getting close to 11, and I would guess that Laurenson is going to make an appearance in the next half hour or so. They'll be a self-congratulatory wankfest in some hotel suite where the many producers and studio heads all fall over themselves to tell him how fucking fantastic he is, and while he waits for Lucy to get changed from one ridiculous dress into another. If it wasn't for the fact that she was there I wouldn't bank on him making an appearance, but she won't be able to resist an opportunity to be stared at, and she'll no doubt drag him down to cement their role as the golden couple of the moment. Not much longer.

A band starts up on the small stage on the other side of the jetty. Our bar is still heaving busy, and people are knocking back the drinks like they're going out of style. The Margaritas are extremely popular, and Jimmy looks as I open our last case of Triple Sec. He ducks back down to speak to me.

"Charlie. I need you find Jenny. She'll show you where to fetch another couple of cases."

Fuck. Fuck. Fuck. Fuck. Fuck.

I don't want to venture out into the party. It's packed full of fucking journalists, who are a nosy bunch of bastards at the best of times. My new haircut may have thrown off Jimmy, but if I run into someone who I've been interviewed by before then they may start asking all sorts of awkward questions, and I can't afford for that to happen just yet.

I've no choice. This is what I'm here to do, so I nod and tell Jimmy no problem, then walk across the jetty, across the dance floor towards the main bar where I hope I'm going to find Jenny. I keep my gaze locked on the middle distance and try and look as non-descript and innocuous and possible. I walk past some fat fucker who I'm pretty sure works for the Daily Mail, who interviewed me about eight years ago when I still had a career. Patrick something-or-other. He looks over at me for longer than a couple of seconds, and I think I catch a quizzical look as I keep walking. Shit. Not yet. It could be just that he fancies the skinhead look, but then I'm not sure.

I reach the bar, and there's no sign of Jenny; but the guy who's running the bar lets me take a case of both Triple Sec and Tequila back with me and I make my way back across the dancefloor, taking a different route and moving as quickly as I can just so I don't run into the journo again. Everybody is half watching the three pretty boys on stage, one of whom I recognise as an actor, so this is probably some vanity side project.

I cross over the jetty and back to our bar where there are still people swooping past to grab the cocktails. No-one else seems to pay me any attention, but then they're all too busy trying to find the next person to schmooze; and a cocktail bar-back is about the lowest you can find on the food chain. I duck back down into my position behind the bar and go back to keeping everything in place.

I check my watch. 11.10. The jetty is full now; people mill around wandering up and down checking each other out. For the plan to work I need to make sure that I catch Laurenson's entrance on the stairs. If I miss him coming in, and he gets off the jetty onto the main dance floor, then everything is going to start to get really complicated.

I cut some limes. Refill the ice buckets. Put fresh pitchers down on the bar.

It's 11.15. There are some camera flashes on the top of the stairs, and a flurry of activity. My heart leaps into my mouth, but then a couple of Hollywood A-listers come down the stairs, and I calm down again. Danny Ward is in the movie and is squiring his new girlfriend Emma Chase to the party. That Danny's here is a good sign. Everyone immediately pretends not to notice them while simultaneously scrutinising their every movement. They come to the bar and Jimmy is all smiles as he passes them over a couple of Margaritas. He's the perfect schmoozy fucker in situations like this, which is why I'm sure he keeps getting work with all the party organisers. Everyone loves a charmer.

Every minute seems to drag past like an hour, and I can't help but feel twitchy as each second moves me closer to destiny. The band finishes and is replaced by a DJ who immediately starts off with some funk. The bar is still mobbed, and I'm pissing about behind, trying to seem busy while never looking away from the top of the stairs.

Then I see her. More camera flashes at the top of the stairs, and the security stands aside to let Lucy Fontaine through. She pauses at the top of the stairs like Ginger fucking Rogers, all teeth as she surveys her party, almost like she's expecting a fucking round of applause. She turns round to grin at who's following her, and my heart sinks as I see it's a woman I don't know, and not James Laurenson.

Lucy reaches the bottom of the stairs, and I duck out of the way to make sure that she doesn't catch my eye as she approaches the bar, but I don't need to worry. I'm still invisible. She grins at Jimmy as he hands her a drink, but no-one else is noticed. She's wearing a diamond necklace that probably cost more than I'm getting for my flat and is looking as hot as ever. I'm still looking at her when I realise that James Laurenson is halfway down the stairs, following Jake Hunter who's starring as the retired MI5 guy in the movie. Laurenson is laughing at something Hunter is saying and is looking about as pleased with himself as it's possible for a man to be. His face looks fuller than recent photographs, so either he's been having them photoshopped, or he's been eating a lot of fancy dinners. Just goes to show the allure of power, because I somehow doubt anyone as drop dead gorgeous as Lucy Fontaine would normally look twice at a fat fucker like that. He reaches the bottom of the stairs and is immediately beset upon by several fawning minions from the studio who are all no doubt telling him he's the Second Coming, and a shoo-in for the Palme D'Or.

My palms are sweating. I rub them on my trousers, then reach down between the limes for where I've stashed the boot bag, and grab hold of it. Maybe it's the adrenalin, but it feels lighter than ever, and I unzip it just to check it's still there.

And I pull it out. I don't know that much about guns – I've only worked on a couple of films where I've ever had a chance to use one – and this seems tiny to me, but I'm sure it's going to do the job. It's certainly loaded with real bullets, and real bullets kill. I keep the boot bag in my other hand, crouching down by the bar to wait for the optimum moment.

Then it happens. Laurenson peels away from the acolytes who are talking to him, and heads along the jetty towards Lucy, who's deep in conversation with some blonde. I jump up onto the jetty, and it though it must only take me about three seconds to come up behind Laurenson and jab the gun in his back, I feel as if time slows right down.

"Watch it," he says, turning round to see who's just barged into him.

"Hello maestro," I say. My heart is hammering in my chest. He looks startled, but clearly doesn't recognise me.

"It's a fucking gun in your back, cunt. Keep walking. Eyes front."

People are looking confused as we pass; first registering what is clearly a petrified look on his face, then looking at the skinhead who is marching him along the jetty towards the sea. Lucy smiles as he approaches, then looks back in a double take; and searches my face for a second. Then she recognises me, and her jaw drops.

As soon as we pass her I raise the gun in the air. There's only about twenty people this far along the jetty, and I say a silent prayer as I point the gun at the sky and pull the trigger.

It fires, and Laurenson jumps. Thank fuck for that, I think. Elijah's man came good. I would have looked like a right cunt if it hadn't worked.

I fire the gun again, and a weird silence falls across the party as people look at each other trying to work out where the sound of gunfire is coming from; the only sound is the music coming from the DJ, and that stops a few seconds later. I'm still marching Laurenson towards the sea, and a woman sees the gun and screams. She sprints back down towards the party, and this sets off a chain reaction of panic; everyone screaming and trying to escape up the stairs.

A couple of partygoers this end of the jetty look at me, dumbstruck.

"Move!" I growl, and they run back down towards the beach. I keep checking over my shoulder to see what's going on behind me, and so far, so good: it's pandemonium. People are panicked, running up the stairs trying to get away, while some other, braver – or more stupid – individuals are trying to get a look at what is going on.

"What do you want?" Laurenson says. He's trying to sound brave, but there's a tremor in his voice like he's shitting his pants.

"Don't you recognise me?" I ask the back of his neck. He shakes his head. "You're not looking at me," I tell him.

I keep the gun to his temple as he turns round to look at me.

"Fucking hell," he says. "Charlie? Charlie Reed? What the fuck are you doing?"

"Having some fun."

Two of the security guys from the entrance to the party are making their way slowly along the jetty towards us.

I jam the gun in Laurenson's temple.

"Stop there," I tell them. Behind them is a guy straining to get a good look at what's going on.

"Oi. You." I shout at him, and he looks over, nervous. "You know your way around a camera?"

He nods. I pass the bag to Laurenson. "Get the camera out for him."

Laurenson nods and undoes the zip to pull out my video camera.

"What's your name?" I ask the guy. He's looking like he could shit his pants at any moment, yet excited at the same time; he's clearly aware that he's part of some kind of event.

"Patrick," he says.

"Hi Patrick. Turn the camera on. OK, first things first. Patrick, I'd like you to just say now that you're happy that I own all rights to what's filmed in that camera. Just in case there's any confusion."

Patrick looks momentarily thrown by this, but says, "Sure. Of course."

"Good. Can you just swing round, get a view of the party for me?"

Patrick does so. His hand is shaking a little as he pans around, but then I guess that's par for the course.

"And back on me," I tell him. I jab the gun firmly into Laurenson's temple. "I'm Charlie Reed, and I'm here to tell you exactly what it's like to work with the great James Laurenson."

"You're fucking crazy," says Laurenson.

"You'd better believe it," I say.

The Croisette is beginning to flash blue and white and the air filled with sirens as every police car in Cannes seems to be arriving outside the party.

"You're never going to get away with this Charlie. You know that, right?"

"Why do you think I want to get away with it? Why did you pull the funding on the film?"

"What the fuck are you on about?"

I can see Lucy Fontaine crying, and the blonde girl she was talking to earlier has her arm around her, trying to lead her away. She probably thinks that she's in danger. Fair play to Lucy though; I thought she might play the hysterical wife and make it all about her, and at least she's not doing that.

"Donovan's film? Finding Jessica? The one that you said I'd be perfect for? The film that you were exec producing?"

"Jesus, Charlie. I was only doing that as a favour..."

"Because that's what you do, isn't it?" I interrupt, changing the position of the gun to jam it into his ribs. "You fuck with people."

Two policemen are now making their way slowly along the jetty to join the security guys who are hovering nearby, as several of their colleagues behind them are trying to evacuate all the other guests.

"Don't come any closer! Ne bougez pas!" I scream to the police, who immediately stop in their tracks. I look past them to see if I can catch a glimpse of Jimmy D and the others. He's going to be seriously pissed off.

There's a huge crowd milling around along the top of the Croisette, all straining to get a look at what's going on. The police are trying to hold them back, and I can see the tell-tale lights on top of the TV news cameras flick on as they swarm to try and get a better view.

"I'm sorry, Charlie," says Laurenson. "I just don't get it. What exactly is your problem?"

"It's you. You're my fucking problem. You ruined my fucking life, you evil cunt. You made my life hell, and I've been paying for it ever since. And now it's payback time."

Patrick has still got the camera fixed on both of us, and Laurenson is all too aware that he's being filmed.

"You okay?" I ask him, twisting the gun in his ribs. "You don't seem very natural to me. It's a shitty feeling isn't it. Someone fucking with you on camera. Trying to get an emotional reaction."

"Jesus, Charlie. Grow the fuck up."

I raise the gun in the air, and fire quickly into the sky again. The police react immediately, waving their hands at me trying to get me to stop. A gasp ripples all the way down to the end of the jetty and up the Croisette. Laurenson whimpers.

"Don't tell me to grow the fuck up," I stage whisper in his ear. Patrick's hands are shaking as he tries to keep focus on the pair of us.

"What is it you want?" asks Laurenson. His voice is really shaking now, and he believes I mean business.

"First, let's recognise that I'm the one in charge for once. Not you. And I want you to tell them all to move back, or I'll fucking shoot you."

"Please," he says to the police. "Move back."

"Du calme, monsieur! Du calme!" One of the policemen is holding his hands outstretched and is motioning to the other one to put away the pistol he has trained on me. He's probably thinking that shooting one of the key talents who's visiting this year's Festival is not going to be a good look.

"Why did you cancel the funding on Finding Jessica?" I ask Laurenson. "Is that why you recommended me to Donovan for Roy? Just so you'd get another opportunity to humiliate me?"

"I don't know what you're talking about. I didn't make any casting recommendations at all. All I said was when they got you was that I was sure you'd do a good job."

"I don't believe you."

"Why would I lie?"

It sounds like he's telling the truth. And I'm sure there's nothing like a gun in your ribs to inspire you to be honest.

"So why did you cancel the funding? Fuck, with the amount that that film was coming in at, you could have written a cheque single handed to cover it."

"And why the fuck would I want to do that?" asks Laurenson. "We got fucked by the Germans. Plain and simple. The production company doing the co-funding pulled out. And I haven't got the money to start splashing around on funding features."

"You're fucking loaded, you cunt," I shout.

"I wish I had half the money that I read about, Charlie. Fuck, it's not easy. I've got two ex-wives and four kids in public school. It all adds up. The last thing I can do is drop a quarter mill on seeing a film get made. Even my own, let alone another fucking director's. I said I'd exec to try and help him raise the money. Not so I'd get stuck with the fucking bill at the end of it."

His voice sounds like he's telling the truth. I feel a little disappointed, as I thought he'd be more belligerent than this. But he seems a lot smaller than he did twenty years ago. Maybe it's just that I've got taller. Grown up.

"You know you made my life a living hell on 'The Twelfth of Never'. You know that right?"

"What do you want me to say, Charlie? Jesus, it was a fucking lifetime ago! You want me to keep apologising for it?"

I'm almost tempted to fire the gun again. "Keep apologising? What the fuck do you mean?"

"I told you I was sorry, Charlie. Really I did. If you choose not to remember, then I can't help that. I know it was hard for you. It had to be, to get the performance that I was after. That I knew you were capable of. Pain is temporary. The film is forever."

"You fucking tortured me! I was just a boy. Just a fucking teenager."

"I know. I know! I spoke to your mother, and she said that you'd be able to handle it."

Pat fucking Reed. She really has fucked my life up pretty spectacularly.

"I wasn't. I wasn't able to handle it." I can feel my eyes sting, and blink hard to stop myself from crying. This is about me being strong, being in control. Being the hardman. Blubbing away with a gun in my fucking hand is not the look I'm going for.

And yet, there's something about this situation that seems to take me back to that time. Whether it's the fact that every pair of eyes in a half mile radius is fixed firmly on me, or whether it's that I'm stood, once again, right next to James fucking Laurenson; but suddenly it's like I'm fourteen. And I don't want to be here anymore.

One of the policemen about ten feet away must sense some weakness and takes a half step forward. I wave the gun at him quickly. "Don't fucking do it, Frenchy. I've got enough bullets to take us both down. Don't think that I won't do it."

"Fuck, Charlie. Calm down. Please." Laurenson is sounding a lot calmer than I'd like.

"You don't think I've got the balls. Do you." I'm tight in his ear as I stage whisper this, hoping that the shitty microphone on my video camera is going to pick it up. "How you doing Patrick?"

Patrick gulps, nods. I bet that this wasn't what he was expecting when he rocked up to the party tonight.

"Why did you never want to work with me again?" I ask Laurenson.

He sighs, deeply. "Jeez, I don't know. It just didn't happen. I'm sure I would have used you if there was a part for you. If you'd been right for something. But..."

He clams up. "But what?" He stays silent. I prod him again in the ribs. "The man holding the gun wants to know what you were going to say."

"What I was going to say," says Laurenson through a tight mouth, "is that it's not always all about you."

I drop a hollow laugh. "Well, kind of is right now, isn't it?"

"What do you want from me, Charlie? You after work, is that it?"

I laugh. "No. Not really. I just want you to tell the world just what a shitbag you really are."

"What?"

"I think you heard me. I want you to look into the camera, and tell the world that you're a manipulative, emotional bully."

He swallows. "I'm a manipulative, emotional bully."

"Don't just fucking parrot me, you cunt. Say it like you mean it."

"Sorry Charlie. It's just... presently my improvisational skills are a little off. What with the gun in my ribs and everything."

"You don't think I'll do it, do you? Let me tell you, James. I've got nothing left to live for. Thanks to you, my agent is dead, and my career is in the toilet. And seeing you here is the one thing that's stopped me from losing my mind for the last fortnight."

"Jesus. You really are a fucking loony."

I grin, and mug for the camera. "You know us actors. We're a very flighty bunch. No, we're just going to stay here until you decide to apologise. Properly. And then maybe I'll kill you. Or maybe I'll let you live. I haven't decided yet."

The chopping blades of two helicopters thunder overhead, and a search light beams down, adding to the swirling spots that circle where we stand at the end of the jetty. I grin to myself. I'm betting this looks pretty fucking spectacular on all the cameras that are trained on me right now.

Another policeman has turned up behind the two who watch me at close quarters along with the two security guys from the gate. He's clearly senior, and must be some kind of negotiator, as he calls out to me by name in heavily accented English.

"Are you alright, Charlie? You are not harming Monsieur Laurenson, no?"

"We're just fine," I say. "Just having a chat."

"Do you want to give me the gun Charlie?" he continues. "Then we can all go home to bed. It's been a long night."

"We're okay, aren't we?" I ask Laurenson, who says nothing. "Thanks anyway, though."

"Can I get you anything? Perhaps you would like some water?"

"Water would be good. Do you want some water?" I ask Laurenson, but he's silent. I nod to the cop. "Yes, we'll have some water."

He turns and speaks to a policeman next to him, who immediately disappears in the search for water. The negotiator just smiles calmly at me. He looks a bit like a fatter, shorter Bruce Willis; with the spotlights bouncing off his bald head.

"My name is Jacques, Charlie."

"Hi Jacques."

"What is it that you want?"

I nuzzle the butt of the gun into Laurenson's ribs again. "That's what I was just telling James. We go back a long way, you know?"

"Can I come closer to speak to you?" Jacques starts moving very slowly towards me.

"I'd rather you didn't. And in fact, I'd rather not get into a big chat thing with you, if it's all the same. Just stay there and shut up. I want to hear from James."

Jacques raises his arms in a non-threatening gesture and stops moving.

"Charlie, listen." Laurenson's voice is low and steady, like he wants me to believe whatever it is that he's about to say is an important truth. "I'm sorry for the pain that I put you through on 'The Twelfth of Never.' Really, I am. But what you must understand is that I honestly thought that you'd be able to handle it. I did it for the film, Charlie. For the good of the film. That was all it was. There were times when I knew I was being tough on you, but only because I could see that that was the only way to dig the performance out of you. Because it was in there all along. I'm proud of the film, and I'm proud of your performance. I still think it's the best portrayal of adolescence that's ever been on screen, even if I say so myself. I don't know what else you've got going on in your life right now, but this isn't the answer. You know that, right? This isn't the answer. I'm sorry to hear about your agent, and I'm sure you can get another one. You're a fucking good actor. It sounds like things have hit a bit of a rough patch for you, and I'm sorry. But things will get better. You have to believe that. But whatever you've built me up to be in your head for the last twenty years – that's not me, Charlie. That's not me. I was always on your side."

Fuck me, he's good. Listening to him I have to fight to stop from screaming out loud. My eyes start to smart and fill with tears. Because, despite not wanting to, despite my deep-rooted desire to keep hating him, I actually believe what he's saying.

I try and cast my mind back, and I just can't seem to remember what happened anymore. Perhaps some of the suffering I felt was only magnified through the fog of adolescence; perhaps he isn't the person I am truly angry with after all. Given the chance, maybe it would have been better to have held a gun to Pat's head; but then it wouldn't have been quite the drama I was looking for.

"How long have you been filming Patrick?" I ask.

He looks at the tape counter in the flip-out screen. "Nine minutes."

Shit. It feels like a lot longer than that. I wanted to try and string this out for at least forty-five minutes, even an hour. But I just don't really have the stomach for it. Laurenson has apologised, which is partly what I wanted. I think I've made my point, and I'm hoping that the stage and the location will make up for the shorter duration of the kidnapping. Plus, the last thing I want to do is end up fucking shot. I'm not that crazy.

"So, you're sorry?" I ask Laurenson.

"Of course I am," he says.

"That's all I wanted to hear," I say. And I slowly raise my hands, holding the gun aloft, and let it fall to the ground behind me.

The next seconds are a blur. The policemen move with lightning speed to jump on me and wrestle me to the ground. My arms are wrenched behind my back, and everyone is screaming and shouting as I'm frogmarched up the jetty at top speed.

My arms feel like they're about to pop out of their sockets as I'm dragged up to the top of the stairs, and suddenly there's a sea of people shouting my name, and flashbulbs explode white among the swirling blue of the police lights. Every cop car in the south of France must be here.

I raise my head as high as I can, and just before I'm bundled into the back of a car, I grin at the cameras.

And then we speed away, and I try to look over my shoulder, trying to catch a last glimpse of the havoc I've created; knowing that this will always be the Festival that's remembered for me.

NOVEMBER

Charlie. I know this shoot has been difficult for you, but I just wanted you to know that you've been incredible.

I'm sorry for a lot of what I've put you through, but when you see it on the screen, I'm sure you'll understand.

You've got a long career ahead of you, you know. If you want it.

You just need to be careful what you take on.

This business is all about choices in the end, Charlie.

It's all about choices.

Seven a.m., and the alarm sounds. I've already been awake for at least an hour; but then this place isn't exactly conducive to lie-ins.

I stare at the paint flaking off the ceiling for a moment and wait for it: I've only been in this cell six weeks, but you could set your watch by the fart that Sabah lets rip every morning. He's in for a four stretch for robbery but should get life for the noxious fumes that leak from his arse every day.

I'm down for three years. I thought I'd get more that that; and was kind of figuring that I'd be away for double that, but Laurenson turned up to the trial and actually spoke in my defence, claiming that circumstances had led me to have some kind of breakdown, and that given the choice he would not even press charges. That was never going to be an option after embarrassing the whole of the French police and the organisers of the Festival though. After I managed to hold a gun to the head of one of the world's premier directors, and a guest at Cannes, I think they would have brought back the guillotine for me if they could. I may have misjudged Laurenson slightly; as he seems like quite a decent guy now – and if the director is God, then he's definitely erring on the side of merciful rather than vengeful.

I was front page news for a good couple of days after the party, and according to my lawyer he could barely get into the court on most days due to the overwhelming number of TV crews all fighting to get a piece of the action. The papers had already gone to town, speaking to my family and everyone I'd ever worked with. Only Pat remained silent. She wouldn't say a word.

Sales of 'The Twelfth of Never' rocketed, and the studio brought out a new edition of the film especially. There was a short doc about me on it, a cheap rushed job by all accounts. They might as well have called it the Charlie Reed's A Fucking Nutbag Special Edition. But on the film front things have taken an interesting direction; Laurenson is producing a documentary about the whole hostage situation, kind of like a Bus 182 *sur mer*, and is of course keen to use all the footage that I got Patrick to shoot on my camera. He says he's going to be kind to me, but what-fucking-ever; I'm sure he's smart enough to know that that was always part of my plan anyway.

It's like the 'they' you hear about always say: when life gives you lemons, make lemonade. No-one's hiring me? Then fuck it. Change the game. Make yourself the story. Once I get out of here, I've got my pick of agents, and I'm going to have work coming in for the rest of my life. Guaranteed, most of the roles will probably be playing crazy people, but I certainly won't be worrying about money anytime soon.

Prison was always on the cards, and I'm not an idiot. I've seen 'A Prophet'. I knew it was going to be no picnic. But it was a calculated risk. Besides, after living in that fucking bedroom at Churchill Road with Pat, prison is almost a blessing – even with the state of Sabah's arse. Sure, I've taken a beating a couple of times, but I've stood up to it, fought back and not grassed. If things go according to plan I could be out of here in six months and spending the rest of my sentence in an open prison. At least, that's what Laurenson is fighting for.

Jimmy D wasn't happy. He got hauled up in front of the police and questioned for hours, and they eventually believed him after both of us told them he had nothing to do with it. The class act that he is, he never ended up selling his story – unlike my dad, who must have sprinted to the Mail on Sunday with indecent haste as soon as he found out about the whole affair.

I got a letter from Nick, which I wasn't expecting. He told me that I was a twat. He also mentioned that he's managed to nail work on a horror that's going to be shooting out in Prague for a couple of months, and if he gets a chance will come and visit. He didn't mention Alex once, and I might be wrong, but the way he described looking forward to getting out of England for a bit leads me to think that maybe he's realising she's actually a fucking midget cow after all.

I kind of hoped that I'd hear from Callie, but then there's no reason why she should. She's married with children; I've got to accept that. Besides, it's not like I've exactly displayed the character traits that might win myself a mate. Although some of the fan letters I've received in here need to be seen to be believed – there seems to be a lot of women who go crazy for crazy.

The one thing that really surprised me was the letter from Elijah. Naturally one of the first things that the police wanted to know was how I'd got the gun into the party, and moreover, where I'd got it. I said the same thing every time. I found it in the park. I'd never give Elijah up. Not after he stuck his neck out for me.

So, I was surprised when the letter arrived, halfway through the court case. He'd nailed his GCSEs (they must be giving them away, because with the strength of his reefers I was barely able to stand up, let alone take an exam), and had got himself a new agent of the back of the St Anthony's episode. It had got him a lot of attention, and he was waiting to hear back about a lead in a new West End play that sounded interesting. He told me to be careful, now that I was the Bad Man.

I swing my legs over the side and rub my face. Nice Prison is pretty fucking hardcore, and although I knew this was going to be hard, I didn't think it would be like this. Some days I just want to curl up into a ball and disappear. But then I think back to the lights on the Croisette, and a thousand voices shouting my name.

In a couple of years, I'll be out of here. With a new agent, and a whole new career waiting for me.

But fuck London. I'm going straight out to LA.

Hollywood loves a bad boy.

Acknowledgments

The Last Audition was born in my last days of living just off the Portobello Road, when I passed an actor who had made the shift from being a child star of sorts into a successful adult actor (and now director), and after a split second of eye contact my imagination did the rest. We've never actually met, but I owe him my thanks.

I moved out of the area in 2007; many of the places mentioned in the book were open then and I tried as much as possible to make sure that they were still open at the time the book was set.

The avid readers amongst you may think the name 'Charlie Reed' is familiar – I read Stephen King's 'Fairy Tale' this summer and was gobsmacked to see that the hero of that book is Charlie Reade. I did consider changing Charlie's surname for a while, but then as we live in a world where two very different Brian Coxes happily co-exist, I figured there's probably room for both Charlies. While I'm on the subject of other authors, there's waaaaay too many to give a shout out to, but I'm not going to let that stop me trying – John Niven, Matt Haig, Alan Moore, Mick Herron, John le Carré, Emma Jane Unsworth, Colson Whitehead, Richard Osman, Emily St. John Mandel, Ted Chiang, James Smythe, Amitav Ghosh… I could go on. And on.

I'd like to thank my early readers who helped give me such

invaluable feedback that (I hope) have made the book better. Olly Wicken and Paul Allen were both brilliant in helping temper some of Charlie's already awful misanthropic tendencies to make him at least somewhat sympathetic. Katy Hanley and Andy Tomlinson also made some invaluable suggestions, and Caroline (dearest Cazzles) was as encouraging as she always is.

A special thanks to Sam – she knows why.

Thanks to the Coolbox crew who I spend my days with and who continually work their lovely bottoms off and create wonderful things for all our fabulous clients. Bob, my right-hand man and business partner, Toby, Jade, Maya and Amy (Ambles) who also did the cover for the book you hold in your hands.

Fortunately, I'm nothing like Charlie (I'd hope that would go without saying, but you know, just in case), and so huge thanks to all my lovely friends – I'm not going to list you all here as being the nob that I am I'd miss a name and never hear the end of it. Nonetheless, you know who you are, and I love you all. And if you're reading this, you're a new friend. Come find me on Instagram and say hi! I'm @coolhilldesigns.

And finally, a word of thanks to my family. To Gid and Sue, who nurtured a love of reading, and who I woke up with my first story at a very early age (Once upon a time there was a boat...) and my sister Emma, plus Stephen, Anna and Lucy.

Noah and Lottie, you are wonderful, loving, funny and creative human beings and I'm proud beyond measure to be your dad. And to Lou, who is the most gorgeous, funniest, kindest, strongest and best woman I know – I love you very much.

Brighton, October 2024.

ABOUT THE AUTHOR

Tom Bainton is an award-winning filmmaker and creative director with Coolbox Films. He designs the occasional T-shirt, and still loves to DJ. He lives in Brighton with his family, a chatty cat and a completely mental dog.

This is his first novel.

Printed in Great Britain
by Amazon